"Some people think I'm a hero."

Daniel desperately needed to share himself with her, to make her understand. "But heroes are not often what they seem to be," he said sadly.

"I don't understand what you mean," Jamie said, moving closer to him, her voice gentle.

"When I trained to be a border guard, my superiors grilled me for weeks. 'Can you send a hungry child back across the border? Can you resist payment or bribery to allow people of your own heritage into the United States?' Being a Texan, I wondered if Davy Crockett had ever had to be unkind to a hungry Mexican child. It isn't easy, being the hero."

The mariachi music was playing again, a lilting love ballad that sounded vaguely familiar to Jamie as she looked at Daniel and suddenly comprehended all the questions in his eyes.

"Maybe...maybe someday you can just be a man. Maybe someday you won't need to be a hero anymore," she said. "Except, perhaps, to me."

ABOUT THE AUTHOR

Even a hurricane couldn't deter Debbi Bedford from researching her fourth Superromance, *To Weave Tomorrow*. Caught on the Texas-Mexican border when the notorious storm Gilbert struck, Debbi interviewed border guards and local citizens who were no doubt as impressed by her "true grit" as her editor. A Texan by birth, Debbi makes her home in Wyoming with her husband, Jack, her son, Jeffrey, and her baby daughter, Avery. When she's not at her word processor, Debbi spends her time fly-fishing, square dancing, doing cross-stitching and teaching Sunday school.

To Weave Tomorrow

DEBBI BEDFORD

Harlequin Books

TORONTO • NEW YORK • LONDON
AMSTERDAM • PARIS • SYDNEY • HAMBURG
STOCKHOLM • ATHENS • TOKYO • MILAN

Published December 1989

First printing October 1989

ISBN 0-373-70384-8

Printed in U.S.A.

You are a border
within me,
drawing a line between
who I once
was
and who I
will be.

Your love marks the difference
between
my yesterday
and
a forever,
a place where I stand
as a child,
waiting,
until you take my hand and,
together,
we weave
tomorrow.

To Avery Elizabeth, my new, tiny daughter.
May you find a love as precious and fine someday
as the one I have found
with your father.
—D

Acknowledgments:

To David Portillo,
Chief Patrol Agent, INS McAllen Sector,
and to Ludivina Ybarra,
principal of F.J. Scott Elementary School.
Thank you for helping make the story real.

CHAPTER ONE

THE CHILDREN MADE NO SOUND.

"I want to meet each of you, to learn your names." Jamie's eyes met and held the gaze of a boy in the front row. She pointed to him. "What is your name, please?"

He did not speak. Instead his huge, dark eyes communicated volumes. He reminded Jamie of herself as he assessed her, as if they were both poised on the brink of some transition, not knowing whether to express trust, disbelief, flight or quiet fear.

Jamie thought back to her years in North Texas, the times she'd spent drilling her third graders on their Spanish vocabulary. *The mother wears red. The cow gives milk. The postman delivers the package.*

She was at the opposite end of the world now, far away from everything she had once depended on and held dear. Sometimes it was as if she was viewing life through a photographic negative—the bright objects dark, the dark light, all the shapes eerie, only vaguely familiar.

Jamie rose from her desk, her eyes holding the boy's, smiling, yet feeling her mouth tremble. She knew he was frightened, too. "Please. Tell me your name."

"Me llamo Gilbert," he answered, and Jamie was satisfied, even though he had spoken in Spanish.

"Fine." She leaned forward and touched his hand, willing him to be brave and to accept her. "Now, say it in English, please. 'My name is Gilbert.'"

His voice was timid and tiny, the voice of a much younger child. "My name . . . is Gilbert," he repeated slowly.

She squeezed his hand hoping that, eventually, he would trust her. "Very nice." And then she walked down each of the aisles, meeting her students, as they shyly told her their names. Juana. Miguel. Three Pedros. Sarita, Rudi, Diego, Tomás, Eva, Inez, Francesca and Soyla. There were twenty-five of them in all, crammed into a classroom where bright yellow paint on cinderblock walls tried to balance the effect of several broken desks and tattered books.

"Okay now." Jamie returned to her desk and pulled a stack of flash cards from her drawer. She had brought them with her and she was glad she had. Her students in Richardson, a suburb of Dallas, had always responded to them. And, she knew now, she wouldn't have much of a budget to spend on additional visual aids. "Here is a colorful drawing of a clown," she explained. She wanted to prod them, to make them relax enough to laugh with her. They were children, after all. "Who can tell me about the picture? What color is the clown's hair?"

It was a hilarious sketch, a depiction of the clown tumbling head over heels while his hair flew in all directions and his shoes fell off and landed on his hands. Jamie was hoping it would make her students smile. And, to her relief, several of them did.

One hand moved into the air in the back of the room. "Yes? Say the entire sentence for me."

"The clown's hair is yellow," the little girl named Sarita answered timidly.

"Yes." Jamie nodded her approval just as the door to the classroom swung open.

"Hello," a uniformed man said as he walked in.

She stood abruptly, torn between her pleasure at Sarita's correct answer and annoyance at the uninvited interruption. "Do you need something, sir?"

"I do."

The children were silent again, the funny clown forgotten. The picture was laying on her desk, and the man glanced at it briefly before he introduced himself. Jamie thought it odd that he seemed bothered by the formality of an introduction, as if he was used to whisking into classrooms without one.

"Daniel Salinas." He did not extend his hand.

The students were deathly quiet. Jamie had the horrible feeling they knew what was happening before she did.

"United States Immigration and Naturalization Service." The patch on his mud-brown cap said U.S. Border Patrol.

He was moving toward the children, but Jamie stopped him with an extended hand. "Hello. I'm Jamie Forrester. I'm the teacher and I'm in charge of this classroom."

She was sharp with him because he frightened her. Actually, she had been frightened all morning. Probably more frightened than the children. "I'd like to know why you find it necessary to interrupt my class."

For a moment, as she watched him, she caught a glimpse of regret in his eyes. But then it was gone, and in its place was a guardedness as he spoke to her. "Don't tell me," he said lightly. "Another new teacher. From *el Norte*." The north.

"Yes," Jamie said proudly. "Dallas." The city had been her home all her life, and she loved it. But she was saddened by it, too, by the materialism of people who had too many things and by the apathy of their children. The aimlessness of urban life was one reason she had come to Roma.

"I won't distract you further," he said coolly. She noticed a holster at his side and wondered if he was carrying a gun. "I have a job to do, just as I'm sure you do." The man's eyebrows knitted together as he spoke to her, and he angered her now because he sounded so sarcastic. "I've no doubt you've come here to change these children's lives."

"Perhaps I will try."

He stepped around her and surveyed the children. "I am looking for Gilbert Muñoz. I must take him with me."

"What business could you have with a child, Mr. Salinas?" She knew the one he wanted. The first little boy in the first row. The boy who had said, *"Me llamo Gilbert."* "Must you take him away now?"

"Yes."

"I can't let you do that."

"Miss Forrester." He was growling at her now, like a dog who had sensed her fear and was preying on it. "I suggest you refrain from asking so many questions. Some of them are very hard to answer."

"I am the child's guardian while he is here." Jamie was proud of herself. She was so angry, her fright had faded. "I have a right to ask questions. I have a right to protect my students. I have a right to talk to Gilbert's parents, if need be, before I let him leave with you."

Daniel Salinas glared at her. "I have a lot to do today. You are obstructing a government agent. Perhaps you should reconsider."

"Perhaps you should tell me why."

He glanced at his watch. If he didn't hurry, the boy would have no family left in the United States. The INS bus that crossed the border left from Rio Grande City in an hour. "I will."

Daniel was furious. This Anglo teacher was like all the others who thought they were so grand, coming from a place where life was so easy, where people had jobs and dreams and a chance. As far as life on the Texas-Mexican border was concerned, it was he who was the teacher and she the student.

"We picked up the boy's father this morning after the child left for school. His entire family is undocumented. They are Mexican nationals. They have each signed consent papers, and they will be shipped back across the border in an hour. Since it is our policy not to break up families, I came to your classroom to retrieve their son. Do you have any questions or objections?"

The little boy named Gilbert was rising from his chair, and Jamie moved toward him. The boy cowered behind her skirt.

Daniel Salinas didn't move closer. He was speaking to the teacher, but his words were directed to the child.

"If he stays here, he will go home to find no *madre*, no *padre*, no *hermanos*. They are all going back to Mexico."

"The entire family? You just *move* them with hours' notice?" Jamie was shocked. "This is heartless, Mr. Salinas."

"Move away from the child, Miss Forrester."

She stared at him. She could feel Gilbert sobbing into her legs. But he made no sound. It was the first time she understood their silence this morning. Children like Gilbert Muñoz spent months learning to cry, to play, to live without attracting attention, silently.

Daniel Salinas touched his gun in its holster. He did not draw it. He just wanted her to know the weapon was there.

Jamie felt as if she was teetering on the edge of a chasm, not knowing whether to step forward or back away. The man said nothing more. He just watched her, waiting for her, sizing her up, his eyes jet black, emotionless.

At last she turned to Gilbert. She bent to his level and gathered him into her arms. "Ah, *niño*," she said to him in Spanish. "You must go with this man. It is better that you stay with your family."

"Sí, maestra." Gilbert disentangled his limbs from hers and walked toward the man with the cap and the gun.

Daniel Salinas shifted his weapon at his waist and then he nodded brusquely, without saying more. And, as she got up from the floor and watched them leaving, Jamie thought it odd, how gruff the man had been with her and now, how gently he took hold of Gilbert's hand.

Dear Grandaddy,

I wish you could have seen the look in the little boy's eyes in my class today when the border patrol officer came to take him away. I would have done anything to not have to let him go. I felt so helpless. I guess it won't be the last time I feel that way here.

His name was Gilbert. And he could have been just like all the boys you told me about you used to teach in Renner, the really mischievous ones who invited you to play hookey with them that one summer when the bass fishing was so good.

Only this little boy was so scared. And I can't help thinking that maybe now, his childhood is over.

The officer that came today said they were taking his whole family away. I don't know if they let them take any belongings across the border or not. Gilbert left all his pencils and notebooks here. But he might not have been thinking fast enough to take them. I had to clean his desk out this afternoon after all my other students had gone home. I've decided I'll wait awhile to see if anybody sends for his things. If not, I'll keep them and give them out to some of the others. Hardly anybody has much money for school supplies. Frances Ybarra, the principal here, says that most of the children's parents work picking crops that grow year round in the valley. Most of them send money to families in Mexico. And they still have more, economically, than if they lived on the other side of the border.

I have so much to tell you. Already, I find that the time is going quickly. I found a perfect little house. I wish you could come down here and see it. But since you can't, I promise to send pictures of it. It's near the historical district and it's made of adobe. It's homey and cool and old, with red bougainvillea blooms on a trellis that covers almost the whole front wall. It belongs to some "winter Texans," a retired couple from Kansas who come down here in January to spend most of the winter where it's warm. So I don't have to worry about moving out before my temporary teaching contract is over at Christmas.

Mrs. Ybarra has hired a permanent teacher to come in then. She's a new graduate from Texas A&M. So it works out well. I can come home then and be with you just like I promised.

I miss you so much, Granddaddy. I know you said that the nurses would take good care of you. But you've given me so much during the past years, and I just think you deserve to be taken care of by somebody who loves you. (And if you tell me that any nurse there loves you as much as I do, I won't believe you—so there . . .)

Did you win the domino tournament the day after I left? Was Mrs. Crenshaw's birthday party fun? Did they really get ninety-four candles on one cake?

Well, I'd better close. I have lesson plans to write tonight. (The first of many. Ha!) I think you were right about the kids teaching me as much as I can teach them. I haven't really gotten to know them yet. There's something about the way of life here, everything seems so old and steeped in tradition. Even the children seem so very wise.

I really do have to go.

Much love,
Jamie

P.S.—I'll send you a picture of my class as soon as I can take one and get it developed.

Jamie lay down her pen, walked outside to the patio and stretched. The September heat of the Texas Rio Grande Valley shimmered through the air in waves, the late evening sun moving in ripples behind it as it traveled toward the horizon. She stood gazing up at the undulations of the heat and the endless sky, missing her grandfather.

William Forrester was eighty-seven years old. He had been her legal guardian since her parents had died in a rock-climbing accident in West Texas the year she was thirteen. He had been her best friend and her partner during the past decade. He had cared for her when she was alone and needed him. And now their roles were flip-flopping the way the roles of parents and children often do, but it was happening so much faster with him, because he was so much older.

Jamie walked inside her little house and stared at the outline of tomorrow's lessons plan, scattered across the kitchen table. She was haunted by the day's events. It was the saddest thing she knew of, thinking of children like Gilbert Muñoz, children who deserved and needed an education but who were dragged away.

How often would the INS officer come into her classroom and take one of her students away? The children had recognized the man today. She had sensed their discomfort the moment he had walked through the doorway.

Jamie uncapped her pen and made a note to call the INS offices in Rio Grande City during business hours tomorrow. This time, she would meet him on his home turf. The idea of facing him across a desk again frightened her more than she cared to admit. But she owed it to her students, and she owed it to herself. She had to find what she could expect from Daniel Salinas during the months to come.

DANIEL PARKED the Dodge Ram Charger beside the pay phone on Grant Street and dialed the INS office to get his messages. "Your mother called," the office manager, Martina, told him. "She needs tortillas and vanilla for dinner. She was hoping you would purchase them for her while you are in *la ciudad* today."

"Fine." His mother sent him shopping for something at the markets in Mexico almost every day. The ranch where they lived wasn't too far northeast of town. But his mother used to make the trip when she was a little girl, leading the family's mules. And now she was taking every advantage of modern conveniences. He smiled. "Anything else?"

"Jamie Forrester called."

"Who?"

"She says she met you yesterday. When you took one of her students out of her classroom."

Daniel's smile disappeared. "What does she want?"

"She made an appointment to see you Thursday afternoon before your patrol shift. She says she needs to know what to 'expect from you.'"

"Thank you, Martina." *Great.* Daniel hung up the phone. *Here comes one more brilliant schoolmarm bent on easing the burdens of the border people.*

This section of Texas was like a third country. Everyone accepted it that way, and loved it, too. The area teemed with families who were trying to get along; where tradition meant everything, but reaching for a new beginning did, too. That's one reason it had been so hard for him to whisk Gilbert Muñoz away from Jamie Forrester's classroom yesterday. He hated sending them back. After all these years, the expressions of the people he returned to the dirt-poor *colonias*, to hunger and hardship, continued to haunt him.

Daniel drove to the market then back again, crossing the International Bridge back into Texas from *Ciudad Miguel Aleman*, barely slowing at the customs house. He only needed to nod his head at the inspector inside and he could pass. And when he pulled the truck in across the front cattle guard at *Los Ebanos*, he could see his mother, Harriet Salinas, waving to him from behind the wrought-iron latticework on the patio.

"Thank you, Danny." She laughed as she hugged the son who seemed almost twice as tall as she was. "We had to have vanilla. Lúpe is making flan for dessert tonight. And I can't believe I let us run out of tortillas."

He bent to kiss her. "Where's Dad?"

"Out back with Pedro. They've been dipping cattle all afternoon. Harvey Ragsdale found a fever tick on one of his heifers." His mother shook her head. "It's going to be a big project."

"Let me go inside and get out of this uniform. I'll do what I can with them before dinner."

Los Ebanos had been the Salinas home for a hundred and fifty years, since before Texas won its independence from Mexico. Daniel's great-grandfather had served as the *patrón* of Roma once, a mayorlike position that came to him because his family was held in the highest esteem locally.

The Salinas men had worked the ranch for over a century—Daniel's great-grandfather, his grandfather, his father. And, someday, *Los Ebanos* would be Daniel's, the vast acreages of high brushland that had always been his home, the purple sage on frosted stems, the tangy smell of salt cedar, the sun-warmed arroyo bank carved into layers of sandstone that he had explored as a boy.

The ranch was known for its Simbrah beef cattle and quarter horses. Daniel's father grew melons and cotton, too, on the land that could be irrigated with precious water from the Rio Grande.

The elder Salinas hired extra workers during the months the cotton went to gin. But the operation had dwindled over the years, like many of the smaller ranches, which were less productive now. Daniel helped in the evenings when he could, but *Los Ebanos* couldn't support two owners. So Benny Salinas did the work with the help of Pedro Canales, his one *vaquero*.

Pedro and his wife, Guadalúpe, lived in the ranch-hand's quarters with their son, Miguel. For ten years, Pedro had toiled beside Benny Salinas, tilling the soil and branding the cattle as if the ranch were his own. And it might as well have been, for the security the job afforded him. Guadalúpe, whom they all lovingly called Lúpe, worked in the sprawling house every day, helping Harriet with the cleaning and the bookkeeping on the computer while Miguel was in school. She cooked superb meals for the family every evening.

"Smells good, Lúpe." Daniel kissed her, too, after he donned a worn cotton shirt and jeans. He was on his way to join Pedro and his father in the corrals.

"Get back," she said, laughing at him as she pushed him away. "No food yet. Stop trying to compliment me. I won't feed you early."

"It was a good try, though."

"Out. Out!"

Daniel was laughing now, too, all thoughts of Jamie Forrester forgotten as the kitchen door slammed behind him and he made his way outdoors to help his father.

"Darned fever ticks," Benny shouted as he climbed over the mesquite fence. "They'll kill a cow within two weeks sure. The tick riders must have missed some wet stock." He called the cows that wandered in from Mexico wet stock because, somehow, the animals found their way across the river. It was a way of life they all lived, had lived forever, always knowing of the boundaries and the forbidden things that crossed them, the parts of each place that permeated the two countries here and stitched the two cultures together. Like fever ticks. *And little boys like Gilbert Muñoz.*

"I'll take over for you out here, Dad," Daniel volunteered. "Lúpe will have supper ready soon. You should rest. Pedro will help me."

Benny tipped his Stetson back and mopped the sweat from his forehead with a shirt sleeve. "I'll take you up on that, son." He was tired, but he wasn't exhausted. Still, he welcomed the opportunity to turn work over to his son. He knew the mental toll Daniel's job with the border patrol took on the boy. He was proud of him, of the olive-green uniform he wore, of the danger he faced sometimes because he wasn't afraid to protect the community that had been so good to them all. But, still, Benny watched often as the lines on Daniel's face softened while he worked the cattle, the physical labor a welcome respite from the questions Daniel never asked aloud anymore. "I like to watch you work, Daniel. It's good for you, I think."

Daniel winked at Benny. "Whatever you say, Dad." He turned to the next cow. "Yah!" he shouted as the animal began to move into the chute.

Benny didn't go inside. He sat atop the corral railing, watching his son and his *vaquero* working, calling in suggestions, laughing every time they struggled to dip a particularly stubborn cow into the vat.

"I took over so you could rest," Daniel called to him.

"No," Benny called back good-naturedly. "You took over so *you* could rest."

They worked for a while in silence then, Pedro flapping his arms and moving the heifers into position. And it wasn't until Benny had left his perch beside the corral and had gone to wash up for dinner that Pedro spoke to Daniel.

"Miguel says you came for a boy in his class today," he commented in Spanish as they worked side by side. Pedro never spoke anything but his native tongue. He had decided it was a denial of his heritage to speak anything else.

Daniel prodded the cow. "That's right."

"Miguel tells me the teacher fought you."

"She did."

"Why? Why would a woman question you when you were in uniform?"

Daniel smiled again. Pedro's question was an innocent one. In the culture Pedro had always known, it was not a woman's place to question a man. Daniel was amused by the question's double meaning. *A woman can't say no to a man in uniform.* But this one had. "The teacher is new. Another one from *el Norte*. She is from Dallas."

"Miguel likes her. He likes her because she was not afraid to be angry and to help Gilbert, his friend."

"Miguel had better watch out when he grows up, if he finds himself attracted to women like that."

"He says she is *muy hermosa*."

Muy hermosa. Very beautiful. Daniel hadn't thought of Jamie Forrester as very beautiful. Actually, he hadn't looked at her at all. He remembered only how angry she had been with him. "I wonder how long she will stay here. Not long, I'm betting. She will be like the others."

"She taught Miguel mathematics yesterday. How to add long columns of numbers. He showed me last night. He is in her class because he tests well in languages even though he does not speak English. The new teacher teaches a class where only forty-five minutes is in Spanish. And Miguel learns. Numbers, my son can learn on paper, without the use of words."

They didn't speak for several moments while they worked another animal into the chute. They wrangled with it for a while before it would move in the right direction.

"Miguel says the new teacher's lips are like roses," Pedro said out of the blue. "Red roses."

Daniel threw back his head and guffawed at the typically Latin-American way the boy had expressed himself. He hadn't noticed lips like red roses. "No wonder Miguel learned so much math yesterday. It sounds to me like your son is ready to fall in love."

"He is eight years old," Pedro answered in Spanish, laughing all the while. "Perhaps it is time."

CHAPTER TWO

DANIEL HATED HIMSELF. He was staring at her lips.
He couldn't help it. *I have Miguel to thank for this.*

"Mr. Salinas," she was saying to him, "I cannot
lose control in my classroom again."

"So—" he was frowning more at her lips than he
was at her words. They *were* lovely. "You think you
lost control."

"I want to know how many times this is going to
happen," Jamie demanded as she leaned across his
desk toward him. "How many times are you going to
waltz into the elementary school and take my students away?"

"As many times as I have to. It is my job."

"We have to arrange something then," she said. "A
way for you to contact me, something, so I can prepare the children. You frighten them."

Daniel turned his attention from her lips to her eyes.
"I am sorry, Miss Forrester. And do I frighten you, as
well?"

It was her eyes that impressed him. Round and gray,
the doe color of a morning just before the sun rose,
lined by lacy lashes a shade deeper than her brown
hair.

"No. You don't scare me."

Her nose was nice, too. Long, with just a tilt at the end, perfect with the full lips that were frowning at him. He would have to tell Miguel that he agreed with him. The new *maestra*, though angry, was very beautiful.

He turned his attention to defending himself. "It often has to be," he told her. "You are from Dallas. You take these things for granted. But I am here on the battlefront, winning or losing an immigration war one person at a time. This country has always been my home. It was my great-grandfather's home. My duty is to protect its borders."

"That's a nice, patriotic speech."

He held his ground silently, waiting for her to acquiesce, but she didn't. It was the same speech he had had drilled into him when he was training to become an INS agent—the one most people accepted. Looking at Jamie, watching the storm clouds gather in her eyes, Daniel decided to be brutally honest. "There are times it isn't easy to do. But I don't break the rules."

"But Gilbert Muñoz was just a child, for God's sake. He was sitting in my classroom, learning English. An innocent child reaching for a future."

"How easily you classify innocence. And guilt. You make it sound as if I sent him to a concentration camp. I just sent him back to his home."

"Home to a place where he will be hungry. Home to a place where he will have to work so he cannot learn."

Daniel sat at his desk and began drawing ticktacktoe squares on the notepad beside the phone. He didn't have time for this.

Jamie sat across from him, although he didn't offer her the chair. "Do you have bad dreams about the things you do?"

His pen paused momentarily on the paper. She was way out of line. And, for a moment, he wanted to tell her. That he did have bad dreams sometimes. And the people were often very cruel to him, the Mexicans crossing the river who threw bottles and spit at him and the Texas bureaucrats who always thought he could be doing a better job. "Miss Forrester..." He didn't finish his sentence.

"What is it? What were you going to say?" She had seen something in his eyes, a hint of sorrow, a vague warning, and she wondered if she might have pushed him too far.

"Nothing. It doesn't matter."

"You were going to tell me I was wrong."

"Perhaps I was going to tell you that you were right."

She stood and turned away from him. "Do people cross the river every day?"

Daniel recognized the reprieve and took it, gladly. "The valley has a fairly stable work force. Most of the Hispanics living here have ancestors who were a part of this country long before Texas joined the union. Many of the others, the ones who have come in my lifetime, were productive long enough to have been eligible for amnesty under the new Simpson-Rodino immigration laws."

"But there are others?"

"Some of them didn't apply. They didn't seek legalized status because they were afraid the amnesty was a trap to bring them out of hiding. Or because not all the members of the family were eligible and, if they had applied, the others would have been found out. The amnesty period was a circus...trying to make them trust us, when they had run from us for so long."

"Who comes now?"

"Those who want to live here. And those who smuggle contraband." Instinctively, he touched the gun on his belt. Daniel didn't usually wear the weapon in his office, but he was already late to take his position beside the Rio Grande.

He would work the river until midnight. Each of the agents took turns with the shifts and the duties, so that no one could watch them and predict where they would be from day to day. He found himself wishing he didn't have to go just yet because, for some reason, he wanted to make Jamie understand. "The smugglers are the most dangerous of all."

"Tell me about the Muñoz family. Had they been here long? From my records, Gilbert had been enrolled at Scott Elementary for at least six months."

"We aren't certain. But they weren't here long enough to apply for legalization." It was often hard to spot undocumented Mexican nationals when they had lived on this side of the river for several months or longer. Illegals learned not to attract attention to themselves, and they learned to fit in. They showed counterfeit documents purchased in Mexico—social security cards mostly—and they took the driver's tests in Spanish and obtained a Texas license with no questions asked. "We were lucky with them. We detained Gilbert's father during a routine traffic check this morning. He was driving to work in the fields before sunup with a headlight out on his car. His driver's license was in order. The sheriff ran a check on his social security card. It was forged."

"I guess—" Jamie hesitated, gazing at her hands, not wanting to meet his eyes, "—I can only teach these kids and care for them during the time I know I have them. I suppose I can't ask for more than that."

It was the first time he could agree with her. "You are right, Miss Forrester. In a place like Roma, that is the very most you can ask for."

Dear Grandaddy,
I went to see the border patrol officer who came and took Gilbert Muñoz from class. He asked me if he frightened me. And I told him no. But he did, and I think he knows it. Anybody who has that much control over someone else's life and uses it that way frightens me.

I think he always carries a gun.

I don't know if I did any good by going to him. I asked if he would contact me before he came again to take one of the children. I just feel so responsible for all of them.

The nurse I talked to on the phone this week told me you won three domino tournaments in a row. I can believe it! Not many people around here play dominoes. So I guess I'll just have to wait to come home to play forty-two again. After playing so many years with you, I don't think I'd want anyone else as a partner anyway.

Writing about dominoes makes me think of all the late evenings we used to spend, sitting on the porch at the old house on Greenville, while the water sprinkler was on, waiting for some poor unsuspecting neighbor to walk by so we could play shoot the moon. I still think Larry Crosser used to walk by on purpose so we would invite him.

The katydids don't sing in the trees here the way they do at home. Every so often I'll hear one, and it makes me so homesick for you. There aren't many teenagers in this world who got to grow up like I did, with somebody to listen to them every time they needed someone to hear them. I feel so lucky.

Remember when you went to the Berkner High School football games and learned all the cheers that year I was a sophomore and in the pep squad? I don't know if I ever told you, but there were some girls in my squad whose parents never came to a game. (Of course, there were some girls whose boyfriends never had to listen to your old farmer jokes at the door, either. But I think I've forgiven you for that. Ha!)

The children here are so different from the ones I taught in Dallas. They all want to learn so badly. I guess, for me, all the studying was worth it. One of these days, I'm going to take the time to write my elementary-ed professor at SMU and tell her how exciting it is to teach children who really want to learn. I know the kids in my class really do want and need what I have to give them.

I read over that last paragraph and laughed. It makes it sound like I'm going to stay here forever. But don't get worried. I know you need me, too. (Right. I can hear you now arguing against it. But you and I both know it's true.) I miss you so badly I just want to sit down and cry sometimes. But writing these long letters helps me a lot. And it's better this way, I think, especially since you can't hear me very well over the telephone.

Oh, I've got to finish telling you about the school and the kids and everything. Believe this or not, F.J. Scott Elementary boasts fifteen hundred students, all just in kindergarten through the third grade. Frances Ybarra says they don't even know where all of them come from. Most of them are from families working on the outlying farms and ranches all around Roma. And others come from across the border, although we don't talk about that much. We just teach them for the little time we have them. And I think others must just crawl out of the woodwork. There are so many!

Some of the children speak English well, and others don't know it at all. When a student comes in, he is given a test and rated on a Language Assessment Scale. If the child ranks high in Spanish but not in English, chances are very good he will be able to speak English well some day, too. The test mostly measures their skills in communicating—in any language.

There are fourteen other third-grade teachers here besides me. Some of the teachers conduct their classes almost entirely in Spanish. Then they review the lessons for forty-five minutes in English. Mine is the opposite. All English except for forty-five minutes in Spanish to make certain they are comprehending everything. That way I am sure the kids learn the language *and* the content of the lessons. Last week we worked in science and learned that, when it is cold, water will freeze. So, that way, they learn *words*, but they also learn the concept of tap water turning into ice cubes in the freezer. (That's the closest these kids will ever get to ice down here.)

Right now, we're working on prepositions, pronouns and possessives. And, as soon as I can buy some plastic magnifying glasses, we're going to start on some of the more elaborate science projects. I submitted a request for some to the district last week but I haven't gotten an answer. Judging from everything the other teachers say, I might never get an answer. So I'm going to buy supplies myself. None of the schools around here has much of a budget—the high school doesn't even have a football team! But don't misunderstand what I am saying. There's money enough for the essentials. You should see the room full of computers these kids use. I can't help but get excited when I see eight-year-olds already familiar with a computer keyboard. They are using skills I didn't even learn until I was in college.

I'd better close now, Grandad. Please, take good care of yourself. And know how very much I love you.

Jamie

FELIX GALINDO SAT in the corner of the darkened family room listening to Sarita chatter to her mother in the kitchen.

"Silence, Sarita," he wanted to shout. "Don't even talk of it." But he didn't dare frighten her, not now, while she was telling the story about the boy the INS had taken away.

"It was Gilbert Muñoz, *Mamacita*. He's been in my class since last year. He was really quiet all the time. But he was really nice all the time, too. And when the man in the uniform came to take him away, the teacher almost didn't let him go. She stood in front of him and argued, even though he had gun."

Oh, niña, Felix wanted to say. *I thank God every day that it will not happen to you.* He and Elena had given her such a gift the day they had crossed the Rio Grande into Texas so that Sarita could be born on the other side. But at such a price. In his mind, Felix traveled back over the miles they had trod northward to the shanty in Mexico City, where the little boy would stand forever in his memory, his only son, Jorge, barefooted, toes gritty from playing in the streets, the tears leaving clean streaks on his face, as Elena hugged him goodbye.

"We will send for you soon, *niño*," Felix had called to him. "We will find a home for you and we will make money to buy food. We will save every *centavo* we can save and send it so you can come join us."

It was the only way they knew how to secure a better future. Jorge stayed behind, safe and well cared for by his grandparents and aunts and passels of cousins, while Felix and Elena walked what seemed like hundreds of miles each day with very little water and hardly any food, the sand beneath them so hot it felt as if their skin was adhering to their shoe soles.

They made it across the border three weeks before Sarita was born.

A women's society at a church put them up for several days. It didn't seem to matter where the Galindos had come from, only that they didn't have a home. Felix had heard the stories about the United States for years, how the streets across the river were paved with golden opportunity. Only he couldn't have guessed how long it would take him to prosper, or how many years it would take him to save the money to send for his son.

And even now, eight years later, he feared that he and Elena might be discovered by the immigration authorities and sent away.

In a few months, Felix would have the money to send for Jorge at last. But, meanwhile, he had Sarita to think of. And meanwhile, he prayed for the day when his family would be reunited.

Elena walked into the room, her hands twisted inside the towel she had been using to dry the dishes, with Sarita right behind her, still talking of Gilbert Muñoz. And from the grim expression on Elena's face, Felix knew she was afraid again, too.

"Are you hearing Sarita's stories?" she asked.

He nodded. And then they both stood silent as Sarita went to pick up a pile of schoolbooks and, with a wave, went out into the yard to do her homework.

"It could happen to us, too," Elena said softly after Sarita had gone.

"I know."

"The INS might suspect us when we try to bring Jorge here. If we send too many letters. Or too much money."

Felix agreed with her. "We must be careful. There may be other ways."

"So much is at stake, Felix. Sarita's future."

"And Jorge's, too," he reminded her gently.

Tears filled her eyes. "I could not forget that. My dear tiny *niño*, who has grown into a man without me. I write him, always, and tell him we are sending money for his travels soon."

"I think often of the ways we can provide for Sarita if we are deported," he said. "She would not have to go back with us. She is a legal resident here. We must find someone who will agree to become her guardian in the United States."

Elena was shaking her head. "I will not think of leaving a child behind again. In Mexico City, we had family. In Texas, we have no one."

She was right. The Galindos had many friends in Roma. But they had no family. There was no one who shared their blood whom they could rely on to raise Sarita. "We have no choices, Elena. We began this a very long time ago," Felix said. "Everything moves forward. We cannot let them send us back."

THE CHILDREN STOOD in a line at the front of the room. Jamie called on them one by one.

"Juana, please turn off the lights. Pedro, put the book on the desk. Inez, tell Tomás to draw a circle on the chalkboard. Soyla, tell Sarita to walk to the wall."

They were all busy giving commands and taking them. They were giggling and happy, and Jamie couldn't keep from smiling, too.

It's working! Even the most quiet children are laughing.

Then she saw Miguel Canales standing alone beside the door.

He was staring at the floor. "Miguel?" She went to him. "What is wrong?"

He shook his head and said nothing. He was shuffling his feet and watching his classmates so he wouldn't have to meet her eyes. Jamie swallowed the urge to kneel and hug him.

"Miguel," she said as gently as she could, as all the other children looked on. "The lights." She pointed toward the ceiling, where the lights were still extinguished. "Tell Diego to turn on the lights, Miguel."

Miguel remained silent, looking at her as if he was lost. And then he turned to Diego while Jamie held his hand. He whispered one lovely, clear sentence. "Diego. Please turn on the lights."

His sentence was perfect, his pronunciation almost accentless.

"Very good, Miguel. I'd like to hear you speak more English." Jamie did hug him then, but he was crying, and she didn't know why. "Miguel? What is it? What is wrong?"

He shook his head again. "I am sorry, *maestra*. I do not speak English well."

"Who told you that? You're doing fine."

"I would like to go back to my seat now."

"Your pronunciation is wonderful, Miguel." Jamie nodded. She would not make him stand before the other children and speak a language that reduced him to tears. She didn't understand his unhappiness. Her heart went out to him as she hugged him once more and told him what a good job he had done, then she let him go.

THE RANCH-HANDS' QUARTERS had always been one of Daniel's favorite places. When he was a boy, he had come down here as often as he could sneak away, to hear the *vaqueros* telling their stories about wild mustangs that eluded them or rangy coyotes that had never been caught. It had always been a favorite subject here. The things that got away.

"We never caught the scoundrel," Pedro was saying in Spanish. It occurred to Daniel that the stories never changed. Only the people who told them. "No saying how many chickens that coyote made off with during his lifetime. And you know, when it came time for him to die, he slipped back over the border into Mexico so his spirit would be at rest. A coyote. At rest. I say never."

Daniel didn't comment. He had grown very good at listening. Slyly, he slipped one of Lúpe's pralines off the plate beside him and popped it into his mouth.

"You eat too many of those, Daniel, and they will kick you out of the INS. You cannot chase illegals if you weigh three hundred pounds."

He winked at her. "It will be your fault, then. You should only make these at Christmas."

"I *do* only make them at Christmas."

"It's September, Lúpe."

"Yes. Almost Christmas."

It was true. She made all the Mexican delicacies she could think of at Christmastime. Pralines and gingerbread men to hang on the salt cedar tree, and her own secret recipe of homemade tamales with corn husks. She was as much an innocent in some ways as her son, Miguel. Each year they teased her about her childlike enjoyment of the holiday season and, each year, she started her cooking earlier.

"Pretty soon," Daniel said, chuckling, "you are going to have us celebrating Christmas the year round."

"And Daniel will be too round for the border patrol," Pedro commented, laughing.

Daniel stretched out in his chair. "But what a way to go. Three hundred pounds of Lúpe's pecan candy."

He was relaxed here with Pedro and Guadalúpe, and happy. They would always seem like an extension of his own family to him. Pedro had first come to work for his father when Daniel was a junior at New Mexico State University, studying law enforcement. He had fallen in love with a young woman from Santa Fe that semester. She disapproved of his career. He had been so vulnerable then, and it had been Lúpe who had talked to him for hours, soothing his pain.

"She's right, Daniel Salinas. If she is frightened by what you do, you cannot ask her to marry you and then expect her to sit at home waiting for you to be killed. You must let her go and find someone who will trust you more."

Lúpe's straightforward words had helped Daniel gradually face his pain. But it had taken months for him to lay aside the bitterness over Sandy Matson's rejections. She had asked him to choose between the two things that had meant the most to him, and he had been trapped in an emotional cul-de-sac.

"I won't make love to you at night and make breakfast for you in the morning and send you out to get shot at by desperate men who know no laws on either side of the line," she had told him, handing the little black velvet box back to him unopened. Inside the box was the daintiest, most brilliant solitaire diamond he had been able to find while he was shopping in McAllen. She wouldn't even look at it. "I can't live my life that way, Daniel."

And so it was over. Soon, he'd left both Sandy and Santa Fe behind.

Daniel's first position after graduation was on the border in Douglas, Arizona. He was homesick for Texas, and the INS officers put him through horrible mind-bending drills. They asked him questions he hated, questions he still heard in his sleep after years... *Salinas? Are you tough enough to send them back across the border even though you perceive Hispanics to be your own people?... Are you strong enough to take children or old women back into Mexico even though you know they will be hungry?... Are you smart enough to deport someone even though he may offer you money not to do it?*

Knowing Lúpe and Pedro and the infant Miguel had given Daniel his only grasp of reality during those difficult times. Lúpe sent him tin canisters filled with baked goodies, and Pedro offered him advice even his own father couldn't give, because Benny Salinas had never lived in Mexico. The entire time that Daniel was learning to harden his emotions, the Canales family remained one of his only links to the child he had once been, growing up on the ranch near Roma.

At last, when he was transferred to Rio Grande City, Daniel felt as if he could help them. He gathered the papers together and, after the new amnesty laws took effect, he helped Lúpe and Pedro obtain legalized status in the United States. And, as he guided them to a safer, freer life, he imagined being able to assist others, too—the desperate people he had to turn back as they stood knee-high in water in the river, wearing polyester leisure suits and three frayed shirts, carrying everything they owned and weren't wearing in a brown paper bag.

Daniel reached across the chair and took Pedro's hand. "You are a good friend to let your wife share your pralines with me."

Both men chuckled.

"My day off is Tuesday. Let's dip cattle again that day."

"A good plan," Pedro agreed.

Miguel swung open the screen door and came in.

"Hello, son," Pedro greeted him. "Where have you been? Out exploring the brushlands?"

The boy shook his head but he did not speak.

"Come." Pedro held his arms out to his son while Lúpe looked proudly on. "You can show our friend Daniel what the new teacher at the school is teaching you. You can show him the long rows of numbers."

"I do not feel like numbers." The child's voice was quivering. He had answered his father, as always, in Spanish. But he could have expressed himself better in English. Lately he had even caught himself thinking in English.

"Didn't you learn mathematics today? More addition?"

"No." Miguel's eyes met his father's as he spoke for the first time, in perfect English. "Miss Forrester didn't teach us numbers today. She only taught us how to speak English."

Pedro jumped from his chair. "What are you saying? I don't understand you." But he had comprehended enough. "She should be teaching you your native language. She should be teaching you about yourself." The *vaquero* was angrier at Miguel than Daniel had ever seen him. And Daniel found himself wishing he could slip away.

"No. Spanish means nothing. I will never amount to anything as long as I am a Mexican."

"Did your teacher tell you this?"

"It is what I know."

"You will not deny yourself or your heritage. You will not deny your father. I will not have you speaking English in this house. You must be proud of who you once were."

"I will speak English." Miguel's voice was calm. "In school, everyone speaks it but me. And, in my heart, I already know it. In my mind, I am thinking it."

Pedro raised his arm to strike his son.

Lúpe grabbed Pedro's arm. Years ago, when they lived in Mexico, she would not have dared. But she was an American now. "Wait, my Pedro. Let your son finish speaking. He is growing up. He has a right to take the things we have always wanted him to have."

Pedro glanced back and forth between them, his wife and his son. "He does not have the right to forget who we all once were."

"You are right," Lúpe agreed. "But he will only remember his past if you let him love it for what it was."

"I know who I am, Father," Miguel said, softly. "But I want to speak English, too."

"Not in this house. Not ever again. Spanish is your native tongue. You will use it when you speak to your father."

"I won't." Again, the boy spoke in perfect, unaccented English. Then he bolted for the door. His mother reached out one arm to stop him, but he wrenched free. Miguel was running away from them all, away from the horrible house where his father couldn't see anything positive, down toward his hiding place in the arroyo. His legs were bleeding, for he was scraping them against thorny bushes, but he couldn't even feel the tiny wounds on his legs, so great was the one in his heart.

"I'm leaving." Daniel rose from his chair. "I'm sorry, Pedro." He couldn't think of anything more to say. He was sorry for both of them. He knew what Pedro thought he was up against. But Daniel agreed with Miguel.

As he walked toward the main house, Daniel reconsidered. Perhaps he could talk to the boy. He knew where Miguel had gone. There was a grove of mesquite trees beside the corrals that marked the edge of an arroyo, a chiseled spot in the sandstone where a tiny stream had once run. Daniel had loved to hide once, too, when he was a boy.

As he moved closer, he heard Miguel sobbing beneath one of the gnarled mesquite trees that shaded the corral. "I am sorry, *niño*." He lay his hand on the child's shoulder.

"I hate who I am. I hate being from Mexico."

"Pedro is your father. You must obey him. Trust him, Miguel. There are parts of old Mexico that he loves, traditions he wants to share with you."

"I don't want to share them."

"Can I ask you something? Did Miss Forrester urge you to speak English at home?" He had to wonder whether the boy had been motivated to challenge his father by his infatuation with the new teacher.

"She talked to me. She said she would like to hear me speak more. She says I am very good, almost as good as I am at math. I was hoping, if I did well, it would make my father proud, as proud as he is about my numbers."

"You are a part of two places." Daniel stroked his hair as Miguel continued to cry. "I do not know if your new *maestra* understands that."

"I like my teacher. She is very smart. And beautiful."

"But I don't think she knows about the people here," Daniel said carefully. He did not want to undermine Miguel's respect for the woman, but he had to be honest. Miss Forrester's naïveté had placed a child at odds with his family. "She is an Anglo. She has not lived the culture we live here on the border. She does not know the slow, lazy afternoons, the traditions, the stories. All these things are not a part of who she is."

Miguel got up slowly from the ground and grasped Daniel's hand. "I like her, Daniel. Will you tell her this? That she has made my father angry? Will you talk to her? It would help her to know, then, wouldn't it?"

"Yes. I suppose it would."

"And you could tell her that you are my friend."

"Maybe it would be better if your father went to talk to her."

But, even as Daniel suggested the visit, he knew it wouldn't work. Pedro was so proud and single-minded. And, from their two brief meetings, he suspected that Jamie Forrester was the same way. "Do not forget how much your father loves you, Miguel."

"But perhaps you should be the one to talk to *Maestra* Forrester," the boy suggested, as if he'd read Daniel's mind.

"Yes," Daniel agreed, in spite of his better judgment. "Perhaps it should be me."

CHAPTER THREE

DANIEL WAS NOT IN UNIFORM when he knocked on the classroom door.

"Come in," Jamie called.

Daniel swung the door open and stood there, facing her somberly.

"Mr. Salinas."

The children had all left for the day. He moved toward her, and she rose. "This is not an official visit. Call me Daniel. Please."

"It is going to be hard for me to call you by your given name when you are in uniform." Jamie didn't smile. "You always look so ominous." But he did appear more approachable today, in faded jeans and a soft Western-cut shirt that flattered him. She extended her hand. "You can call me Jamie."

"Fine." He took her hand, and she liked the way his skin wrinkled around his eyes when he smiled at her. But his eyes were ice cold. Beneath the smile, his expression was still controlled. "Jamie, then."

"Thank you."

"I'm here to talk to you about Miguel Canales."

Daniel expected her to be taken aback because he had come to her to discuss one of her students. Or to be frightened, thinking he wanted to take Miguel away. He hadn't anticipated the relief he saw on her features. "Do you know something about Miguel?" She had worried about the child for days now. Miguel had remained sad and unresponsive since she had first urged him to speak aloud in class. Even his math was slipping.

"He is my adopted friend. His father is my father's *vaquero*."

She was shaking her head, still wary of him but pleased because she hoped she had found a kindred spirit who was as concerned for the boy as she was. "Miguel speaks English beautifully. But he will not do so in class. I pushed him once. He did as I asked, but when I praised him, he cried."

"Miguel is not allowed to speak English in his home."

"What sort of person would do that to a child?"

"A father who doesn't want to lose what he had once. A heritage. A very stubborn man. Pedro Canales." Daniel felt like a traitor saying so, but it was true. And Jamie likely had other students in her class whose parents held similar views. "Miguel and his father have had an argument. Miguel asked me to come and talk to you. Since the day you first encouraged him, Miguel has been happy about his English. Yet he is defying his father. I don't think you can ask him for that."

Daniel had expected Jamie to be angry. Instead, she just stared out the window, her eyes huge, and he was suddenly sorry for her. It was as if he saw himself in her eyes, long ago, before he had learned it was painful to care so quickly for people. When she spoke, her tone sounded very bleak, her voice very small. "My grandfather used to be a teacher, too. He used to visit each student in the student's home. I thought perhaps I should do that, too. Miguel's home is first on my list. But the past two nights I've been working on lesson plans..." And she had put the visits off because they frightened her. But she didn't tell him that.

"It would be good of you to visit Pedro and Lúpe Canales. They are very proud of their son."

"He is a gentle, smart boy."

"As are his parents." Daniel's voice was soft, more tender than Jamie had previously heard it. "Here on the border, they call it the brutal bargain. Parents want their children to adapt by picking up drive and aggressiveness from the Anglo culture. But they also want their children to respect the slow pace and the richness they left behind in Mexico. Some, like Pedro, find it harder to let go than others. And the children find that they disobey their parents by obeying them."

"Why did you come here? Do you care that much about Miguel?"

"I came here because Miguel asked me to." He smiled at her then, for the first time, wanting to make amends. "From what your students tell me, the kids in your class are happy with their new *maestra*. You have already been able to teach them many new things."

He couldn't know how desperately she needed encouragement. And, as he grinned at her, it was the first time Jamie had seen anything but hardness in his eyes. She was startled by how handsome he was. His smile was wonderful—kind yet sexy. His skin was burnished bronze by the sun and smooth, the same texture as the wet sand she had seen lining the banks of the river.

His coloring was the only thing that hinted at his Hispanic ancestry—his raven-black hair, his huge, dark eyes, his olive complexion. Daniel's features were typically Texan; angular and strong, yet soft in a way, hinting at vulnerability and boyishness, now that she had seen his generous smile.

"I'm curious—" she noted "—as to which of my students you have been talking to."

"I won't divulge my sources," he told her, laughing. What could he tell her? *You are going to succeed because Miguel Canales likes the looks of your lips.*

She was laughing, too, her anger gone. And there was something about Jamie that made him like her, something about the way she cared for Miguel that made him willing to confide in her. "It's hard for me to accept it, too, sometimes," he told her. "It's as if we live in a third world governed by two major powers that are far, far away. There is a frightening duality on the border. People feel both frustration and delight. Shame and pride. Guilt and satisfaction. But when you are born here, you just learn to accept it."

"Why are you telling me so much, Daniel?"

"So your hopes will not rise too high."

"I can't help it if my hopes are high." She found herself being honest with him, too. "That's why I am here. There is so much for them to learn in so short a time."

"It doesn't work that way. You can't get too involved."

She stared at him. "Is that what you do, Daniel? Monitor yourself and, when you find yourself hoping for too much, turn away?"

It was a brutal way to put it. "Yes. It is something I must do." *To stay sane. To face reality.*

"It doesn't have to work that way."

"It does." Jamie would get hurt, eventually, if she let herself care about the children, or anyone else, too much. He knew it all so well. "Sometimes it's the only choice you have."

She was startled by his callousness. And by the fact that he was telling her to be like him. He was telling her to give her students her guts one day and turn off her feelings for them the next. It was an insane, impossible way to deal with people. "I can't do that."

Daniel put on the brown cap that read U.S. Border Patrol. "I just hate for you to have to learn the hard way."

As he spoke, his voice had gentled once more. Jamie sensed something odd about him, as if there was a border within him, too, a reason he had drawn a line within himself he wouldn't let anyone cross.

"I'll talk to Miguel when I can get him alone," she said.

"It would help the boy."

"You *do* care about him." She followed Daniel to the door. "You are his friend, and he depends on you. Could you pull away from him if you had to?"

Daniel faced her. "Yes. I could." But it wouldn't be easy. It never was.

"Tell me something." Her eyes met his. Suddenly he reminded her of the children in her class when they were frightened. He was stoic...silent. And perhaps sad. "Why do you do this? Why do you act so fierce with people?"

"You don't know?" He returned her level gaze. "I am fierce because I have to be. I am *la Migra*." Slang for the border police. "I am to be feared."

Dear Grandaddy,
I found out this afternoon that there is a child in my class whose father doesn't want him to speak English. The man believes his son will become too assimilated, that he will lose touch with his Hispanic heritage.

I guess this is the first time I've seen how trapped some of the Hispanics are. And I wonder. Can you hang on to the person you once were and still grow into what the country around you dictates you must become? Does that make sense? Sorry. I'm being philosophical.

This little boy's name is Miguel. I can see in his eyes that he comprehends the words I teach him. But if he never has a chance to practice speaking English in his everyday life, how is he going to speak naturally enough to find a job and work and fit into the Texan life-style one day?

I know he can survive down here without speaking English. There are radio stations that broadcast nothing but Spanish. There are Spanish language signs and shops and churches, too.

And yet, Frances Ybarra told me there are some children whose parents complain because their kids are in a bilingual class. They don't want their children in the classes because they think we are teaching Spanish.

The only idea I can come up with is to visit all the families, like you said you used to do. I'll go to each of their homes and meet all their parents, and then maybe I can convince these people to trust me. Can you send me any advice? I guess you just take every day as it comes and care for the kids as much as they'll let you care. Although I've been told differently. I've been told that it hurts too much to do things that way. But you know me. I often have to find things out the hard way.

Thank you so much for sending your old globe. I had been dying to have one. But after Frances had to turn down my request for the magnifying glasses, I didn't want to ask for anything else. I know how much you love that old globe and how many years you used it. I almost didn't let the children touch it at first. But then I started looking closer, and I saw all the places at the bottom where the lettering was worn off from little hands turning it. How many children from Renner used it? So I decided my kids could use it, too.

They were so excited when I showed them Texas on the globe. Then I showed them Rio Grande and tried to pinpoint Roma. Several of them wanted to find Mexico, too. And one little girl, Sarita, found Mexico City for us. She says she has some family living there.

Once again, I must close. Is it cooling off any up there? It is so warm here all the time. It's hard to believe that the fall is going so quickly. I love you so much, Grandad. Send me any advice you can think of. I need all I can get!

Take good care of yourself for me.

Hugs,
Jamie

IT WOULD HAVE BEEN DARK in the old shanty, except
for the moonlight. It poured in through the cracks in
the old roof and fell in eerie patchwork patterns
against the weathered floor. An ancient dog wandered in through the open door and plopped down
with a groan onto the rag rug beside the bed.

The dog's sounds did not awaken Jorge. He had already been awake for hours. His limbs were aching
from lack of movement. But he didn't want to stretch
or turn and risk waking the cousins who were flank-
ing him.

Eight years ago, this sleeping arrangement had been
fun. But they had all grown since then, from tiny boys
into teenagers. And now the bed was filled with a tan-
gle of arms and legs and an occasional chicken or two
that wandered in from the coop outside.

Jorge didn't move now. He scarcely let himself
breathe. If he woke the rest of them, they would be
mad at him the entire next morning. They were like his
brothers. And their mothers and fathers were like his
own parents, too. They had welcomed him into their
extended family long before his mother and father had
left and gone to Texas.

He couldn't help the tears that escaped from beneath his lashes. He felt so alone sometimes. And he
was supposed to be so grown up now. He was supposed to be a man. But his sadness was never as strong
as it was right now, just after he had heard from them
again.

The letter from his mother had come today. And, as
always, she had written in it that they were making a
way for him to travel to *el Norte*.

He hated himself for giving up hope. His father had always said that they would send for him soon. *Soon.* That had been eight years ago, when he had almost been too little to understand. And, still, he remembered everything.

He remembered his father standing in the road, scarcely daring to look at the shack where they all lived, never once meeting his son's eyes, as he waved goodbye. It was his mother who had hugged him one last time, and he would never forget the smell and feel of her, the firm, encompassing arms as she reassured him, the scented mixture of salt from her tears and cinnamon.

She wrote of Sarita now, how his little sister was growing. He supposed his *mamacita* had been fat when she left, from carrying the baby. But he only remembered her as soft and warm and loving him. She had provided a security he had never felt since.

And, now, his childhood was gone, too.

"Oh, *Mamacita*," he whispered just barely, needing to say the words aloud, needing someone to hear them. "Oh, Papa. I know why you left me behind. They have told me over and over again here that you did it to keep me safe." The bare mattress beneath his head was wet from his crying. He did not have a pillow. "But I would give away all of my safety just to be with you."

JAMIE WALKED TOWARD Grant Street, taking stock of the tiny houses and the storefronts, pausing every block or so to check her progress against street signs. As she surveyed the little town that seemed so different from the suburb of Dallas where she'd grown up, she couldn't stop thinking of Daniel Salinas.

Why should I fear the man?

It was a question Jamie had asked herself often since she'd met him.

She didn't know the answer. There was something about Daniel, something about the sadness he seemed to carry around with him like a burden, that made her unwilling to judge him according to his own words. He had come to her trying to help Miguel. Somewhere, some place deeply beneath the intimidating olive-green uniform, was a flesh-and-blood person. The Daniel Salinas she wanted to know.

She finally came to the address she had been looking for. Jamie had decided to visit the home of each of her students, but it was a long, grueling process. She had already kept appointments with many of the families. Miguel's family was too busy on the ranch where they lived, dipping cattle, to see her. Today, she was visiting Sarita Galindo.

The girl's parents both worked all day, her father at a furniture factory in Rio Grande City, and her mother in cauliflower fields that belonged to one of the larger corporate growers in the Rio Grande Valley. They didn't have a telephone. Jamie had written a note in Spanish for Sarita to deliver home to her family and she'd received a lovely reply in return. Tonight at six-thirty, she would have supper with them.

Jamie had wanted to decline the meal. But Sarita had been so excited all day, flitting around the class-room and raising her hand to answer questions so many times that Jamie had to consciously call on the other children, that it had been impossible not to accept.

"Thank you for letting me come meet your family." She hugged Sarita when her student met her on the front walkway. "I've been excited about it."

A woman appeared behind Sarita in the doorway, a beautiful woman, although weathered, with kind, dark eyes like Sarita's. "Welcome. I am Elena Galindo." The woman's lilting Spanish accent made even her English sound melodic. "Come. Come."

The house was a small one, much like Jamie's, the cool adobe interior a respite from the constant heat outside. In the foyer, a statue of the Madonna praying stood in a tiny alcove.

"It's beautiful," she whispered to the child, who was clinging to her hand.

"Thank you." Sarita beamed. And then she nodded at the man who waited quietly in the next room for them to enter. "*Está mi maestra,* Papa. Miss Forrester."

"Hello," he said, and Jamie was struck by the fact that Sarita was the only one who spoke loudly in the house. Her mother and father always whispered. "I am Felix Galindo."

The house smelled wonderful, like cinnamon and chocolate and *chili ristras*. A massive loom with spools of brightly colored yarns stood in the corner of the family room.

Sarita saw her gazing at it. "Mama makes serapes," she explained. "She sells them at the stores here in Roma."

One hung on the wall beside the loom, a huge orange and brown serape with spidery fringes at each end. "The people in my family who came before me taught me how to weave them," Elena said. "It is a part of who I am. My past. Yet the money I make selling them helps buy clothes for Sarita to wear to school. It is my future. Now, I am teaching my daughter."

Jamie fingered the wool beside her, so tightly and perfectly intertwined. "It is lovely work." There was something about the garment that made her think of her life with her grandfather, of the parts of his life he had shared with her. There was something about the obvious craftsmanship that intrigued her, as well as the idea that the skill had been passed down for so long, from an ancient family perhaps, from mother to daughter.

Jamie had noticed many serapes decorating homes in Dallas. And she knew they cost a fortune at the little shop in Olla Podrida and at the West End Marketplace. None of the serapes she had seen in the city were as pretty as Elena's.

"Have you thought of selling these in Dallas or Houston? Your work is better than what I've seen there. You could make more money..."

"Oh, no." The woman was horrified, and Jamie didn't understand why. "I couldn't do it. Ever. I would be too..." She stopped.

What word had she been searching for? Vulnerable? Visible? Jamie began to realize what Elena must be saying. Adeptly, she changed the subject.

"My family didn't have a tradition like this one. My mother and father died when I was just a little older than Sarita. I lived my teenage years with my grandfather. He's the one who taught me how to play dominoes and how to fish."

She missed him so much. It was hard to make other people understand how close they had been. "I wish he could meet you. He would love to see both of you working at your loom."

Sarita grasped her hand again. "Would you like me to teach you? You could do it, too. You could make one for him."

"Ah, *niña*." Felix Galindo came up behind his daughter and hugged her. "Do you think you already know enough to teach someone else how to weave?"

"I can try." Sarita was practically jumping up and down.

"We'll begin after supper then," Elena called from the kitchen. "The meal is simple, *Señorita* Forrester."

They sat down to a kettle full of fragrant dark stew thick with fresh vegetables and cinnamon gravy and chunks of beef and a huge plate of corn tortillas. And afterward they went to the massive loom, while Felix sat in the one fat chair in the corner to read the newspaper.

Sarita manipulated the three sets of strings on the vertical loom with a bowed wooden tool. She identified it as the shuttle. "What color should we make it? What does your grandfather like best?"

"He likes red. Can we make it red?"

Elena handed her the red yarn, and Sarita began sliding the shuttle between the rows. "You do it this way," she explained exuberantly while her mother watched and she demonstrated. "This makes either the front or back row of yarn pull forward. Then it makes the wool go between the rows."

"Do you always know what it's going to look like when you begin?"

"No," Elena answered. "You work in your mind. And as a pattern begins to appear in your head, you change the yarn. You start with an idea...use intuition...let the pattern show you itself what it wants to do."

"It sounds like life."

"A weaver learns much about life while she works."

Sarita worked for a while longer, then moved back, beckoning Jamie to take a turn. Jamie fumbled for minutes, concentrating on the things Sarita had told her about the yarns. She moved the shuttle the exact way she had seen Sarita do it...in...out...in...out.

"You have seen serapes at places in Dallas?" Elena asked while she worked. "What do people pay for them there?"

"About forty dollars," Jamie told her.

"In the markets here, all sizes sell for six dollars."

"You could do better than that, Elena. You could start your own business, contact buyers in Houston or San Antonia or Dallas, show them your work..."

"It would not be possible for me," the woman said, her musical accent softening her words. "I cannot bring attention to myself that way."

"Elena." Jamie turned from the loom and gripped the woman's hands. She didn't know if she dared ask the question. But she needed to know the truth, to help Sarita, if someday Daniel Salinas came to the classroom to take her, too. "Are you a legal resident?"

Elena did not lift her eyes. Instead, she reached her arms toward her daughter. "Sarita is a United States citizen. We crossed the border while I was pregnant. It was the best gift we could give our new baby."

"We have learned to live our lives quietly," Felix joined in, although Jamie hadn't realized he'd been listening. "If we are robbed, we can never call the police. We have driver's licenses and our own home. My employer deducts social security and income tax from my paycheck. It is money I will never see again."

"But you could be sent back."

"We will not be sent back unless we are caught crossing the border or are stopped for some reason. The INS agents here ask us no questions. They question only those who are suspect."

"Thank you for telling me." Jamie felt as if she was beginning to see why Daniel had told her that she couldn't understand life in Roma.

"I have a brother who lives in Mexico City with my aunts and uncles and grandfather," Sarita said. "Mama and Papa knew he was too little to make the trip on foot when they came to Texas. Sarita was eight now. That meant the boy had been only five when they'd left him. "You've been here a long time now," Jamie commented, not asking, just wondering what it must have been like to travel to a different world, as they had, and to have left a beloved son behind.

Quietly, she prayed that she would never have to know.

MORE THAN ANYTHING, Daniel hated feeling inade-quate.

He hated knowing there would never be enough INS officers to stem the tide of Mexican nationals. The border between the United States and Mexico stretched for nineteen hundred miles from the Pacific Ocean to the Gulf of Mexico. Thousands traveled across it each day. The INS employed thirteen hundred men.

As Daniel walked the dusty stretch of high brushland this morning, his mind was on the futility of many things. He thought of Pedro's life before he had come to Texas, a life that didn't exist any longer...of Miguel and the things he wanted to find for himself...of the things he had said to Jamie. And, because he was thinking of so many things, Daniel missed his cue.

He looked up from his hiding place to see at least fifty men crossing the river. Daniel was too far from his truck to radio for a backup. And one wouldn't have gotten there in time, anyway.

He did the only thing he knew to do. He stepped out from behind the thorny bush and trained his handgun on one of them. "You are crossing into the United States illegally," he snarled. "Turn back immediately."

They laughed at him. They laughed at the gun. It was the way more and more of them crossed recently. Together, their strength was in their numbers.

"You are breaking the law. Do not come farther. You will be detained."

One of the men at the front of the group shouted something obscene in Spanish. Then he spit on Daniel. And, this time, when Daniel continued to hold his ground and brandish his gun, the other men spit, too, then they bent to throw rocks and their shoes.

It wasn't until Daniel fired a warning shot that they began to run toward him, crashing around him like a herd of stampeding antelope, the water flying from their feet. They scattered in every direction, smashing through the underbrush like frantic animals. Daniel was helpless against them. Other than shooting a few, he could do nothing.

He managed to round up four of the older men. He handcuffed them and marched them to the truck while they swore at him. And after he drove them to the Rio Grande City station, he trudged to his office to finish the paperwork.

In his neat printing, Daniel explained how forty-some-odd men had escaped him into Texas. And, as he wrote the report, he could feel the men's saliva running down his face once more.

Daniel decided not to mention the spitting or any other indignities. Several of the shoes and stones had grazed him in the shoulders and on the groin. He knew his chest was bruised.

Daniel set the pen on his desk and ran fingers through black hair that would have been shiny as gunmetal if he hadn't been covered with dust. God, what was he doing? *Being who I have to be. Doing what I have to do.*

When Jamie knocked on his door, he didn't bother to look up. "Yeah? What?" he asked roughly.

She almost gasped when she saw him. He looked gaunt, haunted. And she had to swallow the urge to run to him and hug him to her, the way she would have hugged a child. "Daniel? Are you okay? What happened?"

"I'm fine," he told her abruptly. He frowned. "Just nursing some war wounds."

Why does the woman make me feel as if I'm fighting for myself against her?

"Do you get war wounds every day?"

"Only when I'm lucky."

For some reason, Jamie wanted to touch him, to make everything better for him, only she didn't know how. He slumped against the desk, his fatigue evident. And she was surprised, for even though she wouldn't have wanted him to know, she felt sorry for him. "I can come back."

He glanced at her at last. She looked every bit the maiden schoolteacher just then, with her wispy brown hair swept back into a French braid, a few unruly strands escaping around her ears. She was wearing a tailored linen suit that must have cost a fortune at some exclusive Dallas store.

Unconsciously, Jamie swiped a stray hair away from her face. "You will want me to stay, though. I figure you're going to enjoy this. You might not want to wait for it."

"Wait for what?"

"My apology."

"I wasn't expecting one." He was thinking of Miguel again. Maybe she had thought of something he could do to help the boy. "It is Miguel?"

She shook her head. But her heart softened. "It's all of them, Daniel. Every child in my class. I've been visiting their homes as my grandfather suggested." For a moment she was tempted to tell him about Sarita's

family, about the hardships Elena and Felix Galindo
had endured for the sake of their daughter. But then
she remembered who he was.

He could send them away if he knew.

She was overwhelmed as she thought of it. There
must be hundreds of them here, people like the Galindos, who quietly fit in with life in Roma, who knew
Daniel. "The last time we talked," she said, choosing
her words carefully, "I accused you of being insensi-
tive. Maybe now I understand some of the reasons you
have to cut yourself off emotionally from them."

"So you're beginning to agree with me."

"No. I do not agree with you, Daniel. But I think it
only fair to try to understand you. That is what I am
doing. Trying to understand."

He sat in his chair without speaking.

"I wanted you to know. Daniel..." Jamie suddenly wanted to tell him more, but she didn't know
what else to say. He looked ravaged. And, when he
noted the indecision in her expression, he smiled at
last.

"It's okay, Jamie." He didn't know why, but he
found himself wanting to detain her. Being with her
made him forget things—his fatigue and the futility of
his job and the way it felt to watch forty illegals
scramble away from him and vanish into the Texas
brushland. "It's enough for me. Enough that you're
trying to understand."

"I did the right thing, then."

"You haven't visited Miguel Canales yet." He knew
she hadn't come to *Los Ebanos*. Miguel and Pedro
would have both told him about it.

"No. Miguel keeps telling me his father is busy dipping cattle."

Daniel raised his eyebrows. The boy had come up with a good excuse. "He is. He and my father have been running cattle through the vats late into the evenings. Fever ticks." But he had to wonder how much of the snub to Jamie was because of the cattle and how much was because of Pedro's stubbornness.

"Miguel was one of the first children I wanted to visit."

Daniel picked the pen up from his desk and rolled it between his palms. "I may have an idea." He studied her, then grinned. "I say we give Pedro Canales a surprise." He was looking past Jamie now, out the window, thinking of a boy who deserved at least as much as Jamie was willing to give him.

"Just what idea are you proposing?" It was impossible not to respond to Daniel's sudden shift in mood, the mischievous gleam in his eyes.

"Next Saturday is a national holiday in Mexico. November second. *El Día de Los Muertos.*" The Day of the Dead.

"Oh." She had been expecting something cheerier.

"Many Hispanics believe that, on *El Día de Los Muertos*, their deceased loved ones come back to earth to walk among them. They plan everything wonderful they can think of that day so the departed ones will have a good time and know how much they are missed."

"Sounds interesting."

"We'll eat like there's no tomorrow at the main house, then we'll go to the cemetery for a picnic. There'll be music and games and dancing." November second had always been just a holiday for Daniel, a day when he stopped more people than usual crossing the river, both going and coming, because many of the illegals traveled to cemeteries in Mexico to visit their dead relatives. But this year he had finagled a day off. And it suddenly sounded like a celebration to him, thinking of sharing it with Jamie. "It would be good for you to see it. It will give you the opportunity to talk with Pedro Canales about his son. Perhaps he will soften toward you if he sees you enjoying a Hispanic holiday he holds dear. I think it's worth a try."

"I think so, too." Jamie sat in the chair opposite him, gripping her purse in her hands, her composure gone. "I'm willing to do anything to help Miguel, Daniel."

She won't be willing for long. This is going to help her. But it may hurt her, too.

And, as Jamie stood to go, she didn't notice, but he suddenly looked sad.

CHAPTER FOUR

FELIX KNEW HE COULDN'T do anything to arouse suspicion. That was the most difficult thing of all. Contacting people without contacting them. The future of his family was at stake. If the wrong person found out what he was doing now, everything he and Elena had worked for would be gone.

He picked up the telephone receiver and dialed the number. A man he worked with at the furniture factory had given it to him. He was standing in the phone booth outside a fast-food restaurant. He didn't want to be where anyone watching could trace him.

"Elizando here," a gruff voice on the other end of the line answered.

"Yes. Ah..." Felix hesitated and suddenly realized he was very, very afraid. "A man I work with gave me your name. I am trying to...reach...a relative in Mexico City."

"And you want me to reach this person for you?"

"Yes. I do."

"Do you have money?" the voice asked.

"I do. My wife and I have been saving it. It is for our son."

"And how do you know who I am? Who gave you this number?"

"Someone else who used your services." Felix did not want to give his friend's name. "Someone who works with me at the furniture factory." He was willing his voice to sound calm. "We have waited for eight years to bring our son home."

The voice was unrelenting. "And how do you prove that to me? How do I know you are not with the INS?"

Felix wondered if the INS had called on Elizando before. "Why is it that you do not trust me?"

"I do not trust anyone."

Felix didn't know if he trusted anyone, either. But something about the way the man said the words made his gut seem to curl up inside of him, to crouch in warning, like a snarling cat. "I will not give you my money, then."

Elizando was instantly cooperative. "We must make some arrangement. You can meet my men in Brownsville. They will determine the extent of your trustworthiness."

Felix was ready to hang up the telephone. But he had no choice but to place his faith in the voice of the man he could not see. He and Elena had fought too hard to back away now. And, if Elizando would not help him, he did not have anywhere else to turn. He was silent for a long while. And then, at last, he spoke. "Very well, then. I will meet with your men. You name the time."

"Listen carefully," the voice told him as Felix's emotions moved in a cycle of apprehension, then excitement, then relief. "Do you have a pencil? Some paper? I will outline the plan."

Dear Grandaddy,

I'm sending you a picture of my class. I took it last week. Be sure to find everybody. Look for Miguel and Sarita and Diego and Juana. Maybe, if you memorize everybody's name, you can hang it on the wall in your room and tell all the nurses you have twenty-five great-grandchildren. Ha! Although you might have trouble convincing the nurses of that. The children are darling, but they don't look a thing like you.

I am making you a Christmas present. Sarita is teaching me how to do it. I can't tell you anything more or it won't be a surprise. But I think you'll be very happy. Now I really can't wait for Christmas to come! (Except I still have so much work to do.)

I'm visiting my students in their homes. And I'm really finding ways I can help them. That takes lots of time. But soon I will have made my way through all of them. I'm going out to a ranch called *Los Ebanos* to celebrate *El Día de Los Muertos*. I will meet one of the last families then. Daniel Salinas, the INS agent who took Gilbert Muñoz out of my class, has invited me. Miguel's parents live on his family's ranch. Miguel's father is Daniel's father's *vaquero*. It is strange how people's lives are intertwined here. People who should be enemies are friends. And the other way around, too.

I talked to Frances Ybarra not long ago, and she told me all about her life. She used to be a student right here at F.J. Scott. Her parents were migrant workers at one of the little farms. And

she vowed to study and come back and help other
children the way her teachers had helped her. So
she went to Pan-American and then got a job
teaching here. Now she is the principal. She loves
these children so much. And she's done so well
with her life. She has two children of her own at
this school right now. We were going down the
walkway together the other day and her little boy
jumped out of the school lunch line and came
over to hug her. I think of that and I see her living a very rich life. Around every corridor, there
are children and other people she has helped who
love her, all waiting to hug her. I stop and think
that that kind of life is the kind of life I want to
have, too.

I must close. Know how very much I love you.

Hugs,
Jamie

DANIEL MOTIONED TOWARD Miguel. "Why don't you
get that baseball bat your uncle sent from Chihua-
hua? We'll practice a bit. I know I can find an old
softball around here somewhere." He still had one
tucked away in his closet that he'd kept since boyhood. He knew right where it was. And maybe it was
time he brought it out again. "We'll practice hitting
before lunch."

Daniel had played on a team once, a long time before, when he was in junior high. He and his best
friend, Raphael.

Raphael had been the best pitcher in Starr County,
even when he'd been just eleven and the older boys

thought he was too young to play in the Roma league. But they had cheerfully invited him to join the team after they saw him throw his lightning curve ball. In fact, they had *begged* him to play. And Raphael had told them he wouldn't join the team unless they invited Daniel to join it, too.

He would have played in the major leagues some day. Raphael had that look about him, the wiriness and the tenacity. In school, he talked of it all the time. "If the INS sends us back," Raphael had whispered to him one day, "I will not stay in Mexico. I will come back again to play ball."

One day, Daniel had stopped by Raphael's house to walk to school with him. The house was empty. And so Daniel waited. But Raphael never came back.

There were rumors. An INS officer had tried to hurt his little sister. Raphael had fought for his sister's honor. The agent beat Raphael. Raphael was injured. He did not survive the long trek by foot to his home in Durango, on the central plateau of Mexico.

Through the window, Daniel saw Miguel running onto the front lawn, bat in hand. The baseball program in Roma had died not long after Raphael was sent away. No one had seen fit to resurrect it since. Boys Miguel's age only dreamed of playing on a team.

"This is it." Daniel dusted off a spot in the Bermuda grass with his shoe. "This is home plate. Stand like this. That's right. With your hands on the bat, right one above the left."

Miguel concentrated and positioned his hands.

"That feel okay?"

The boy nodded.

Daniel pitched to him for twenty minutes. Miguel whacked some of the balls soundly, some he missed and some were just bad pitches that made them both laugh.

He saw Jamie's car turn in through the black wrought-iron gates just as he threw a low ball toward Miguel. It swerved off to the right. Miguel missed it.

Benny lay down his latest edition of *Southwest Farm Press* and eyed Jamie's funny old import. The vehicle was pinging loud enough for all of them to hear it coming.

"A friend of Danny's." Harriet patted her son's arm. Then she whispered to him. "You are doing the right thing. It will be good for all of them."

"I hope so," he whispered back.

Jamie cut the engine and waved at Daniel.

"Está mi maestra!" Miguel ran to the car as soon as he recognized Jamie, with Daniel right behind him. And when she swung her jean-clad legs from the front seat and stood to greet him, Daniel couldn't keep from staring at her.

"Hello, Miguel," she said in soft English, her eyes remaining on Daniel's, reflecting all the uncertainty she felt. "Are you enjoying the holiday?"

"Yes." The little boy was jumping up and down at her feet. *"Señor* Daniel is teaching me to hit a ball with a bat."

"You look nice." She looked different than Daniel had ever seen her before, softer somehow. Her jeans were worn and faded, and they traced her tiny waist, her hips, her long, coltish legs, with precision. "Welcome to *Los Ebanos.*" He wanted to reach out to her, to take her hand, but he didn't.

"Thank you for inviting me."

She had worn little, if any, makeup. Her lips and cheeks sported a glow that seemed to set just below her skin, and her complexion was an interesting blend of pink and tan. Her hair was pulled away from her face with a pink band that wound halfway down her back on her long ponytail.

As she reached out her hand to Miguel, Daniel found himself wanting to shield her from what was coming. She looked so innocent and small. She smelled like jasmine to him, and citrus. And her hair shone in the sunlight the same way water would shine. Daniel found himself wanting to feel the satin texture of it. But he didn't dare.

Together the three of them walked toward the sprawling ranch house and the group on the patio. "So...did you warn them beforehand?"

"Only my mother. I was afraid I might be the next one they were welcoming back on the Day of the Dead," he quipped.

"Maybe I shouldn't have come, Daniel." Jamie stopped walking and touched his arm. "If this doesn't work, I'll leave."

"Nonsense. You are my guest." It was going to be easy to pretend that was the only reason he had asked her here, because he had wanted her company. He was vitally aware of the way she was walking beside him. She was willowy and graceful. Just now, he felt as if he was leading an innocent into a lion's den. The introductions to his friends and family were no doubt going to be uncomfortable for her.

Miguel continually jumped up and down by her side. The child was gripping his teacher's hand as if he was gripping some sort of lifeline. Lúpe dutifully presented Jamie with a cup of coffee and a dwindling plate of pecan pralines. But the woman kept glancing at her husband, who was perched, silent and stone-faced, on a porch glider beside them.

Daniel introduced her to them all in Spanish.

Jamie lapsed into the melodic language she loved. "I have been wanting to meet Miguel's family," she said evenly, with a slight smile. "I have Daniel to thank for including me in such a celebration."

"I invited her here—" Daniel said carefully, as he stood at her side, "so she can experience *El Día de Los Muertos.*"

"She needs to know nothing," Pedro growled from his seat while Miguel's eyes pooled with tears. "What does she care about the way we live?"

"I care about Miguel, *Señor* Canales," she said respectfully, holding the pleading from her voice with difficulty. "Isn't that enough?"

Daniel couldn't restrain himself any longer. He reached out to her and brushed the sleeve of her blouse with his fingers. He could feel her trembling beneath the linen.

"Give her a chance, Pedro," Daniel said slowly, his voice tempered with anger at the man's rudeness. "Think of the things Miguel is learning in school. I know how proud you are of his mathematics." He was indignant for Jamie, who was standing there, helpless and frightened, beside him. "You speak of it to everyone. But what good is your son's knowledge if he doesn't speak the language of the new country that is his home?"

"My son speaks the language I want him to speak."

"I am frightened for you. You are an obstinate fool, friend," Daniel said evenly. "Your son is the one who regrets your decision. I fear Miguel will hate you for it some day."

"Daniel," Jamie whispered to him. "Don't . . ."

Several trucks pulled into the long gravel drive as Pedro and Daniel stood facing off. As a mariachi band climbed out of one of them, waving salutations and holding their guitars high, Daniel dropped his hold on her arm.

"I shouldn't have come," she said so softly that only Pedro and Lúpe and the others near her could hear.

"Do not go now." Lúpe touched her then, a gesture ageless in its kindness, with fingers as gnarled as the bark on the mesquite trees that covered much of the grounds around them. "Only remember this. Beliefs can only come from within our hearts, from a place we once have known. Think of the remembrances that are dear to you. Think of the ones who gave them to you. We hold within our hearts the memory of a heritage that haunts us. Mexico is a country that knows much sorrow, yet much beauty. It beckons us, yet frightens us with who we are. And so Pedro fights."

The band began playing then, its black-clad members each wearing huge sombreros. The men trilled their tongues and sang a song called "Maria Isabel." Jamie stood motionless, listening to the words. It was a romantic song that told of a lonely man on the beach who sees a lovely girl with brown eyes coming toward him, her hat in her hand.

"Let's go inside, Jamie." She felt Daniel at her side again before she saw him.

Wordlessly, she followed him across the patio, away from the strumming guitars and the obvious disapproval of Pedro Canales.

Daniel didn't speak again until they were behind the sliding glass door, in the darkness of the cool adobe living room. "I'm so sorry." He was apologizing for a great many things, for Pedro's response to her, for the disappointment he could see in her eyes.

The protective feelings she evoked in him were not foreign. He encountered them often...when he was talking with Miguel...when he encountered a particularly frail grandfather or a big-eyed child on a frugal trek across the Rio Grande. And now, Jamie.

She has to find her own way like the others. I cannot...cannot protect her, either.

"You don't need to apologize, Daniel." She inclined her head toward him, her pink-wrapped ponytail draped across one shoulder, her mouth in a wry smile that caused tingles of warning to shoot through his body. "It isn't your fault, and you know it. I'm glad I came." She was honored, almost amazed, to be here in his childhood home, seeing parts of the man that *la Migra* never would have dared to show.

"Are you?"

"Yes."

"We haven't long before the picnic." His tone was suddenly abrupt. Daniel was having second thoughts about having defended her so fiercely to Pedro, when his feelings for her were so ambiguous.

"I'd like to see the house," she countered, not understanding his withdrawal. "Is it very old?"

"This original adobe went up in 1866. My great-great-great-grandfather, Agustín, built it. The Salinas family had lived here since long before that, when the land was still a part of Mexico, before the Treaty of Guadalupe Hidalgo gave most of what was north of the *rio* to the United States.

"The Comanches raided the ranch that year, in broad daylight, just after noon. Agustín Salinas was out on one of his horses, searching for a calf that had gotten lost in the black brush. His wife had ridden out in search of him to take him his lunch. The Comanches took all the cattle in the corrals and the horses, too, and they killed the three older children left behind. They burned the old house. Agustín built this one. And my great-great-grandfather was born later that year."

Jamie ran one hand along the old wall, the tempered adobe kept from crumbling by years of whitewash and care. "It scares me when I think of how strong people had to be back then. Everything they built together disappeared in an afternoon. Yet they came back to the same place and claimed a future for themselves.

"Is it strength? Or is it just human nature?" he asked. "I see people who do that every day." Jamie was that strong, too, or she would be, he guessed, only she didn't know it.

"I've always taken this for granted." It was something you would read in a storybook or a tale you would hear in a museum. She had sensed already, standing on the International Bridge between Roma and *Ciudad Miguel Aleman*, that this was the place where most of Texas's history had begun. And the people who lived here now continued to cherish that history in an almost tangible fashion. "You must come to my classroom and tell the students about the Salinas family. Or maybe we could have a field trip, we could bring the kids here and let them touch the walls and feed the cows."

She was suddenly very excited by the possibilities of the things she could share with the children through him. It was perfect. She was dealing with parents like Pedro who were afraid their children were losing touch with their heritage. She was dealing with parents who didn't want their children in bilingual classes at all because they were afraid their children were learning too much Spanish. These stories, this shared history, were the things that could bind all of them together. But when she turned her eyes toward his eagerly, Jamie was surprised to find Daniel shaking his head.

"I came to your classroom and took a child away. My duty is as a member of the U.S. Border Patrol. I would scare the children to death if I came and started telling them tales out of history books."

"You wouldn't. They would love it."

"But maybe I wouldn't." For a moment, Daniel let himself think of what it would be like, standing before a sea of expectant faces, telling them about a state that, for some of them, would never be their rightful home.

Jamie saw the look of distaste on his face. She had seen the same expression before. "Don't feel sorry for yourself. It doesn't become you."

"I have a job to do."

"You have a life to live. You are a human being, too," she said, knowing full well the things he must be hiding from, and angered by them, because they were the things she most wanted to give the children.

"I am just a man," he said bitterly. "I can't change the rules."

"You are also Hispanic, Daniel. You are just like any of the others who live here and do not wish to go back."

"The people from across the river are different." But take away subtle things he couldn't put his finger on and she was right, Daniel thought. He'd reached the same conclusion himself many times. It might have easily been him who'd been born on the other side of the border. *There, but for the grace of God, go I.*

"How can you take a child like Gilbert and lead him away from every opportunity you lucked into?"

From somewhere deep inside him, the answer to her challenge came. It *had* been more than just luck for him. Agustín Salinas and his son and all the others had fought to make a life in Texas for themselves. He was a product of that fight. Somewhere, won by the blood and sweat of his ancestors was a balance of sorts.

He gazed out the window at the group of family and friends gathering in the yard. When he spoke at last, Daniel's voice was level, revealing none of the questions she had forced him to face. "I will never forget how it felt when I was ten years old and I first decided what to be when I grew up. Every Tuesday, my grandfather and I drove into town to get the mail. The border patrol officers were always there, milling around the lobby right at ten o'clock.

"It was a shift change for them. We don't have them now because there are people on this side of the river we know of, drug smugglers mostly, who wait for the trucks to come back to the station at shift-change time. They radio across the river to tell smugglers they can cross without being apprehended. So now, we stagger our hours. Back then, the stakes weren't always so high.

"I remember staring up at their uniforms, their belts and guns, their neatly pressed shirts and the pocket with the badge. I've known ever since that I wanted to be one of them." It had been Texas he wanted to serve, just like the heroes he'd learned about in school…the Texas Rangers…Sam Houston…Davy Crockett. But since Raphael had disappeared, his boyhood dreaming had turned into a much larger vision.

If I had been an agent, I wouldn't have let it happen. I would have been fair to them. I would have respected their honor even as I had to send them away.

He couldn't tell Jamie about Raphael's death now. The pain within him was too deep to voice the reason for his vocation, too tied to his soul for him to articulate.

"I didn't wait to graduate from college," he told her simply. "I was in my first senior semester of law enforcement at New Mexico State when the INS offered me a job. I took it. And you can't imagine what it was like at first. I hated Arizona. It was hot and dry and almost as dusty as this place." He couldn't keep from smiling at her then, just because she was there beside him, gazing out the window at the ranch, too, listening to his story. He was grateful for that. There were times he desperately needed to share himself with someone. "With my initial INS training came the re-alization that heroes are not often as they seem to be."

"What do you mean by that?"

"My superiors grilled me for weeks. 'Can you send a hungry child back across the border? Can you resist payment of bribery to allow people of your own race into the United States?'" And then he couldn't resist adding his own touch of humor to it all. "But I couldn't help thinking of Davy Crockett and wonder-ing if the man had ever had to be unkind to a hungry child. It isn't easy... being the hero."

"Maybe..." Jamie moved up closer beside him and spoke, her words gentle, her voice strong. "Maybe someday you won't need to be a hero anymore."

The mariachi music was playing again, a lilting Spanish ballad that sounded familiar to her as she re-garded him and, at last, comprehended all the ques-tions in his eyes.

"I don't think so." The timbre of his voice matched her own. "I have to be the person I am."

"The same way Pedro Canales must be who he is."

"Yes."

Jamie thought of William Forrester then, of the things her grandfather had shared with her, a past and a knowledge that she had been cared for by a man who had given life to the man who had fathered her. He was alone now, in Dallas, waiting for her.

This time it was her turn to grasp Daniel's large, rough hand. "You're right," she said. "It is the same way with me."

She seemed so tiny beside him as she slipped her hand inside his, and Daniel felt his guts wrench with a fresh onslaught of protectiveness toward her. And there was something more, as well. He wanted to kiss her, to feel her head leaning against his shoulder, to unwrap the long tassel of hair still draped around her shoulder.

It would be an amusing incident. Daniel Salinas. *La Migra.* Kissing Jamie Forrester. The teacher who had come to fight against him for their futures.

He studied her for a moment, scarcely daring to consider indulging his fantasy. He couldn't turn away from the honey texture of her full lips, which were once again drawn into a smile. He wondered, for one insane moment, what it would be like to taste her, to run his fingers along that stubborn jawline and bury himself in the scent of her, the faint mixture of flowers and lemons that surrounded him whenever she stood nearby.

"Daniel?" she asked, her eyes full of some secret emotion.

He stepped away from her, leading her, their only connection the length of her arm as she reached forward once more to touch his hand.

CHAPTER FIVE

"PICNIC'S PACKED," Harriet called as they made their way through the sliding door to the patio. The band members and a great tumble of people were already loading into the vans, singing. "It's time to move this party to the cemetery."

Jamie climbed into the van with Daniel right behind her. Miguel was with them, too, bouncing along on Daniel's knee and talking about baseball, as the vehicles backed away from the long, low house and made their way across gray-washed yellow sandstone and the sand-dusted road.

They arrived at their destination in minutes, *Los Ebanos's* final resting place, a small fenced plot in a beautiful stand of mesquite trees and ebonies and succulent, white-blossomed huisache.

"This is why they named it *Los Ebanos*," Benny told her as they both helped Harriet carry food to the place the blankets were spread. "So many ebony trees. A long time ago, traveling saint makers used to stop here to buy ebony wood so they could carve patron saints for the ranchers."

The graves were inside an ornate wrought-iron enclosure with a little gate. "Mom and Lúpe came up early this morning to decorate," Daniel told her. They had worked for hours making huge crepe flowers.

They had used layers and layers of paper from Gonzalez Mercantile. Lúpe had spent most of the morning twining ribbons into the fence. The colors were brilliant, blues and purples and pinks and crimsons. The handmade flowers were grouped with them, lining the fence and marking each grave.

"I don't know when I've ever seen anything so beautiful."

Daniel stood beside her while the others readied the chicken and honeydew melons and potato salad, and pointed the graves out to her, the headstones of the people who had carved *Los Ebanos* out of the thorny brushland, the family that had become so real to her as he'd told her his history. She saw the markers of Agustín Salinas and the children who had died, Daniel's grandfather, and Lúpe's father, who had walked seven hundred miles from central Mexico to join the Canales family in Texas. Many of the memorials were marble, but the older ones were made of wood. Names and dates, lives, carved into weathered ebony.

"Look at them," Daniel whispered to her. He motioned toward Pedro and Miguel. As Jamie watched, the man said something to the boy, then they stood without moving, the angles of Pedro's face and Miguel's small body pronounced distinctly in the shadows of the white-hot sun.

"They are remembering other ones, beloved ones they left buried in Mexico, family members who may be searching for them today."

"Somehow," she commented gently to him, "I believe their loved ones will know they have come to a better place."

"Come on and eat, y'all." Benny was quartering melons and slicing grapefruit while Harriet passed out napkins and plates filled with fried chicken.

Jamie was devouring her chicken when Daniel bit into a ruby-red grapefruit half and juice dripped down his chin. "This way of life is contagious," she said, laughing again, as she ceremoniously dabbed at Daniel's chin with her napkin. It was strange how natural and right the motion seemed, when she had only done it to tease him. His chin was clean-shaven and smooth, and a slight dimple appeared as he grinned at her. Jamie couldn't keep from tilting her head and giving him an impish smile.

Daniel had a fine leathery-clean scent about him that she liked. His lips were wet with juice. And, as she eyed his mouth, wondering at the flavors she would find there should he ever lower his lips to hers, he gripped her shoulder.

"Don't look at me like that. It will get you in trouble."

She pulled her gaze away, realizing too late what she had been thinking. "Your chin is still sticky," she said evenly, ashamed he had read her thoughts so easily. "This napkin will stick to it if I rub any more."

"And then I'll have little pieces of paper all over my chin." He licked his lips to clean them.

"You had best go find some water."

"I will."

The mariachis were tuning their guitars once more. As he walked toward her with a thermos in his hand, they broke into a rousing rendition of "La Cucaracha." She spun around, desperate to be silly and break the tension between them. "This music makes me want to twirl my skirts and dance with a rose in my teeth.''

"So do it.'' How like a little girl she seemed with the wistful sparkle in her eyes, when she talked of twirling skirts and dancing. Daniel reached up and snapped a twig off the mesquite branch that hung above them. "Here is your rose.''

"*Sí, Señor,*" she said, giggling, as she did her best to bare her teeth. "I shall dance for you.''

"Has anybody told you that you look like Mr. Ed when you bare your teeth like that?''

"No one has been brave enough to be that honest with me.'' She put the twig in her teeth and then hissed through it at him. "But I probably *do* look like a horse when I dance.''

She threw her head back then, holding the mesquite in place of a rose in her teeth as she spun in a circle before him, pantomiming skirts. And Daniel couldn't keep from thinking she was nothing like the lumbering animal she had mentioned, but more like a deer, graceful and delicate as she pivoted to the music on pointed toes. She stopped herself, then wobbled slightly because she was dizzy, before she laughed with him.

"Ah,'' he teased her, half wanting to reveal the things he was thinking, half wanting her not to guess. Their lives were built on two different systems of beliefs, beliefs that could either unite or divide them the same way the border life often tore apart families. It was dangerous to be drawn to her the way he was. Very dangerous. "The beauty of a graceful woman dancing with mesquite twigs in her mouth.''

Jamie put the branch behind his ear then cocked her head to admire it. "A nice fashion accessory for any man."

He pitched the offending twig away. "Get this slobbery thing away from my ear."

"It isn't slobbery."

"It is. It has been in your mouth."

"I don't slobber."

"How do you know?"

"I'm not a slobbery kind of person." Jamie threw her head back, enjoying the game between them, not thinking where it might lead. "The millions of men who have kissed me don't think so, anyway."

"Well—" Daniel drawled slowly, the teasing smile gone from his face, the thoughts he had fought against before back again full force "—maybe I'll just have to form my own opinion on that one."

Jamie froze. She wished he would kiss her. When the realization hit her, it gripped her with a staggering force in the bright sunlight where they both stood.

I have no right to want this. Not here. Not from Daniel Salinas.

He saw it in her eyes and knew it, too. "Jamie . . ."

She didn't answer.

And because Daniel was the one so certain, so accustomed to the necessity of pulling away when he knew caring would cause pain, he was the one who turned away from her now. "Pedro's been watching you." He and Miguel had been walking beside the memorial stones, placing food on them and little gifts and tiny handmade wooden toys on the ones where the children lay.

"This is a beautiful tradition."

"I know I've given you a hard time, Jamie. I can't really apologize for that."

"I know." She was staring off over *Los Ebanos*, feeling very much a part of it all now after spending the day with him. "I wouldn't ask you to. It's been good for me. I've had to face reality quickly. It's been good for the kids, too."

"I just wanted you to know how much I respect what you are doing. For the children. I know enough to know that it isn't easy."

She turned toward him then, her eyes sweeping the terrain around them before they met his gaze. "Thank you, Daniel."

"You bring an entirely new world to them. You are an Anglo. You bring ideas from children who live in Dallas, who have a life-style these children can only dream about. People like you don't usually stay here long. It's been a long time since a teacher has come from *el Norte* and has been as dedicated to these kids as you are. Usually the children just learn to trust newcomers and then they go away."

He wasn't watching Jamie or he would have seen her face go ashen as he spoke. "Why would they all leave?"

"I don't know. Seeing these kids scares them or hurts them. And so they run away."

And I am running away, too.

The truth seared her.

Only I don't want to. Or am I only being proud, thinking I should stay here and prove I am better than the others have been?

"Usually," he commented offhandedly, "It takes someone who grew up here to care enough to stay."

Jamie fingered the glass of lemonade she was drinking and then set it down on the low table beside her. She took great care to set it right in the center of the coaster Lúpe had laid out for her. "You can't say that someone doesn't care for the children here if they do not stay," she said, and her voice held the same iciness as the cubes in her glass. "What about those of us who only signed a temporary contract?"

He stared at her. "What are you talking about?"

"When I applied for this job here, I was only offered a temporary teaching contract. I wanted it for personal reasons. But you can't accuse me of leaving because I don't care." She hated telling him she was leaving, especially now, after the things he had said and the parts of himself he had shared with her. But she had to be honest. And, even as she defended herself, she saw in his eyes that a portion of himself was closing to her, like the gates at night that kept illegals from crossing a bridge.

"I'm sorry to hear it," he said stoically.

She didn't think she could make him understand the incredible pain she'd experienced when she'd admitted to him, and to herself, that she was really leaving. So she didn't try. But until now, she hadn't realized how much she wanted to stay.

"Don't lump me in the same category as all the others," she said quietly, not knowing if she should raise her voice or cry out to him so he could know that she was pleading. "Please, Daniel."

He did not reply.

Jamie sat beside him then, gazing out over the land that his ancestors had settled, wanting to weep. She had come here today to learn about her students' past, a past she was determined to tie to their future. But, when it came to the future, she knew hers was already decided.

ELENA GALINDO STOOD on the high hill at the entrance to the old plaza in Roma, just outside Our Lady of Refuge Parish Hall. She was facing what had once been the old ferryboat landing on the Rio Grande.

"Elena."

"I will come, Felix."

The couple had walked to mass together, hand in hand, while Sarita followed. The old entrance to the church, where Elena stood now, faced west, toward the *Camino Réal*, the old military road that had been abandoned when the highway was built through town. It also faced the river. Always, the river. The boundary between Elena's daughter and the son she had left behind.

Felix stepped beside her. "It has been a hard week for you. I know. And I am sorry."

"Yes."

They had received a letter from the boy just yesterday. Jorge wrote them faithfully, and every so often he sent a photograph when he could coax someone in Mexico City into taking one for him.

"We will have enough money to send for him soon." Felix gazed across the river, too, its muddy waters golden in the late-evening sun. Three teenage boys were swimming in the center of the *rio*, a black horse beside them as they cheered and splashed, the water sparkling against their olive-skinned backs and the horse's mane.

It should be so easy to bring Jorge across that quiet stretch of water. But nothing was ever as easy as it looked. The trip from Mexico City was a long, perilous one. Felix had never wanted to bring his son to *el Norte* until he was certain he could get him into Texas safely. If the attempt was unsuccessful, it would be a long time before he and Elena could afford to try again.

"Will it really be so soon?" she asked. Jorge was a loyal son. He had not complained that he was the one who had been left behind with aunts and uncles and grandparents so many years before. Yet, in his letters, Elena could feel his sorrow, and she sensed his innermost wishes. She knew her son, if not by sight, then by his words. He wanted to join them in Roma as desperately as they longed for him.

Felix lowered his voice. He did not want Sarita to overhear their conversation. But Sarita was running through the dust with friends in the parish-hall yard playing tag. "I have found a family in Brownsville named Elizando. They have cousins across the river in Matamoros. One of them is a coyote, a man paid to smuggle people safely into the United States. He charges many pesos. Four hundred dollars. I have talked to this man. We are making a plan."

"Four hundred dollars for a ride across the river?" Elena scoffed. "It is too much."

"We almost have that, Elena. And isn't our son's life worth it? The fee is fifty dollars more if we want documents. The coyote makes false papers for the people he brings across, papers that look very real. He makes social security cards and rent receipts and paycheck stubs."

"And so, is the man honest? Or is he dishonest? Do we trust him with our son's life? He is disobeying the laws."

"As are we. I believe the man will be fair with us," Felix reassured her. "It is his business. That is all."

She stared over the muddy water again, toward *Ciudad Miguel Aleman*. The town on the other side was a mixture of cement high-rises and rickety shacks. It seemed like a distant eternity to Elena, bridged by an old suspension crossing no longer in use and a newer, safer expanse of steel and pavement right beside it, with customs inspectors checking papers and vehicles on both sides. Yet, on the opposite river bank, she could see someone's laundry flapping in the gulf coast breeze. "I will trust your judgment, husband. I only hope it is as simple as you make it sound."

DANIEL WAITED until the men were almost upon him before he moved. He rose from his hiding place, gun pointed. "Hello, there," he called out in English.

"Hello." One of the men called back and waved.

"I am a patrol officer for the U.S. Immigration and Naturalization Service. May I ask if you are United States citizens?"

The men looked at him. Not one of them replied.

Patiently, Daniel repeated the information and question in Spanish. This time, one of the men answered. "No. We are not."

"Do you have documents to allow you to be in the United States?"

The men looked at one another then shrugged. The same spokesman answered for all of them. "No. We do not."

"I'll have to take you to the station for paperwork," he called to them, not unkindly. "We will fill out the necessary information for your voluntary return to Mexico. This way please." He motioned with his gun toward the vehicle he was driving today, which stood parked out of sight several yards away.

"Oh, well," one of the men joked as he climbed into the back of the van. The passengers were separated from Daniel by bars. "The aloe vera plants will not rot in the fields today. I can come back tomorrow and find a job to pick them."

"I will be waiting for you tomorrow, too." Daniel knew he probably wouldn't catch these men a second time. But he didn't want the comment to go unchallenged.

"Ah, we shall see," another man joined in. "We have come a far way to find work for the men in our village. We have walked many days. We will not give up until we have money to send back to our women."

Daniel couldn't help thinking of Jamie. "Oh, yes. The women. Where in Mexico have you come from?"

"We are from *La Escusa, Michoacan*. It is our home. We will not stay in Texas. We have only come to make money and take it home with us."

"How many men stayed behind in *La Escusa* to protect the women there?" Daniel asked lightly, thinking it ironic that he had thought so much about Jamie during the past few days, since she had told him she was leaving. And yet, here was an entire community of men come to *el Norte*, men who had left their women behind. For some insane reason, the whole idea made him want to laugh at himself.

"These women are strong," the men behind the bars were telling him. "They will take care of themselves. We left behind only a few old men who were too weary to walk."

Daniel couldn't help teasing them. "Think what it would be like to be the only man with all those women. Perhaps I should let you all work here and I should began walking to *La Escusa*."

And, suddenly, he knew it was because of Jamie that he was able to laugh at himself today. Because of her and in spite of her. He remembered the light-hearted way she had danced with the mesquite twig in her teeth. She was right. She *did* care about the children, even though she had told him that she had to go. Perhaps he had no right to wish that they could spend more time together, that she could become an important part of his life. But he couldn't help it. And maybe the friendship and the respect they had only just found for one another would be enough.

Daniel glanced at the men behind the bars and grinned. "Maybe next time, when you come to work, one of you will have second thoughts and stay behind." An entire community of women left to fend for themselves. Daniel knew it happened often, and the practice had its dark side. But it didn't make the thought any less amusing. He and the men were all still laughing as he turned into the parking lot at the station and prepared to send the men from *La Escusa* away.

Dear Grandaddy,

Last night, all night long, I dreamed I was able to bring you to Roma so you could see it. I know I've written you about it and sent you pictures. But I would love to just bring these kids home, and the school and the little town, and share them all with you. I would give anything if the doctors would only let you come.

I fixed broken desks again yesterday. You would have been proud of me. I went around with the screwdriver and tightened everything and even glued some of the tops together. One of these days, maybe the school district will budget some extra money for new desks. But I won't be here then. So I decided to do what fixing I could do now.

I'm still working on your Christmas gift, Grandaddy. It won't be very long before I come home. I find myself really having to hurry to squeeze everything in that I need to finish. I go to Sarita's house often so I can work on this little project for you. Can you tell I'm excited?

I love you so much.

Thank you so much for urging me to come and spend this little part of my life here. I find that it is meaning so much to me. And, even though I want to come home to be with you, I know I will carry a portion of these children and this place around with me for the rest of my life. I only wish that there were more parts of it that I could share with you.

Fall is moving on. It's almost winter, although it doesn't feel like it.

We have learned a lot about geography since we have been working with your globe. Right now, the kids are learning all about Africa. One of these days, I'm hoping they will all be able to do oral reports. Maybe about the animals that live there. Or maybe we will do some on Texas history. I'll have to leave a note for the next teacher. And I have some other ideas to give her, too. I have to be honest with you. I am almost envious of her. I can only hope she will come and will find the friendships just the same as I have. These kids really deserve a teacher who cares for them.

I must close. It won't be long now before I am with you. Christmas in Dallas. I'm certain it will be beautiful. It always is.

Take care and know how much I miss you,
Jamie

She lay down her pen and stared at the ceiling. She hated writing letters that didn't tell everything. She had tried her best to tell her grandfather everything she was feeling. But she didn't think it fair to burden him with all the emotions that were tugging at her.

Jamie would have given anything just now to be able to bring her grandfather here, to show him a life that she was beginning to learn to love. But the doctors in Dallas had told her a long time before that it was almost impossible for William Forrester to travel. Because he was so elderly, it would have been hard for him even if he hadn't fallen down the front porch steps at their old house and broken his hip.

He had been in Parkland Hospital for weeks. He couldn't remember if he had stumbled or why he had fallen, and before they released him, Dr. Rankin had suggested Jamie move him to the retirement home. It was the first time she had considered that possibility. He had clots in his legs, the doctor told her, and they were giving him a blood thinner. But William Forrester would have trouble walking, and it was going to be very hard for him to be moved.

"Jamie," he had told her when she went to him to discuss it. He could tell she was on the verge of tears. "You are a wonderful granddaughter. But I think it's about time I started hanging out with women my own age."

When she moved him into Oakhaven, she thought her heart would break. Everything was so white and antiseptic. Even the things he brought with him seemed too clean, the underwear she had washed and folded for him, the shirts and one Sunday suit so that he could dress up for special occasions.

He clucked at her mercilessly when he saw the tears in her eyes. And she had come back at him, teasing him, the way she always did. "Don't you dare lose any of your underwear while you're staying at this place. I should have written your name on all the labels with an indelible pen. That's what moms do when they send little boys off to camp."

But she wasn't sending him to camp. The vital parts of him remained at the house: the fishing gear propped against the front doorjamb, the crappie lures, his hunting rifle, the old trumpet he had played in some war that he had used to get her out of bed every morning when she was in school. Jamie had kissed him goodbye. Then she drove back to the house, her eyes so full of tears she could hardly see the road. And when she arrived, it was even worse. The house was so empty it seemed to shout its outrage at her.

Not so much had changed in her life. But now Roma was her place in the world.

She stopped by Sarita's house that afternoon after class and worked at the massive loom, hoping that, somehow, the rhythm of the shuttle as it added to her grandfather's soft crimson serape would prove a balm to the scorching inadequacy that threatened to consume her. But it only made it worse. The weaving was tedious, and she missed several strands of yarn as she worked. Working on it made her miss William Forrester even more. And she couldn't think of the day when she would tell her students goodbye and drive back to Dallas.

She was close to crying as she put the shuttle and the yarns away, then hugged Sarita and Elena before she left.

"*Maestra* Forrester," Elena called out after her. "Do not worry. The weaving will go better another day."

Jamie got to the INS station just before Martina turned the switchboard off for the day. When she walked into his office, Daniel glanced up from the piles of papers on his desk and said her name once. "Jamie..." And the resignation in his tone when he spoke made her feel as if her heart would break. Suddenly, she wondered if he was lonely. Surrounded by humanity as he was, day after day. And alone.

"I don't want to leave. You know that, don't you?"

"I was thinking about it today." He got up from his desk and moved toward her, the papers on his blotter forgotten. She could smell him as he came toward her, the pleasing mixture of spice and sweat.

Even as he attracted her, Jamie knew she had to distance herself. Perhaps it wasn't fair to want him to care for her, because she was leaving. "I only just realized how hard it was going to be for me to go back."

"How long is your contract for, Jamie?"

"Until the Christmas holidays. I just have seven more weeks." There was something about the look of desperation in her eyes that made Daniel long to reach out to her now. She reminded him of a small animal caught in a trap, wanting to run, with nowhere to go.

"Jamie." He moved toward her. And then he smiled. "It's okay."

She stared at him. "You aren't angry with me?"

"No." He shook his head. "Only, tell me why."

"It's my grandfather. I promised him that I would come back to Dallas to care for him. I owe him that, Daniel."

"And so we part as friends," he said quietly. "And it is enough. I enjoyed the day we spent together, Jamie. I enjoyed laughing with you and watching you dance with a mesquite twig in your mouth. You are guileless, honest. I don't meet many people like you."

"I guess I'm just beginning to figure out I'm only human. That there comes a time that you have to step away from something no matter how much you want to remain dedicated to it." She held him captive with her eyes and then, at last, she admitted, "Maybe I'm just starting to realize you were right all along." As she spoke, the tears she had been fighting welled up in her eyes. She hated herself for crying. But it was something she had needed to do for days.

Daniel reached for her then, as the tears wet her cheeks, and pulled her toward him. "Come here, Jamie." At last, he felt the velvet of her skin as he brushed the tears away across her cheek. "Please. Just let me hold you."

She moved into his arms because she needed him. "I'm just one person, Daniel. I wish I could split myself into two different pieces."

"Jamie." He hugged her tighter, comforting her the way he would comfort Miguel if he had fallen. He cupped his huge hand around the base of her head and pulled her closer as he chuckled at her words. "You only want to slice yourself in half? You haven't been here long enough. Sometimes I wish I could split myself into five hundred different Daniels. Then maybe I could do everything I need to do."

She laughed at that, and pulled away just enough to smile at him. "You just want to have enough of yourself so you can form a human chain and stand beside the Rio Grande all day long. If the INS had enough people to do that along nineteen hundred miles of tortilla curtain, nobody would ever get through."

"That's a good idea." He winked at her, relieved to see her smile. "So tell me. If there were two of you, Jamie. What would you do with each of them?"

One of them would return to Dallas to live the life I left behind with Grandfather. And one of them would stay here on the border with the children, and with you.

Somewhere along the way, during their short, stormy friendship, Jamie had decided she wanted to stay in the valley for Daniel's sake, too, to be a part of the history that was *Los Ebanos*. She wanted to teach

Daniel that it wasn't so painful and hard to care for someone. But now, instead, she was proving *him* right.

"I have to get out of here."

"No. Don't go." The gentleness in his voice as he reluctantly released her was so tangible, so different from anything else she had sensed in him before, that it compelled her to stay. The embroidered badge on his shoulder had left an imprint on her face. With one tentative finger, he traced the place where her skin had pressed into his chest. "Your cheek says U.S. Border Patrol on it."

She was standing there, motionless, only a breath away from him. She felt her throat grow tight in anticipation.

"I'm going to kiss you," he said.

She nodded and reached her arms up to encircle his neck. She couldn't deny the physical longing that welled up inside every time she was near him. "I want you to."

Daniel inclined his head and pressed her close again. His fingers enclosed the back of her neck and clasped her hair, tilting her head up. He covered her lips with his own.

His mouth was warm. The sensation of it bound her completely, drawing on hers, caressingly gentle, yet urgent, too, as her lips began to part beneath his own. With her tongue, she felt the smoothness of his teeth, savored the masculine flavor of him, pungent, laced with spice and faint peppermint.

Daniel's tongue played its own rhythm against hers, a primitive dance that made her pulse quicken even more, as she felt his forefinger trace her jawline with feathery strokes. She was frightened. She was ecstatic. She wanted Daniel yet she could not have him, needed him yet knew she had to leave him behind.

When Daniel pulled his mouth away at last, his breath left uneven, warm whispers against her hair at her temples. It was a moment before she could focus on him. And, when she did, he was watching her with charcoal-dark eyes filled with doubt.

"We can't do this, Jamie. Look at who we are." It was too much to ask of both of them now. And Jamie was only just learning how difficult and frightening it could be to care for people when you knew you had to turn away from them.

Daniel thought of Raphael. He knew full well he had built a wall within him since his best friend had gone. There was a border within him, too, very much like the one he guarded with a gun every day. He did not allow many people to push across that boundary within him. And, as he held Jamie, he realized, at last, how easy it would be to let his defenses down with her. And he already knew what that would bring him. Pain. Because she was leaving. "I have to get back to my paperwork. As it is I may be here until midnight."

Jamie saw the warring emotions pass across his face. She knew he had wanted the kiss just as desperately as she had wanted it.

"Daniel?" She said his name. It was the only thing she could say and it was in the form of a question, and they both knew what she was asking. But, for both their sakes, Daniel knew he didn't dare answer. So he turned from her and silently walked to the chair behind his desk.

CHAPTER SIX

THE SALT CEDAR STOOD in one corner, adding a tangy, festive scent to the classroom. The tree had come from the ranch lands. One of her students had brought it in. And Jamie had to admit, even though she was trying to stay detached about celebrating the Christmas season with the children, that the tree was different and lacy and beautiful.

"I've got the star for it right here." Sarita held up the circle of tin foil she had been working on during the past hour in art class. The star reminded Jamie of the tin ornaments that were common in the markets across the river. Sarita had colored it purple and orange and pink. And, even if it wasn't perfectly symmetrical, the star was perfect.

"Put it on," Rudi said, laughing. "Let's see how you make it stay up there."

"I can't put it on yet, you silly. The star is always the last thing. You have to work up to it. The other ornaments go on first."

"Here, Rudi. You can hang these." Soyla handed him three egg-carton ornaments covered with glitter.

"I'll put this on." Eva hung a little figure of the Virgin Mary holding Baby Jesus cut from a Christmas card Jamie had kept filed away from the year before. "This will be pretty, too."

The decorating was going well. All over the Scott Elementary campus, the children were decorating for the upcoming holidays.

"Paper chains go on now," Inez instructed as she held up the end of one long multicolored one. "They should start at the bottom and go in scallops and loop around like this."

"That looks stupid."

"It does not. It's how Mama does it every year at home."

"It's the way *girls* do it."

As Jamie watched the children working, the spirit of the season threatened to take hold of her, too. Christmas in the valley was unlike Christmas anywhere else in the world. A light breeze danced in daily across the delta from the Gulf of Mexico and, except for one Texas blue norther that frightened the farmers and plunged the temperatures into the lower forties, the thermometer was holding at a balmy sixty-five degrees.

Gonzalez Mercantile had piñatas hanging in every window along Grant Street, brightly colored papier mâché ones in all shapes and sizes, donkeys and Santa Clauses and stars, all ready to be filled with candy and hung for parties.

This was the time of year Jamie had always thought things should be blooming. In Roma, poinsettias and Christmas cactus and hibiscus bloomed along sidewalks and up fences and outside the church. Beckoning smells hung in the air from the open markets in *Ciudad Miguel Aleman* across the International Bridge. And the little shops and storefronts in Roma displayed holiday delicacies, too. There were all the

wonderful candy and nut smells of Christmas—
roasted pecans and peanut brittle, divinity and pralines and the beautiful icing-lined gingerbread men in
all the bakeries made for people to take home and
hang on their Christmas trees.

Jamie had worked for hours at Sarita's house during the late weeks in November and in early December. They had almost finished the brilliant jewel-red
serape for her grandfather. And Elena had been right,
the weaving had gotten easier for her. Every time she
made a stitch in the garment, every time she wove a
strand of wool in and out again with the shuttle on the
huge loom, Jamie thought of her grandfather. He had
given her so much.

Frances Ybarra knew Jamie would be leaving Roma
soon. Jamie was waiting until just before the end of
the semester to tell her students. She didn't want to
spoil their fun. Sometimes Jamie thought she was
flattering herself anyway, presuming that the students
would care about her going. Good teachers had come
and gone before. Many of the best ones were natives
of the Rio Grande Valley. But before Jamie told the
children goodbye, she had one last gift to give them.
Las Posadas. The Inns.

The Christmas play was a beloved tradition for the
Hispanics along the border. They each knew the
Spanish version by heart. Jamie decided *Las Posadas*
would be a wonderful teaching tool for the parents,
too. She had worked on the presentation for weeks,
translating key phrases into English and writing a
chorus that would repeat most of it in Spanish. And
she was secure in the knowledge that the words were

so well known that everyone would be able to follow it, no matter if they became lost in the language.

She hadn't told anyone, but this was her way of showing her respect for Pedro Canales and her love for his son. She wanted Pedro to come to the Christmas program and see that she did care about Miguel's heritage. There had to be a compromise for both of them, a middle ground somewhere, a place for Miguel to thrive. The narrative itself would be a choral reading, alternating between English and Spanish. The story was a beautiful one, from the Bible, telling how Joseph and Mary tried to find a place to sleep in Bethlehem the night before Baby Jesus was born. In the play, as in the Gospels, they are turned away from inn after inn until, finally, they seek shelter in a stable.

Elena Galindo had suggested the idea of staging *Las Posadas* to her one day while Jamie was working on her grandfather's serape. The two women had gone over it painstakingly together, making certain that Jamie's translations did not affect the flow or the sense of the story.

The production was now only five days away. And, as Jamie listened to the children recite their lines, waves of apprehension and a growing sense of loss threatened to overcome her. It was all going to be over so soon.

"Poor Maria *y* José" the children in the chorus were singing. "Poor *Niño Santo*. No lodging in any inn nor any room in the hearts of men. Still, still they are wandering."

As the children chanted, Tomás stepped onto the wooden stage they had constructed in the classroom for practices. The boy bent low and brayed, carrying with him the painted cardboard donkey several of them had made. Eva walked beside the donkey. On the night of the performance, she would be draped in light-blue bedsheets to portray Mary. Miguel, who would be Joseph, followed her.

Just as the donkey moved to the edge of the stage, Tomás swung the animal around precariously, knocking books off a desk beside him and ramming into Miguel.

"Aug," Miguel shouted, then he started giggling. "The mean, naughty donkey is attacking me, *maestra*." The children in the chorus began to snicker, too. "Take this animal away."

Jamie did her best not to join in their mirth. "Children," she called out in her sternest voice. By then, the donkey had toppled, and she was able to give Tomás a quick hug. "That was a good try, Tomás. But you've got to let me think a minute and come up with a way to get the donkey turned around on stage without ramming into Joseph and injuring members of the audience. After all, this is a Christmas play, not a bull fight."

She stooped to the donkey's face and whispered loudly into the painted ear. "You are not a bull, sir. You are a donkey. You must be very gentle with Mary and Joseph."

The children surrounding her tittered even more.

"Let me think here. Maybe if Joseph would be willing to move forward just a little bit. Here, Eva. You stand like this. And if Tomás moved back a little bit, it might..."

"He should move forward, Miss Forrester," a voice from the doorway interrupted her. Jamie turned toward it and saw Daniel standing there, holding the door ajar, watching her. His appearance made her feel myriad emotions. Sadness. Joy. Expectancy. Regret.

"Hello, Daniel."

She blushed without knowing it. He thought she was one of the most intriguing women he had ever met. He took such pleasure in the things he had seen her doing, whispering to a cardboard donkey and giggling with the children. "I checked in at the front office. Mrs. Ybarra said I could come see the play practice if you didn't mind." He had come because he wanted to talk to her, to explain why he had pulled away from her in his office. He had so many easy answers. He had come to tell her he wouldn't succumb to the tantalizing force that continued to draw them together. It was too dangerous, and impossible.

"I don't mind," she said quickly, hating herself for how glad she was to see him. "You can critique us. The children are doing very well. Tomás is doing an especially good job. She winked at the little boy beside her. "But this donkey we've hired is a big problem. He's been eating too many oats and he's so fat that he can't turn around on stage without knocking things over."

Her students laughed again.

"I can give you advice." Daniel was smiling, too. It was hard not to get caught up by the children's enthusiasm.

"At this point, I'll take all the advice I can get."

"I think you should move the donkey forward. Have him prance right along the outer edge of the stage. Then, when he turns, have him turn this way so his tail will swing out, and there won't be a collision."

"We'll try it." She turned to her class. "Okay. Let's start from the beginning again. Does everyone understand what we are trying to do?"

"Let me walk through it with Tomás once," Daniel suggested. And, after he did, they were ready to begin rehearsal again.

"Time for run-through number two," Jamie called out. "And this time, remember to walk very, very slowly. All of you. *Muy, muy despacio.*"

"Poor Maria *y* José," the chorus began again. "Poor *Niño Santo...*"

"You are hired," she told Daniel twenty minutes later after the children had filed out for lunch in the cafeteria and she stood alone with him. "You are now the official director of this production."

"Oh, no, I'm not." He waggled his finger at her. "You aren't going to rope me into this one."

"I am," she said, laughing at him. "You can't just come in here and start giving advice without expecting to take responsibility and credit for it. You are stuck, sir."

"I suppose I deserve it," he said, hesitating almost imperceptibly, as if he was teasing her and convincing himself of his new responsibility all at the same time.

Jamie didn't know if she dared to say more. But she wanted him to know what his appearance meant to her, and to the children. "It's good for these kids to know you are touchable, Daniel Salinas. It is good for them to know that you can be a friend to them."

"Do you think so?" The irony filled his voice at last. It was the reason he had come today, to tell her he wasn't touchable, that she mustn't think he was.

"You came for something else besides saving me from my donkey?" She wasn't smiling. And now the way he was looking at her frightened her. She found herself hoping...hoping for the things he might say, but not daring to want them. She *couldn't* want them.

Instinctively, he moved closer to her. "We kissed the last time I saw you..." His voice trailed off. *And I haven't been able to forget the feeling of you in my arms.*

Daniel was trying, as he tried with all the others, to pull himself away from her. But there was something about how idealistic she was that made Jamie vulnerable, something about the bullheaded way she had admitted long ago in his office that she knew she couldn't change her students' lives but that she was going to give them everything she could anyway. That stubborn commitment to the children reminded him of a part of himself he had left behind a long, long time before.

Holding her that day in his office had devastated him. He felt as if he was trying to reclaim a portion of his old self. For days, he could think of nothing except how small, how fragile she had felt when she'd melted against him and he'd enfolded her. "I have come here to fight this off." He addressed Jamie as gruffly as he would have addressed a smuggler trying to bring contraband across the river.

She couldn't help but counter him. She knew the way he was, always obeying the rules and seeing the consequences. "What? What is it you fight, Daniel?"

His eyes locked with hers. "Wanting you."

Jamie's breath caught in her throat. It had been there, all the time, between them, a tangible thing. She knew why he had pulled away from her. She knew it was for the best for both of them. But she couldn't keep from arguing against it for his sake. "And you fight it because you fight everything that makes you feel something and need other people."

"I fight wanting you because caring can be so very painful, Jamie. So very painful when you have to let it go."

She opened her mouth to retort…and shut it again. Jamie wanted to argue his point, but she couldn't. Especially not now, when she knew she cared so much for Daniel and for the children, and she knew she had to go. "Maybe you're right. Maybe it can." But then she tilted her head at him, dared him to prove her wrong, with the defiant angle of her chin. She cared about Daniel and she adored the children and she loved her grandfather. She hadn't severed her emotions from anyone. To her, the caring was worth the pain. "But then, not all people are as intent on guarding their backsides as you are."

"I don't like to take risks." Daniel was furious with her suddenly, because she viewed the things he saw as strengths as such weaknesses. And he was furious with himself, too, for still wanting her although he had come here to tell her he couldn't want her.

Her eyes flashed with fire as she moved closer to him. "If you aren't willing to lose something, you'll never be able to gain anything, either." She jutted her chin defiantly at him a second time, her face, her fury, the soap-clean perfume of her hair, the compliance of her lips, only inches from him. *Step over the line, Sal-*

inas. Prove to yourself you can need somebody with your body but not with your mind. She defied him on purpose, taunted him with her mouth, adding fuel to the fight because, in the end, he would be the loser if he proved himself right. And the effect on him was visible. "Don't you dare come this close and then pull away," she said.

He gripped her arm. And then, as he studied her face, he loosened his hold on her. His touch became the symbol of two parts of him, his toughness, his gentleness, as he released her elbows, and her arms fell to her sides.

Jamie laced her fingers around his back, and he cradled her against him, his hands huge and tan and hard from his days setting sensor equipment up beside the river. They roved over her back, found the curve at the small of it, as she pressed even closer to him. No fight remained in him.

Daniel was lost in the sensations of her, and wondering at her willingness, despite their differences and the things she so often confronted him with. Softly, as if he was touching a miracle in his own life, he reached toward her with one index finger and trailed it to where her smile crinkled the skin beside her mouth. He brought it to a stop at the base of her chin, curving it there, and then used the hook of it to lift her jaw, until the intensity of her gaze seemed to fasten them together. Her lips had fallen open just a bit, softening her features, offering an invitation Daniel could no longer ignore.

He cupped his hands against her head then, one over each ear, and held her there momentarily, just looking at her and thinking how beautiful she was, as his fingers threaded through the satin of her hair.

The moment their lips found one another, when they tasted one other, they were desperate for fulfillment.

Jamie felt as if her feet had left the ground. There was nothing holding her except for Daniel's hands on her neck and in her hair. She wanted to float away, as he traced the inside of her lips, her teeth, her mouth, with a hot, pliant tongue. He might well have been encircling her soul as she stood on tiptoe below him, reaching up to him as if she was reaching up to her destiny. He enveloped her in his arms and his kisses and his life.

She wanted to know more of him, to demand more, to discover more. Her hands searched the vast expanse of his torso, and her fingers found taut, unyielding muscles in his neck, shoulders, arms.

His mouth left hers and traveled to the sensitive hollow just above the collar of her blouse and, as he did it, every inch of her ached for him.

Around them remained the schoolroom where she had come to teach, the bright goldenrod yellow cinder blocks and the brown desks with the little chairs she had repaired herself what seemed like hundreds of times, the salt cedar tree and the green construction-paper calendar that marked off the days before Christmas with fat, red-striped candy canes.

They mark off the days of my existence. Because I want to belong with Daniel now. And instead I will go back home. But I don't think I can ever return to me.

Daniel kissed her once more, as she clung to him, then he straightened and pulled ever so slightly away

from her. He studied her face. "You make me fight
with myself, Jamie. I look at you and feel you near me
and think that maybe you are right, after all."

The level of noise outside was rising. There were
squeals and screams and even shouting as the third
graders who had finished their lunch congregated on
the dusty playground outside the window.

Jamie stepped farther away from him then and
closed her eyes. *What have I done? I am making him
lose his battle against himself.*

She was trembling, feeling more lonely and afraid
than she had since just after her parents' deaths. She
climbed down the steps of the little makeshift stage.
And as she did, her spirits plummeted to a depth of
sadness that she had never known before.

Dear Grandaddy,
The children are performing *Las Posadas* in the
Christmas program next week. They are so
proud. And we *all* still have so much work to do.

I wish you could be here.

All the teachers have worked really hard to in-
corporate both Hispanic and Anglo traditions in
the Christmas program. I am hoping there is
something in it, maybe just one little thing, that
will touch each person in the audience and tie us
all together.

Needless to say, it has been a monumental
project.

I guess it's really my way of saying goodbye to
the kids. More than anything, I just wanted to
share with them something that will reinforce
their pride in themselves.

You should see the boxes stacked all over my little house. The owners come in next week. So I have lots of cleaning to do before I get out of here. If I'm a little late arriving next week, you'll know I'm probably still down here scrubbing something.

The Christmas program is next Friday, the twenty-second. I'll leave here Saturday, the twenty-third. It may take me all day to get there.

I love you so much.

Talk to everybody at Oakhaven and round up a good domino game. Your partner is on her way.

Hugs,
Jamie

CHAPTER SEVEN

"ARE THEY READY for their great debut?" Daniel asked.

"I'll let you know," Jamie whispered. She didn't turn toward him. Her arms were crossed, a barrier between them. She felt safer that way. Her students were taking the stage in the cafeteria, walking in semi-silence, doing their best, but not without an occasional giggle or shushing or stomping as new shiny shoes took to the risers. "They are awfully excited."

"I know. Miguel's been talking about it for weeks now. He tried on the Joseph costume you sent home with him at least a dozen times."

"Did Lúpe mind altering it? It was big. All the costumes were."

"She's as excited about it as he is. And Pedro won't admit it, but I think he is pleased, too. Particularly since you made me honorary director of this thing."

"There's nothing honorary about it. You earned your title."

Daniel stood flush to the wall beside her, watching her profile as the light from the stage etched her nose and her lashes and her lips in a faint velvet outline. She was as proud of her students tonight as he was proud of her, and of Miguel, and of Pedro for coming.

Daniel wanted to reach out to her again but he didn't. Jamie had not learned to mask her emotions like so many other women he had known. He could read her easily. And, even as she stood beside him, he sensed she was far, far away. It was as if she belonged to him without belonging to him, as if she wanted him there yet didn't want him.

On stage, the kindergartners and first graders were singing "The Cradle Song of the Madonna." It was a song all of them had known, Daniel and his parents and their parents, since they had been babies. It was a beautiful ballad, one everyone here could sing in both Spanish and English.

"Then," the three hundred or so voices sang, "You who walk among the palms, holy angels, because my baby is sleeping, hold the branches!"

The second graders took their turn on stage. Their portion of the show was a portrayal of Christmas Eve customs all along the border. This part had been Jamie's idea, too, and she had talked to all the second-grade teachers about it. It was a way to show the children and their parents the heritage of both sides of the borderland.

One child hung his stocking on a cardboard fireplace mantel and waited by the front door for Santa Claus to visit. A second child, on the opposite side of the stage, placed his shoes on the windowsill and watched for the three wise men to ride by on camels and fill them.

The third graders were up next, and both Daniel and Jamie held their breath while Tomás and the donkey trotted perfectly across the stage then turned in the other direction. The chorus stumbled over words twice, but it was to be expected. They were all so excited, they had worked so long for this, and nobody noticed the mistakes but Jamie, as the program drew to a close and Maria and José found the stable with a manager and lovely soft hay in it where they could lay their infant son when he was born.

After the program, the children hosted a carnival for their parents, a wonderful party with game booths and foods and other treats in every room. Jamie served sugar cookies and green punch and hot chocolate spiced with cinnamon, too. It was her concession to the winter season even though it was sixty degrees outside.

"Okay, y'all," she called out to her students after everyone had refreshments. "Time for the fun stuff." She unveiled two piñatas, a blue one with curls of tissue that portrayed a donkey and a red-and-white-and-black one that was a funny, pointed-head facsimile of Santa Claus. She had filled them herself with all sorts of Christmas surprises. Jamie had spent an hour shopping at Riverview Family Center, and had come home to stuff the piñatas with gum and licorice and plastic rings and whistles and all sorts of tiny trinkets she had found.

"We need someone tall enough to pull the ropes. Somebody athletic who can keep these kids from breaking the piñatas open too soon."

Daniel stepped forward. "I'll be your volunteer."

Jamie had attached hemp ropes and pulleys to one of the joists in the ceiling. Daniel reached for one of them. He had consciously stayed away from the citizens of Roma for so long. They had always been afraid of him because he was *la Migra*. But, today, as he joined with them and Jamie, he began to wonder if he might be more afraid of them than they were of him. He grinned at Jamie. "I'd like to be a part of this party, too."

Jamie wanted to cry out to him when she saw the look of expectancy on his face. No one in the room with them knew what he was risking. He had told her himself how easy it had been to cut himself off from everyone since he had gone away to school and come home from Arizona trained and proven, willing to hide himself away from the people he was being kind to now.

"Are you sure?"

Daniel smiled. He was pleased when he read the respect he saw in her eyes. It was a welcome gift from her. "I'm sure."

"Okay. And you better be a good one. I want to see these kids have to work for the goodies they get."

"Yes, ma'am." He gave her a playful salute and then winked at her. "Or maybe I should say, 'Yes, marm.' Schoolmarm."

"Not even funny. Don't try to be cute." She forgot herself for a moment. She was flirting with him. Good, old-fashioned, friendly flirting. It felt wonderful.

"But I thought I *was* cute," he shot back at her.

"Salinas . . ."

The students were already waiting in line. Jamie blindfolded Eva first, and the parents cheered for the little girl. Then Jamie guided Eva by the shoulders to the center of the room where the desks had been cleared away. Eva swatted blindly at the piñata with a long stick as Daniel laughed and deftly bounced it up and down with the ropes, and the children all squealed and shouted encouragement.

"Whack it, Eva. Give it a good one."

"Bash it."

Daniel couldn't keep from chuckling. "Such violence we have here."

Eva smashed the donkey in the leg then. Daniel wasn't quick enough to move the piñata away, because he couldn't stop laughing, and all the eight-year-olds around Eva shrieked and made ready to retrieve the falling candy. But she didn't hit it hard enough to break the donkey open, she only bent his leg a little, and then it was another student's turn to try.

After twenty minutes of bashing and laughing, it was Diego who dealt the animal the final, fateful blow. Seconds later the gum and the candy and little pens had been cleared from the floor and it was time to hang Santa on the rope. Daniel was doubled over, laughing, he was having so much fun.

"These kids are *good*," he said when he could talk at last.

Jamie wanted to hug him. "I've been trying to tell you that for a long time."

The Santa Claus piñata was demolished in no time, too, and, as students and parents began to leave the room, Lúpe moved forward, with Pedro right behind her, and took Jamie's hand. "We are very proud of our son," she said, beaming, while Pedro nodded from behind her. "Thank you for teaching him about both parts of himself. Thank you for teaching him a new language and his heritage, too."

Miguel stood beside his parents and, as Jamie watched, the boy walked over and took Daniel's hand in his own. "Daniel Salinas is my special friend." He announced the fact to his classmates proudly as Daniel gave his hand a squeeze. "My father is his father's *vaquero*. And sometimes, when we are all hanging around—" Jamie smiled at the very American idiom he used "—*Señor* Salinas teaches me to play baseball."

In an instant, a dozen or more children were hopping around Daniel's legs. "Will you teach me to play baseball, too, *Señor* Salinas? Please? Please?"

He glanced helplessly at Jamie and Pedro as the kids danced around him.

"Please say yes. Please?"

For a moment, he pictured Raphael on the pitcher's mound, clapping the ball into his glove once, twice, turning to spit tobacco juice, then his windup, the pitch . . .

"We-ell," he drawled out his answer. "I guess I don't see any harm in putting a baseball team together. We could practice at the park on Saturday mornings. If your parents don't mind."

This time, Jamie pushed her way through the gang of children and she *did* hug him. "It's a great idea."

"I've got two old gloves packed away somewhere," Inez's father volunteered. "I'll get them down this week and dust them off."

"It's been ages since Roma had a baseball team," another father said delightedly. He slapped Daniel across the back as he reminisced in Spanish. "It was probably back during your school days. Remember that Mexican kid who played so well? What was his name? *La Migra* arrested and deported his entire family, and nobody here ever heard from them again.

It was too bad, too. That kid was good enough to be famous."

"I know," Daniel answered. "He was my teammate." And he was surprised this time, when he spoke of Raphael, for he wasn't as sad as he had always been before. Now, with Jamie's students jumping around his legs and parents talking about baseball gloves, Daniel didn't feel as cheated as he had before. It was as if a little portion of Raphael had returned in these kids. They were a legacy to a part of tomorrow his best friend had always dreamed of.

A ball team. A bridge between Raphael's past and these kids' futures.

Somehow, it just seemed right to him.

"Okay. *Okay.*" He held up both hands and gazed down at the sea of anxious faces turned toward him. He waited until the children quieted before he spoke again. "We'll have our first practice this Saturday at ten o'clock. Come to the park and bring all the baseball stuff you can find. Bats. Balls. Gloves."

There were several dejected faces below him, and he saw them just in time.

"And if you don't have any gear, I want to see you there anyway." He was almost shouting now, already overcome by the excitement and the anticipation of becoming a coach. "We'll fix you up with my old stuff. I've got hats and bats and gloves somewhere." He winked at Miguel. "And Miguel and I know where we can find an old ball that's been hankering for some real action for a good, long time now."

JAMIE HANDED DANIEL a pile of dirty paper plates. He dumped them into the trash can beside the door.

"Don't you think you'd better go home now? You'd better get your sleep. You have a wild baseball game scheduled for Saturday. Besides, the janitor will get most of this early in the morning before class begins."

Tomorrow was the last day of school before the holiday hiatus in Roma. Jamie still had piles of work to finish at the little cottage. She hadn't completed the report cards. She wanted to write a note to each of the children so that her students would have something personal to remember her by.

"I know. It *is* late. But I wanted to make sure you made it home okay."

He was right. It was late, and there was no one to meet her at the little cottage. The house was getting emptier by the day. Only piles and piles of packing boxes remained. Daniel kept talking, not quite oblivious to her mood but still so taken by the children's acceptance of him that he couldn't quite believe it. "Just think, Jamie. Baseball practice on Saturday. They want *me* to coach them."

"It is something you should have done a long time ago. But tonight they had to virtually attack you to talk you into doing it."

"I never knew they would want me."

It was the first time Jamie had come face to face with Daniel's horrible aloneness. Sometimes, she mused, he must think people hated him for what he did. There might even be times when he hated himself, and she felt her heart go out to him because of it.

Jamie walked across the room toward him, thinking only of bridging the gap between Daniel and the people he must be so afraid of, and of the uncertainties in him that, tonight, a child's enthusiasm had effectively banished. Children had a way of rejuvenating people. They doled out trust and forgiveness the same way she had doled out candy and treats for the kids tonight. "Did you doubt they would?"

"They had to sit and watch as I pulled that little boy, Gilbert, away from everything his parents had ever wanted for him. His education. His friends. His home."

"You need to learn how to forgive yourself," Jamie told him softly. "The children forgave you a long time ago." She couldn't stop herself from moving even closer to him. She wanted him to know people would care for him because of who he was, Daniel Salinas, and not turn away from him because of the uniform he wore. "Give them all a chance. See what happens."

Daniel opened his arms to her. He needed to hear the things she was telling him. She stepped forward intuitively and slipped her arms around the warmth of his back, wrapped them around the sinew of his muscled torso. He felt so good to her. She closed her eyes and stood silently, absorbing the magic of being with him.

Daniel enfolded her, quietly enjoying her, brushing his lips across the top of her hair, both of them savoring the nearness of one another and of the victories that had come to them during the long, tiring evening.

It was Daniel's tenderness now, his childlike acceptance of her students' friendship, that made Jamie forget that she was leaving. His touch set her tottering over a dangerous edge. She needed more than his tenderness suddenly, she needed *him* with all his power and force. She needed Daniel, the man, the part of him that pressed up against her with urgent passion and bruised her with the hunger of his kisses.

The desperate desire for him erupted in her so forcefully that it threatened to shatter her. She reached up to him then, calling out his name, desperate for a release. She ran frantic fingers through his hair. It was tangled in some places, and she knew she must be tugging at it. But she wanted him to know she was tugging at something inside him, too, something vital and strong he could share with her.

She drew his head toward hers and kissed his face frantically, over and over again, his cheeks, his eyelids, his nose and then, at last, his mouth.

This time, he gave her the caress she had been demanding from him. His body was firm and forceful against hers, and his lips sought their purpose, demanding her soul from her. Just then, she would have gladly given it.

"Oh God, Jamie." He gasped her name. "You mustn't leave. Not after making me feel this way." He had never known anyone could want him, could respond to him, the way Jamie did.

"I don't want to go." It was the first time she had voiced it aloud. She whispered the words against his lips.

Daniel's hands cupped her breasts, drawing a startled gasp from her. Jamie had never imagined his touch, or any man's touch, could feel this wonderful and this right. His hands were gentle at first, light on her skin, like a breath, and then he pressed harder, finding her supple skin beneath the opening of her blouse and her bra, his thumbs circling lazily but purposefully.

The aching his touch elicited was an aching that turned back upon itself, a nameless longing that enveloped her, stung her, filled her with helpless need for him. "I want to stay here forever."

"Oh, Jamie," he whispered against the damp skin of her neck. "Do it, then. Please. Stay for both of us."

It was his words that finally served to fragment her, to separate the two parts of her need cleanly so she could analyze them. Her emotions. Her desperate physical need for Daniel. Her logic. The logic that explained it all away. She wanted to take it with her, this remembrance of him and today. She couldn't be a part of Daniel's life. After tomorrow, she would never see him again.

Jamie felt as if a gigantic, serrated knife was slicing her, severing her from the new world she loved. She might as well be one of her own students, trying to leave behind a country and a life that was beautiful yet would always haunt her, needing a new way, a new place, but never quite seeing how to make it there.

Jamie's logic took over. She wrenched free of Daniel's grip, hating herself for what she knew she had to do, knowing she couldn't wait any longer.

"Stop this," she hissed, her words barely audible, but so forceful and so full of purpose they shocked him. "Stop this *now*."

Daniel halted and stared at her. Damp tendrils of her hair were stuck to her forehead. He brushed her face with the back of his hand to push them away. But she stepped back from him.

"This isn't right. And it isn't fair. Not to you. And not to me."

He started to laugh, a frightening, mad sound that repeated itself in the unsettling flecks of disappointment in his eyes. "Why? Because you're a schoolmarm and I'm an agent for the INS? Or is it just because you are leaving tomorrow and I'll never see you again? I know you feel the same things that I feel, Jamie. I can tell it by the way you touch me."

"I never meant to feel this way about you, never meant to make you . . . *want* me like this."

"But it has happened anyway. No matter where you are going in the morning." He stared at her, hating her for the things she made him feel.

"My grandfather." It was hopeless to think her reasons would make everything right between them. But she had to try. "He needs me."

"There are people here who need you, too." *The children*, he reasoned. *But not me. After today, I won't need you anymore.*

"You think I don't know that?"

He jerked away from her and slammed his clenched fist against her desk. "You don't have to do this. You know that."

"Daniel. Every time we are together, I become so entranced with my life here, with *you*, that I forget I'm going away myself. But I have to remember it. I have to go." She was pleading with him now, and she realized how futile it was, trying to make him understand when, all along, she had been fighting against fate, too. Jamie felt a chasm within her begin to open, a hollow, horrible place that would be empty when she had left him and gone away. She felt as if she was being yanked away from all of them.

"The children in your class. Have you told them yet?"

She stood halfway across the room now, as she talked, and she turned her back to him just before she told him. She was facing rows of candy canes marching relentlessly across the calendar. Her days in Roma had marched by relentlessly, too. "I'll tell them tomorrow. I wanted to give them everything I could give them before I left, Daniel. I wanted to give *Las Posadas* tonight. And now—" she smiled sadly, thinking of the irony of it, how the children had begged him to play baseball with them on Saturday and become their friend "—I am leaving them to you."

"Damn that old man," Daniel roared at last. He counted himself lucky to find some sort of dignity in his anger. "You are a fool, Jamie Forrester. You shouldn't have come here at all. You should have left us all alone. You had no right to come down here and mangle all our lives."

"And what do you think I've ended up doing to my own? You said I couldn't give those kids everything I wanted to give them. You said it would hurt me or kill me trying. And you know what?" The expression on her face was horrible, a twisted, sarcastic smile that echoed the pain she was feeling now because she had to go. "You may have been right about that. You warned me, didn't you? But I'm not the weak one. I'm not the one who holds myself back from people because I am afraid."

What was he going to do without her? "You misrepresented yourself to all of us." He was snarling at her. Daniel felt like a trapped animal. Caring for her had caged him. "You think this is fair to Miguel and Sarita and Diego and all the others? You came in here and you made them *trust* you, damn you. And tomorrow you walk into this classroom and give them your best regards, then you waltz out of here to your comfortable life in suburban North Texas. Jamie, how can you *do* that to them?" *How can you do that to me*?

Jamie had been moving along, undaunted, for days, hiding behind a forced calm and the forced cheerfulness of Santa Claus and Baby Jesus and gingerbread men. But now she had to face the truth as she saw it through Daniel's eyes. It hurts. Badly.

"Daniel. Please. I'm so sorry. Please. Try to understand. I can't just desert an old man who needs me to be there for him. I promised him I would come home to him a long time before I met you." She was reaching one hand out to him, desperate just to touch him, but he was backing away.

"So maybe all my profound advice was worthless. You are the one who has been telling me for four months that I am wrong."

"You are."

"Then you are, too. Because you are doing the same thing. Because, despite your reasons, you are pulling away, too."

"I know," Jamie said, her shoulders set squarely against him, her arms at her side again, her hands clenched. She would not reach toward him again. Her body language was all defiance, as if she dared him to prove her wrong. "But it is my only choice." *And I'm hurting you, too, and I think that's the worst part.*

Daniel turned away from her as if he could read her mind. *And perhaps,* she thought, *I've let him see so much of myself that he can.*

"Don't you see?" Jamie asked. "Maybe neither one of us really has a choice. Maybe both of us are just trapped in a part of our lives so that we can't cross over to the next part. Maybe, for most people, it doesn't have to be this way. Maybe it's just . . . us."

Daniel turned sad eyes to her. "Or maybe it isn't us. Maybe it's the way it has to be for everyone. Caught between yesterday and tomorrow. Like the people who want to come across the Rio Grande and get turned away. Like every kid in your classroom who isn't a legal resident here."

"But it can't be so hard for everyone, can it?" It was the first time Jamie had truly let her defenses down during their heated exchange. And, as she considered telling him how painful it was for her, too, she could feel her strength beginning to crumble. It was the same thing she had been thinking, about yesterday, today, forever. It was uncanny how Daniel could pick up on her perceptions that way. She wanted to step into his arms now and cry, like a little girl. But he wasn't offering comfort to her, and she had no right to want him to, not after the trust she had earned from him then had taken away.

"Perhaps it *is* this way for everyone. Daniel," she said, at last clutching at his sleeve again and wishing there could be any other way to say goodbye except this one. "Someday, try to find it in your heart to forgive me."

"It is over now, Jamie." He pulled his arm away from her grasp, and her hand remained frozen there, as if her fingers were still clutching the woven cotton of his shirt. And, in a way, she was, clutching the fabric of what they had shared together. "There's nothing more either of us can do. I think we both know that."

"Yes. I *do* know," she said, feeling a terrible, permanent sorrow welling up within her and crushing her as he walked toward the door. "And I'd give anything, Daniel, if it wasn't so."

CHAPTER EIGHT

THE TELEPHONE AT Jamie's bedside kept ringing. She groped for it. She found it but she knocked the receiver away when she tried to grab it. For long seconds, she couldn't remember where she was.

"Hello?"

"Jamie? Did I wake you? This is Darlene Simmons at Oakhaven Retirement Center."

Something was wrong. Maybe her grandfather had fallen again and broken his leg. Broken bones became almost irreparable when you got to be his age. Things like that just quit fixing themselves.

Dear God, don't let anything be wrong, not now, not after I've come from so far away to be back with him.

She remembered it now. She was in Dallas.

"...Your grandfather woke up at four this morning. He's just been so excited about seeing you today. We told him you had phoned when you arrived last night but that he was already sleeping."

"Oh, Darlene. I'll be right over. He's okay? You scared me. I forgot...I was here. I can't wait to see him, either."

She hung up the phone and flipped on the lamp beside her. It was morning, and the sun was already blazing. But the old-fashioned brocade curtains were still closed. They managed to cut out most of the sunlight. Relief flooded her as the soft, artificial light illuminated familiar things in the room.

Everything here was just as she had left it, dusty but still arranged perfectly, the perfume bottles and the pictures and the pom-poms. She climbed out of bed and dressed more casually than she would have dressed before she lived in the Rio Grande Valley. She pulled on a pair of pink slacks and a pink sweater, for it was much colder this far north of the gulf.

Jamie pulled her hair away from her face with a pink band and added a touch of blush and pink gloss to her lips. She looked much the same way she had looked the day she joined Daniel at *Los Ebanos* to celebrate *El Día de Los Muertos*. But she didn't realize that now. And neither did William Forrester, when she walked into the front hallway of Oakhaven and he saw her. He only knew she looked young and beautiful and lost as she came toward him with a bundle of Christmas presents tucked under her arm.

"You look just like a Christmas angel," he said and winked at her as he struggled to his feet to hug her. "All pink and sparkly."

Jamie laughed, dropped the presents into his chair and threw her arms around him. "That's just what I needed to hear after my long drive yesterday."

In the corner of the lounge, a minister was performing a service for the elderly who couldn't get out to a church. A very polished children's choir was singing carols in four-part harmony. It was Sunday, the Sunday morning before Christmas Day. Jamie had temporarily forgotten just how close the holiday was.

"I'll take you to Christmas Eve service," she offered. "Think they'll let you out of here?"

"Of course." She was looking at every part of his face, his eyes, his mouth, the pear-shaped freckles on top of his head, thinking it impossible he had aged so much during the past few months. When she had been with him every day, she hadn't realized he was aging so quickly. "They consider you a very proper escort around here. Everybody has missed you, child. Even the nurses are excited about you coming back."

"I'm glad," she said, hugging him again, not quite believing herself that she was here with him again.

"What are these?" He pointed to the gifts she had tossed into his chair. Jamie wasn't certain whether he wanted to know about them because he was interested or because he wanted to draw her attention to them because he needed to sit down.

"Those are your Christmas presents." She gathered them and set them on the floor so he could have his chair.

The Oakhaven staff erected a Christmas tree in the corner of the lounge every year. The seniors had a wonderful time decorating it with pictures of their grandchildren and their great-grandchildren, and satin balls and crocheted snowflakes that the ladies spent hours making with hooked needles. This year there was even a crocheted angel sitting atop it, in place of a star, with a halo and wings starched to spread wide.

"I should have brought you more pictures of Sarita and Miguel and Diego and Eva and all of them. You could have hung them on the tree and claimed them as your own." It was strange, but their names already sounded foreign to her, as if they didn't exist anymore because she wasn't with them. She felt as if she had come from forever away. And she was furious with herself for the tears that were threatening to come to her eyes again. Yesterday, during her drive she had cried all the way to San Antonio. She forced herself to smile cheerfully. "It's a beautiful tree again this year." Jamie knew that her grandfather's domino buddies loved to brag about the number of presents with their names on them waiting beneath the Scotch pine. So she had brought all William Forrester's gifts with her today. "You've got tons of them from me this year. This is the best one." She waggled the huge box with the silver snowmen and the red ribbon. "This is the one I wrote you about."

Elena had helped her finish the serape just three nights before. Sarita had done most of the fringing for her. All three of them had put their best work into the gift, and Jamie felt as if she had brought back a little part of her new friends, too, as she slid the box beneath the huge, pruned evergreen.

Elena had sent her to Dallas with a tin of tiny freshly baked molasses cookies. And she sent a box of divinity, chewy sugar and pecan vanilla candy, to give to Jamie's grandfather as a gift from them.

Jamie had thought it would be hardest of all to tell Sarita goodbye. But the little girl was so excited about going to the first baseball team practice in the park that morning, she scarcely looked at her teacher when Jamie told them all goodbye.

One of the teachers had brought her a cake on Friday morning. Frances Ybarra cut it and served it throughout the day in the teachers' lounge. Jamie didn't think she deserved even that much. She had hardly been at the school long enough to receive any recognition at all.

"But you have given the children a great gift of yourself," Frances Ybarra had told her that afternoon. They were sitting in her office beneath a poster that pictured a kitten sleeping in a pot of yellow flowers. "When you are at peace with yourself, any place is home," the poster read. "I have seen how much you care for the children. I hope you have a fine career in teaching wherever you decide to go next."

"Now," Jamie said, dusting her hands off as if she had just finished hard work. She had placed all William Forrester's gifts under the tree. "You should have more presents under that tree than anybody else in Dallas County. And if anybody argues about that, just tell them that I am your present, too. But I wouldn't fit under the tree."

"MERRY CHRISTMAS TO ME," Daniel said to no one as he crouched beside a thorny bush. His binoculars were trained on the river and on the narrow worn path in the dust on the Mexican side that led to the water.

It would be a busy morning on the Rio Grande. One of the busiest of the year. The Hispanics who were legal U.S. residents used the international bridges or the hand-drawn ferry to cross when they wanted to spend the day celebrating with relatives. The illegals used the river. They hauled wrapped gifts across atop their heads or sometimes piled high on inner tubes. And he, Daniel Salinas, was in a position to stop them. All of them. He was the Ebenezer Scrooge of the day.

He had volunteered to work the holiday. No one in the INS wanted to patrol the river on Christmas Day.

They all wanted to be home eating turkey and un-wrapping gifts and watching football games with their families. But Daniel couldn't stomach a traditional celebration today. He had been hoping to invite Jamie to spend the day with his family. *What a pipe dream*. Jamie was all the way across Texas now. And, for some reason, he hadn't been able to face the party at home this morning, the quiet time spent opening gifts with Harriet and Benny. A fire in the fireplace even though it was too hot for one. Christmas carols on the radio... both English songs and Spanish ballads.

An hour later, Miguel and Lúpe and Pedro had been scheduled to arrive. Harriet had prepared the traditional North American feast: roast turkey and smoked ham with honey mustard sauce. She had decided to give Lúpe the day off from cooking.

Miguel would be ecstatic, displaying the new baseball glove and bat Daniel knew Santa was planning to leave beneath the cedar. Miguel would be excited about the other little presents, too, fruits and candies that the three wise men always left in his waiting shoes each Christmas Eve. Santa Claus and the three wise men. Vying for the final edge in a little boy's life.

Daniel snorted at himself. *Stop looking at everything through Jamie Forrester's eyes.*

He was starting to criticize things he had taken for granted his entire life.

Try as he might, he just wasn't in the mood for happy children today. It seemed much more appropriate to be here, stooped and hiding in the dust with a radio and binoculars, jealously guarding the border

of the United States of America the way he had failed
to guard the boundaries within himself.

Daniel heard footsteps approaching from behind
him. And laughter. His first holiday revelers. In one
fluid motion, he drew his gun and rose from his hiding place. He turned to see an entire clan of men,
women and children coming toward him on the U.S.
side of the river. And, as he spoke to them, he felt his
heart sink. They all looked so happy, both the children and the old women, as they came toward him
dressed in the brightly colored cotton and rickrack
costumes of the holiday.

"Hello." One man greeted Daniel and his gun.
"Merry Christmas."

"INS Border Patrol. Are you and your family legal
residents of the United States?"

"We are."

"And you are preparing to cross the international
border into the Republic of Mexico?"

"Yes. To visit my brother just across the river."

"Are you aware that crossing an international border without declaring yourself to customs is a federal
offense?"

"No." The man hesitated. "We are in a great hurry
to join them and were only taking the shortest route."

"You must go to Roma to the International Bridge
and pass through customs." Daniel didn't lower his
gun. "Otherwise I will have to arrest you."

"We will go back, then."

"Do you have papers with you to prove you are legal residents?" He couldn't look at the children's
faces. There was no telling how far they had already
walked today to celebrate Christmas with their cous-

ins. And he knew from experience the bridge in Roma would be packed. They would probably have to wait several hours to cross.

"We do." The man shrugged in a manner that seemed almost apologetic. But Daniel doubted his honesty. He had been trained to doubt people's honesty. "I have my social security card with me. And my daughter has one, too, if you would like to see them."

"I want to see them." Daniel could radio in and have the agent on duty check the authenticity of the social security numbers. Chances of the man carrying a valid card and trying to cross the river this way were slim.

The man approached him, with card extended, as the remainder of the group stood back. Daniel wondered if they were making ready to run.

Daniel examined the card the man handed him. If it was a copy, it was a good one. He radioed the number in, then attempted to make polite conversation with them all while he waited for his suspicions to be confirmed. "Well, was Santa Claus kind to your family this morning?" He holstered his gun, fully aware he might have to pull it out again and point it at them.

"Yes, he was," the man answered cautiously. "We have found him to be generous every year."

The radio on Daniel's hip crackled to life. Daniel reached for it. "Salinas here." His hand touched his gun. He was ready.

"The card checks out." The voice came over the speaker clearly. There was no way Daniel could have mistaken it. "José Garcia is a citizen of the United States. Here is a description of him. Black hair. Brown eyes. Height is five feet, eight inches. Weight is one hundred sixty pounds..."

Never mind that the description could have fit almost every middle-aged Hispanic male in the Rio Grande Valley. Daniel stared at the card in his hand, printed perfectly with blue, and in red a nine-digit number.

So why the hell had the guy decided he had to cross with his family over the river the hard way?

"Is there anyone else you'd like me to check on?"

Daniel eyed the man again. "All members of your family here are legal residents?"

"They are."

He held the radio close to his mouth. "No. I guess not." He could run a check on all of them. But they would be here all day. "This spot check determines what I need to know." He clipped the radio onto his belt. "You may go. But you must take your family through customs at the International Bridge. That is the law." Daniel checked his watch. He had to change positions immediately. They had created enough of a ruckus here that, if anyone was casing his position, half the Republic of Mexico would know where he was by now. "I can drive you to Roma in my truck. There is room for everyone if the children will sit on the adult's laps."

But the man with the valid social security card was shaking his head. "No. No. We will not accept a ride from you. Thank you." It was the first time since baseball practice last Saturday that Daniel was mindful of how people didn't trust him. "It will take us much time. But we are satisfied to walk."

FELIX GALINDO SAT INSIDE his pickup truck. Even
though it was Christmas Day, it was sweltering inside
the vehicle. But Felix didn't roll down the window. He
sat there rigidly, his arms at his side, thinking of
nothing except the wad of American dollars hidden in
the envelope in his pocket.

He felt as if he was wearing signs all over him,
pointing him out as a perpetrator of illegal activity.
*Man's life savings in right rear pocket. Steal. Steal
while the stealing is easy.*

But stealing this money from Felix Galindo would
never be easy, he decided. He was doing his best to
swallow his fear. He had worked years to save the
money in his pocket. He had sweat blood for it, caning hundreds of chairs that left his fingers raw, and so
had Elena, bending or stretching high to pick the valley crops, standing and bending again, millions of
times, until her back almost wouldn't straighten at the
end of the day. Miles and miles of aloe and broccoli
and grapefruit and melons.

This was the best Christmas gift he could give
Elena. He was bringing their son, Jorge, to the United
States.

Felix had contacted the man named Elizando several times. Christmas Day would be the day for the
exchange of money, a messenger sent to their door-
step had explained to him. Customs and the INS were
virtually in shambles that day, with so many people
crossing the bridges and the Rio Grande to visit relatives, carrying gifts and foods that had to be examined ruthlessly.

A documented citizen of the States with nothing to
declare could cross the International Bridge with al-

most no questions asked at all. Elizando was a documented citizen. It would be easy for him to take the money to his cousin in Matamoros. And, in only weeks, Jorge could join the rest of his family on the other side.

Felix waited quietly. He knew no one was watching him today. The truck was parallel parked with other cars along a main two-way thoroughfare lined with palm trees. It had taken him several hours to drive to Brownsville. And, at last, the vehicle he was waiting for drove by slowly, a baby-blue Ford LTD that looked like it had been rusting on the road for centuries, then it pulled up beside him.

The two men inside glared at him. Then the driver steered the LTD into the traffic lane again. It made a lumbering U-turn. Except for the parked vehicles around them, the street was almost deserted. The car pulled in to park, too, facing the opposite direction.

The two men climbed out of the vehicle, slammed the doors and crossed the street toward Felix languorously, with no apparent sense of purpose. One of them was old, the skin on his face wrinkled and brittle, like old parchment. The second man was younger. Felix guessed he was close to his own age. He was wearing a Mexican brand beer embossed T-shirt and a blue baseball cap. They were all clues, things Felix had been told to look for.

He hurried to roll down the window as they approached him. He didn't want to appear too unfriendly or too afraid. He didn't move to unlock the door, though. Not yet.

"We are in need of direction," the older man said in English with some difficulty. "Are you willing to help us?"

"If I know the directions to the place you are going, I will help you."

They were speaking in codes now, saying predetermined words specified by the *coyote* Elizando so they could acknowledge one another without giving one another away.

"We want to go to the north," the young man said in much better English than his elderly counterpart. "To a town called Roma. Named Roma because it stands on a high hill above the river and once reminded the settlers of the Holy City."

"I will write down the directions for you. I have a pen and an envelope with me." Still, Felix made no attempt to reach for the envelope. He had to be certain of this. Very certain.

"And, in the envelope?" the older man asked carefully. "In the envelope, have you planned for tomorrow?"

He was sure of their identity now. "I have." Felix fumbled for a moment, easing his weight off his torso before he reached for his back pocket and pulled out the folded, fat envelope. It was almost going to be a relief to get rid of it. It contained four hundred American dollars plus fifty more for a forged social security card. "Let me show you the directions."

He pulled the pen out of his front breast pocket and began to sketch the road toward Roma with a shaky hand. Then, in more detail, he drew the streets there and pinpointed his house. The highway he drew would be the one he traveled on his way to Elena and Sarita today. The map he was giving these men today would eventually land in his son's hands, a crumpled, faded connection between a father and his child. It would mark the last portion of the child's journey, the trek through South Texas that would lead him to his family's new home.

"It is very good," the young man nodded, then he smiled briefly as he peered into the open truck window at the diagram. "It will most certainly help us find our way."

Felix handed the envelope to him. It was thick. Four hundred American dollars thick. "Go with God then, my friends." And then he repeated the words in Spanish. *Vayan con Dios.* He said it to the men but he meant the words for his son.

Now he must drive home and tell Elena what he had done. And he wondered, as he watched the two men, the old one and the young one, saunter across the street, if his money was truly safe with them. Here, in a country that was his but not his, there were no laws to protect him. And Felix wondered, as he saw the old car begin to shake then spew the blue smoke of burning oil, if the two strangers who had taken his money had sensed his helpless fear.

"WOULDN'T IT BE SOMETHING," the coach asked them all, "if one of those things fell on our heads?"

"Oh, but you could catch it if it did." One of the female teachers was teasing him, her voice filled with subtle innuendo. "I'm sure they're just empty boxes all wrapped up. Besides, I hear you used to be good with your hands in your day."

"Yeah." The coach gazed up at the ceiling and said the word almost as if he didn't believe it either. "I used to be a pretty fair wide receiver. In my day."

Jamie followed his line of vision above them. There might as well have been a hundred of them, presents hanging in midair, all wrapped in gold, shiny paper, empty and all for show, swinging on invisible nylon lines. There were huge glass balls, gold ones, too, hanging above them, tied at the neck with gold lamé ribbons.

"Oh, it's gorgeous," one of the other teachers said, sighing. "Just think what it would be like if you could afford to decorate your house like this."

A waiter led them to their table. "Welcome to the hotel." He bowed graciously. Jamie scowled at him. What a terrible day to be working. "May I suggest our Christmas buffet this afternoon, roast turkey, smoked ham, hand-picked fresh cranberries from the east coast..."

A well-meaning friend from the Richardson school district had urged Jamie to join this group. They were all single instructors with families far away. And this particular hotel was a spectacular place to see and be seen this time of year.

"But I have a place to go. My grandfather is my family," she had argued.

"Doesn't he rest in the afternoons, Jamie? Celebrate Christmas morning with him, then get dressed up and spend the afternoon with us. It isn't right for you to tie yourself so completely to him."

"It's been months since I've been with him."

"And he did fine without you. We have all been talking about it at school. We are worried about you.

The new coach from Pearce High School is going to be there. He is so good-looking that you won't believe it."

"I'm not interested."

"Jamie, you have to think of yourself, too."

In the end, she had come. It was true. She had spent the four days since she had returned at Oakhaven with her grandfather. She had had very little time to herself.

She and William Forrester had celebrated Christmas at Oakhaven that morning. He had opened his presents one by one. There was a little Christmas book her class in Roma had made him. It told of their holiday traditions in the valley. Several of the children had written in it, and they had colored the pictures in it for him, too.

When he opened the huge, silver package and pulled out the serape, Jamie wanted to weep, her grandfather was so proud of it. He draped it around his shoulders and grinned. "I'll be the only one around this place with one of these," he said, chortling. "So this is the gift you wrote me about? This is the one you were working on for all those months?"

She smiled at him gently. "Now you know how much I missed you."

"Jamie." He stroked the yarn fringe with his fingers. "That makes it all the better. How did you learn?"

"Sarita was a good teacher."

The old man searched her face. "Teachers often learn more than their students." He ran his gnarled hand across the smooth weave of the fabric. "Did you do it on a loom? I am very impressed with your weaving.''

"Yes. And every time Sarita helped me make a row, I thought of you.'' She grinned and kissed him on the nose. "Now go ahead and open some of your other presents.''

"Ah,'' he said at last in his gravelly voice. He pointed a shaky finger at her. "I feel as if I know all these children after reading about them in your letters. It is easy to see that they have won your heart, little one.''

"That they have.'' Jamie smiled at him then, but she couldn't know how lost she looked when she did, like a homeless waif, because she still felt so torn, just missing them. "The borderland is a place where trust doesn't come easy,'' she told him. "You fight against their fear, then you begin to understand it, and then, one day, you look into a child's eyes and you realize a bit of the caution is gone. And when you know you've won their trust, the most valuable thing they have to share with you in their lives, it's like you see part of yourself that you've never been able to see before.''

Her grandfather stroked her cheek. "And to think you loved an old man enough to leave all that, to come back to me.'' He had watched her since she had come home, and she was right; there did seem to be a new dimension to her, some additional quiet strength, that he hadn't noticed before.

"Yes. I do.'' But when she kissed his cheek, William could still see the melancholy in her eyes.

"You know...'' He leaned toward her in the lounge where they were surrounded by people, great hordes of them, in wheelchairs or sitting propped up with their legs wrapped in afghans, and he whispered to her, as if he was telling her a grand secret. "That's how God works with us, too, little one. He always trusts us. He always gives us a second chance. And somewhere along the way, we learn to trust ourselves as well."

CHAPTER NINE

JAMIE THOUGHT OF HER grandfather's words now as she sat at the table with the people who had once been her colleagues, watching the waiter pour ice water into crystal goblets, then use silver tongs to add a twisted sliver of lemon.

"They're already pushing me for next year," the coach was saying. Jamie tried to act interested, to be polite. He was the only man in the group, and it was obvious he was loving it. "They say I've got to give them a winning season. But look what I've got coming in to work with. All those freshmen. And six, count them, *six* departing senior starters."

"You've got some good juniors to work with." Jamie's friend tried to be optimistic for him. "That Eddie Larson is an incredible fullback. He should be fine-tuned and ready to go next fall." She grimaced. "*If* he can pull his grades up in Martin's biology class."

"Oh, Eddie Larson." The coach guffawed. "He's just like all the others, and you know it. I want serious players. That guy is on the team so he can look macho and date cheerleaders. I don't care what anybody says. It's hard to get motivated about driving these kids to victory when they drive to school in sports cars that cost twice as much as mine does."

Jamie lay her gold-sequined evening bag on the table and wished she was any other place right now except this one. She hated the conversation. She didn't like herself much, either. She was sitting at the table with them, listening to the things they each thought important. She was dressed in a cranberry-colored velvet dress that cost as much money as would have taken to feed the Galindo family for two weeks. She felt ridiculous. She felt every bit as gilded and gaudy as the lavish decorations suspended high above her.

"What's wrong, lovely woman?" The coach had turned toward her. He was obviously attempting to draw her into the conversation. "You're the quiet one today. You agree with me, don't you? The kids in the education system are the same way everywhere these days. They take all this classroom hype for granted. They think an education is something due to them, something they get by osmosis every time they walk into my class and start cutting up. We teachers are nothing but high-priced baby-sitters. There isn't a place in the world where kids want to come to school to learn anymore."

Jamie leveled her eyes on his. She was so furious with the man about his attitude that she wanted to strike out at him. "You are very wrong." Her words were soft, but the conviction in them was so strong that the others fell silent at the table. "Yes, there are places where it is all very different. I have just been to one. And I think it could be different in Dallas, too, if some of the teachers would reevaluate their attitudes."

Everyone stared at her. Her friend's fork was poised halfway to her mouth. She smiled then, trying to regain the lost festive mood, as the waiter came and brought their salads. But they weren't smiling back. She had insulted them.

So this is it. They all looked like they wanted to cry for her and laugh at her at the same time. *This is the future I've prepared for myself.*

In an effort to get away from them, she pushed her chair away from the table, leaned back and looked up again, and she faced all the hanging balls and packages suspended high above her. *This is your life, Jamie Forrester. This is what you couldn't turn away from,* she told herself as she glared up at the swinging boxes. *It's all wrapped up for appearance's sake, neatly packaged. And without the third graders in Roma and without Daniel, it is always going to be just as empty.*

DANIEL HAD CHANGED his position three times during his shift. He had stopped four families laden with gifts and one man smuggling parrots and had turned them back to the Mexico side. He had only one hour left before he could go home and eat his share of Harriet's roast turkey.

His radio crackled to life. "Salinas? You still waiting at stated position?"

"I am." He called in to them every time he moved so they would know where he was.

"We've got electronic sensors going off two miles downstream from you. We aren't picking up footsteps. Our guess here is we've got a vehicle parked and waiting on the Texas side for someone to cross the *rio.*"

"I'll get right on it."

"If they're on wheels, you shouldn't go by yourself. I'll contact Johnson and have him join you as a backup. He's three miles north of you. Hold your position until he joins you."

"Fine."

"Roger. Over and out."

Daniel checked his watch. It was two o'clock.

Moments later, he heard a truck pull up and park beside the Suburban. The other INS agent joined him.

"We should take both vehicles," Johnson suggested.

"You call it."

"We'll park in the clearing a mile and a half downstream. We'll have to walk in the rest of the way if we don't want to give ourselves away."

"You have any idea what they're up to?" Daniel was already whispering. His sense of caution was ingrained. It had been ever since his initial training, when the INS had grilled him with questions and sent him through drill after drill of possibly dangerous scenarios.

"On Christmas Day, it could be anything," Johnson answered without cracking a smile. "Hell, it could even be Santa Claus."

"Yeah," Daniel said, his face not quite as deadpan as his assigned partner's. "The old guy has to get across the border some way. And I'd hate to be the one who has to haul all those toys through customs."

"Right." Johnson had to laugh.

The two men checked in with the station via radio and climbed into their separate vehicles. One after another, they drove through the brushland, heading downstream. And, although the two men could have remained in constant contact by radio, they did not do so. There was a chance whoever was waiting in a vehicle on the Texas side of the river had the capacity to monitor their communications. If that was the case, they were playing games with professionals.

Daniel pulled up and parked beside Johnson, and together the two men zigzagged across the rocky terrain. The two guards paused every so often to hide behind a mesquite or a prickly pear and to survey the river and their surroundings. Soon they found the clearing they were looking for, a well-traveled spot in the sand that the INS had decided to mark off with high-tech electronic sensors just a week before. And the radio dispatcher had been right. There was a shiny late-model Jeep Cherokee waiting there, with red trim and shaded windows. The personalized license plate read Pepe.

"Domino," Johnson said triumphantly beneath his breath. "We've got them."

Slowly, so as not to attract any attention to his movements, Daniel drew his gun. "That's a mighty nice vehicle they've got there," he commented. "Too nice for anybody but a doctor or a lawyer to afford on a regular salary."

"You're thinking what I'm thinking."

"Yeah."

"Drug smugglers."

"Blatant ones. Right down to the personalized plates."

Johnson shrugged. "We've got to catch them in the act."

"I've got all night."

"Me, too."

They waited. And waited. And, finally, it was Daniel who caught the movement on the opposite side of the water. He touched Johnson's arm and motioned toward it without speaking.

Two mustached men appeared on the riverbank. They crouched there for a moment, checking upstream and down before standing tall in the grass to wave at the truck that waited for them. Daniel focused on them with his binoculars. They were bending to take off their shoes.

One of the men disappeared into the brush. When he came into view, he was toting two inflatable plastic rafts. He placed the rafts at water's edge and began loading them.

"I bought my kid one of those swim rafts last summer," Johnson whispered. "They cost $4.95 at the discount store in Brownsville."

"Ah. The latest in technology and equipment. I'll take the guys in the river," Daniel volunteered. "Can you handle the truck?"

Johnson nodded. "Keep yourself covered from behind. I don't trust what I can't see behind those shaded windows."

"Thanks for the advice."

The men with their loaded rafts began to wade into the current. Still, Daniel and his colleague waited. They had learned a long time ago that there was a merit in being patient. And, finally, when the men's feet appeared behind them and Daniel could see they were swimming, he gave Johnson the signal.

His partner jumped first, aiming his handgun at the front left window of the vehicle, right where he knew a driver should be. "INS Border Patrol," he shouted, his gun leveled and cocked. "Get out of the Jeep with your hands up. Very slowly."

Daniel straddled the rock they had both been hiding behind and trained his weapon on the two men bobbing in the Rio Grande. *"La Migra,"* he growled. "Come right on across. Let's see what precious cargo you've got on those rafts."

"We've got a problem," he heard Johnson mutter beside him.

No one was emerging from the truck.

Deliberately, Johnson aimed his gun at the vehicle's front left tire and shot it out.

The Jeep's engine roared to life. The two INS agents scrambled behind the rock for cover. The Jeep's window came down three inches. They both saw the shotgun barrel protruding from the crack.

Bullets ricocheted off the rock where they were hiding.

Before they could aim their weapons again, the Cherokee spun in the dust, spitting gravel and throwing dust in every direction. As the vehicle's tires screeched, Daniel fired his gun at the tires over and over again. But he couldn't hit them. The Jeep was moving too fast.

His shots zinged into the dirt.

As the two agents watched the Cherokee escape in a cloud of grime, Daniel remembered the men swimming in the river. He jumped from behind the rock just in time to see them retreating to the riverbank in Mexico. They still carried their rafts, although one had capsized.

"We lost them." His disappointment did not show on Daniel's stony face. "We lost all of them." It was

PLAY
HARLEQUIN'S

LUCKY HEARTS

GAME

AND YOU COULD GET

* ★ **FREE BOOKS**
* ★ **A FREE BRACELET WATCH**
* ★ **A FREE SURPRISE GIFT**
* ★ **AND MUCH MORE**

TURN THE PAGE AND DEAL YOURSELF IN

PLAY "LUCKY HEARTS" AND YOU COULD GET...

★ Exciting Harlequin Superromance® novels—FREE
★ A bracelet watch—FREE
★ A surprise mystery gift that will delight you—FREE

THEN CONTINUE YOUR LUCKY STREAK WITH A SWEETHEART OF A DEAL

When you return the postcard on the opposite page, we'll send you the books and gifts you qualify for, absolutely free! Then, you'll get 4 new Harlequin Superromance® novels every month, delivered right to your door months before they're available in stores. If you decide to keep them, you'll pay only $2.74* per book—that's 21 cents below the cover price and there is no extra charge for postage and handling! You can cancel at any time by marking "cancel" on your statement or returning a shipment to us at our cost.

★ Free Newsletter!

You'll get a free newsletter—an insider's look at our most popular authors and their upcoming novels.

★ Special Extras—Free!

When you subscribe to the Harlequin Reader Service®, you'll also get additional free gifts from time to time as a token of our appreciation for being a home subscriber.

HARLEQUIN'S

With a coin — scratch off the silver card and check below to see how many gifts you get.

YES! I have scratched off the silver card. Please send me all the books and gifts for which I qualify. I understand that I am under no obligation to purchase any books, as explained on the opposite page.

134 CIH KA79 (U-H-SR-12/89)

NAME

ADDRESS   APT.

CITY   STATE   ZIP

Twenty-one gets you 4 free books, a free bracelet watch and mystery gift

PRINTED IN U.S.A.

Twenty gets you 4 free books and a free bracelet watch

Nineteen gets you 4 free books

Eighteen gets you 2 free books

DETACH AND MAIL CARD TODAY

DETACH AND MAIL CARD TODAY

BUSINESS REPLY CARD

First Class   Permit No. 717   Buffalo, NY

Postage will be paid by addressee

HARLEQUIN READER SERVICE
901 FUHRMANN BLVD
PO BOX 1867
BUFFALO NY 14240-9952

NO POSTAGE
NECESSARY
IF MAILED
IN THE
UNITED STATES

the way his life had been lately—he felt as if he was losing parts of himself every time he made another decision, losing faith in the things he had always believed in for himself, losing Jamie.

"We've got to retrieve as much of that stuff as we can." Johnson was pointing to the wrapped bales floating midriver where one raft had flipped over.

The two guards removed their shoes and radios before they waded into the murky water. The bricks bobbed along with the motion of the current. They were all around them, moving downstream toward the Texas bank.

When the water was too deep for them to wade, they swam, retrieving one block at a time, tucking it away, returning to shore when they couldn't carry more and stashing it away there. And while Daniel fished out the very last of it, Johnson went for his truck.

"We'll weigh it when we get to the station." Daniel was still dripping as he loaded their vehicle. "I'd say we've got at least three hundred pounds of pot here."

"And I'd say they got back across to Mexico with twice again that much."

JAMIE HATED SHOPPING after Christmas. People were spending money everywhere on the after-Christmas sales. The decorations in the malls were still up but they weren't as pretty anymore. All the artificial poinsettias looked wilted. They seemed to have lost their life somehow.

Her favorite annual display, the pecan-covered reindeer at Northpark, was dusty and worn. The pecans on their legs were dropping off.

It was the way Jamie felt, too, shopworn, as if she was worse for the wear and tear of the holiday season.

As she turned on the lights in her grandfather's house, the telephone was ringing.

She tossed two packages on the couch, belated Christmas presents she hadn't been able to resist today, a little red plaid dress she had found for Sarita and a Texas Ranger's T-shirt she had bought for Miguel.

"Hello?" She was breathless when she answered. She hoped, as she had hoped for days, that it might be Daniel.

It never was.

"Jamie. Hello. This is Frances Ybarra calling from Roma. How are you?"

"I'm okay." But she didn't sound okay. Jamie was suddenly frightened, for something must be wrong with one of the children to prompt Frances's phone call.

"I've had good comments about *Las Posadas* since you left," the principal told her. "The parents are very proud of their children. And they have been receptive to the English presentation. You put so much work into it. Many have expressed their gratitude to you. They are hoping the children will do it again for them next year."

"I left the scripts filed away in the desk."

"I am sorry you are not here to see Miguel Canales speak of his performance. I believe he is the proudest of them all."

Jamie closed her eyes in an effort to control the emotions raging within her. Until she had heard

Frances's voice, she didn't realize the depth of her loneliness.

She had no one to share her heart with.

"Frances? Is something wrong? Are the children okay?"

"The children are well. But I have bad news. I was hoping…" The principal stopped. She didn't want to push Jamie. She knew her conflicts. They had discussed her grandfather during several confidential meetings in the principal's office.

"Tell me."

"The young woman who was to take your position in January has declined our offer. She has decided to take a better-paying position with a private school in Houston."

"How could she back out now, when she had promised you she would be there all along?" Promises, loyalty, were things Jamie placed great stock in. It was hard for her to fathom any other way.

"It is understandable. It happens often here. They were able to offer her so much more money."

But what about Sarita, who had told her just before she left that she wanted to grow up and be a teacher, too? What about Miguel, who was just beginning to speak English around his family?

"If I don't find another teacher, I'm going to have to split the class up and distribute the students among the other classes. I hate to do it. Some of them will have to be put forward. Some of them will be put back. And I'm already way over the twenty-one to one student-teacher state ratio in every class." Frances had applied for an exemption at the state capital in Austin just after the beginning of the session.

Jamie knew what was coming. She was standing beside the lamp, gripping the telephone as if, in doing so, she could hold on to the children she loved, too. *Don't ask me, Frances. Please don't make me question it all again.*

"I was hoping I could talk you into coming back for a little while. I know your situation there. And I didn't know if you had accepted another position with your old school district. I'm certain they want you back. But I need you, Jamie. It will only be until I can find another permanent instructor."

Jamie's voice was steady over the line, so steady it betrayed her. Her tone proved how much she was hiding. "Thank you for thinking of me, Frances. But I cannot do it. I cannot come back to Roma."

"I was afraid of that. And I'm sorry. I didn't want to put you on the spot. But you understand I couldn't make my other decisions about the class without talking to you first."

"I know that. Thank you."

But Jamie thought about the offer until much later. There were myriad things she didn't understand. How a teacher could desert the class at the last minute for the sake of money. What would happen to the students who had to be pushed ahead or put back? She wondered why God kept flinging doors open for her, doors that led to places she could not go.

As she searched for answers inside herself, Jamie thought of Miguel. He was one little boy in over a thousand.

Almost without thinking, she picked up the telephone and dialed the number at *Los Ebanos*. And when she heard it ringing on the other end, it was almost a relief. It was as if she was holding on to a life-line she hadn't clutched before.

Daniel answered the phone.

"Daniel?" Suddenly, Jamie lost her nerve. Her entire body was shaking. And she was certain he could tell. "It's me."

"Jamie..." Daniel knew he should have shouted at her. But her voice sounded so tiny and sad. And, despite his anger, he was so happy to hear from her that he wanted to let out a whoop right there in the family room. But he didn't dare. He controlled his voice. "To what do I owe the pleasure of this call?"

She couldn't help but flinch at Daniel's sarcasm. "Don't be angry, please. We need to talk about Miguel."

"Miguel is fine." Daniel's tone was acidic. "He will be one of the best players on the baseball team someday."

"Frances Ybarra just called me. She may be splitting his class up. And even though the kids have tested out to an equal level, some will be moved forward to an all-English class and some will be pushed back. I know Miguel, Daniel. He isn't as sure of himself as some of the others. And even though he speaks English well, he doesn't do it often. I'm afraid he's going to get lost in the scramble."

"It's nice of you to be so concerned about him," Daniel said coldly. "It's nice of you to be concerned about all of us."

"Daniel. You have to talk to Pedro. Have Pedro talk to Frances Ybarra. Don't let Pedro sit by while his son loses everything he's gained."

"He isn't my child, Jamie. You know I can't convince Pedro of anything. If Miguel goes back to a Spanish-speaking class, you know it isn't anybody's fault but your own."

"Maybe it is my fault in a way, Daniel." He was making it impossible for her not to stand up to him. "But there are other circumstances, too, and you know it. Don't lay the blame solely on me."

He was being unfair and he knew it. But he couldn't stop himself, couldn't soften, couldn't let her know what her leaving had done to him. "I wish you had considered the consequences of what you were doing before you came here. You got their hopes up, Jamie."

"If I did, it was because I did a good job. My only fault was in not being able to stay."

And, God, how we've missed you. How I've missed you. But he didn't tell her.

"Daniel. Will you talk to Pedro? Can you try? Don't do it to be kind to me. Do it for Miguel. Do it because the boy cares about you."

For a moment, Daniel considered doing what she asked. But he had already interfered with Pedro and his son once. He wasn't going to do so again. "It's too late, Jamie. He's playing on the baseball team on Saturdays. I will do what I can for him then. But that is as far as I will go." He knew that Jamie was right, however. Miguel would be placed in a Spanish class. Daniel wanted to help the boy more than anything. But, just now, he couldn't. "I have to respect Pedro enough to leave well enough alone."

"I'm sorry then," she said, sighing. "I shouldn't have called."

"It will be easier if you just let everyone forget you." This time, he was speaking solely for himself.

CHAPTER TEN

Two BIG-SCREENED TELEVISIONS blared at opposite ends of Oakhaven's lounge. It was shortly after ten o'clock.

In New York, it was the new year already. The huge glittering apple in Times Square had just fallen, the networks had panned their cameras to it briefly and, as viewers were offered a glimpse of the city's streets, all was bedlam.

At Oakhaven the room was quiet, except for two women in the corner who clapped when the apple fell, and except for the dull clack of dominoes as the men shuffled them on the card table near the corner.

It was a soothing sound Jamie had grown up with. Her grandfather's friends were always at the house playing forty-two. She remembered countless nights when she'd drifted off to sleep lulled by the sound of their voices making bets and the click of playing pieces falling together as each player took his turn mixing them up.

Tonight, she was playing the game with them.

"Who shuffled these bones?" William Forrester growled. He was perched across the table from her, looking like a nineteenth-century Native American chief, with the heavy red serape draped around both shoulders. "I bid thirty-one. I'm banking my partner

over there has a trump or two for me up her sleeve."
He winked at Jamie. He had a bad hand. But it was
against his nature to let the bid go by without upping
it.

"I don't know if I can pull you out, Grandad," she
said, laughing, after her turn came and she took the
bid at thirty-three.

As she led out with her first trump, the television
station's logo appeared on the screen beside the table.
"The president's war on drugs—" an announcer's
voice boomed the show's title "—and how it fared on
the Texas border in 1989..."

The mention of the place she loved so well snagged
Jamie's attention.

"...A special KXAS news report from the Rio
Grande Valley..."

"Did you watch the last trick, Jamie?" her grandfather asked after she lay the next trump on the table.
He wasn't supposed to talk during play, but it was a
bad habit he had developed, keeping a running com-
mentary going, because he had taught so many people how to play the game. "You are calling my last six,
and you don't need to."

"Don't talk to your partner," a man named Harold chastised. "Your granddaughter knows how to
play this game. You've told me so many times."

"That I have," Jamie's grandfather said, laughing, enjoying the bite of competition. "Sometimes I
forget she's all grown up and she doesn't need a
teacher anymore." He grinned at Jamie. "She's a
teacher herself."

The game continued in silence. Jamie did her best
to hear the news report. Her grandfather didn't say

anything this time when she played the wrong domino. He only raised his eyebrows. And, in the end, she lost enough tricks for the point to go to the other team.

"Near the little town of Roma," the reporter was saying, "where the U.S. Census Bureau shows the population is ninety-five percent Hispanic and the jobless rate near forty percent, huge houses with tennis courts and a swimming pool stand beside shacks reminiscent of the *colonias* that stand on the opposite side of the Rio Grande. Banks in the tiny community do well..."

"No," Jamie said to the television. "It isn't fair for you to say that." She had seen the huge houses, too. And everyone jokingly called them "marijuana manors." But there were other parts to the community, too. Most people worked hard for the things they had, and most families wanted nothing more than a fighting chance to survive. "They make Roma sound like the whole economy is based on drug smuggling. The people I know down there work so hard." They were like Sarita's mother, agricultural workers, and some, like Felix Galindo, worked in the furniture factory, too.

The commentator continued. "A typical day in the life of an INS agent... or perhaps not a typical day... because today it is Christmas 1989."

The scriptwriter for the show had traveled to the valley to do her research. She had pored through the INS records from the day. She had found Daniel's files.

"For Daniel Salinas and Richard Johnson, the morning began at six o'clock beside the Rio Grande..."

Jamie gasped. "It's Daniel." And, unconsciously, she grabbed her grandfather's hand. He had moved beside her.

As they listened together, the story of Daniel's Christmas Day unfolded before her. She learned about him crouching in the brush alone, about the family he had turned back, the electronic sensors, the rendezvous with Johnson. And, as Jamie heard about his life, the bullets flying from the Jeep and the men crossing the river, she felt her entire body go limp with missing him.

There was so much of Daniel's life she didn't know, so much discord and distrust inside him that she'd never tried to comprehend. As she watched the report, she felt a sense of isolation and insignificance, as if it wouldn't have mattered if she hadn't gone to Roma at all. She might as well not have ever existed, for all the difference she had made in the children's lives, and in Daniel's.

William watched her shrewdly. "I don't know how to interpret the anguish I see on your face, Jamie." He was angry with himself now, for letting so much time go by while he worried about her. He should have confronted her days ago to make her tell him why she seemed so lost and so afraid. "I've been hoping that the sadness you carry around with you is only the result of your loyalty shifting." He knew how dedicated Jamie was to her teaching. He knew how dedicated she had always been to him. "I think it's time you and your grandfather have a long talk."

"You just let us take the lead in this game and now you're quitting," Harold piped up. "If you stop now, Forrester, you forfeit the game."

"I forfeit it." He gripped Jamie's hand beneath the table. "You win, Harold. Put it in the record books." Jamie could feel the playing bones in his fingers. She made a feeble attempt to smile at him but she couldn't. She was tired and afraid and she didn't know what she could tell him.

William pulled the serape tighter around him. He continued to clutch her fingers in one hand. He took his walking cane in the other. Together they walked outside into the darkness.

"We don't have to walk." She knew it was hard for him.

"You talk better when you walk, child."

"Anybody tell you that you're getting bossy in your old age?" she teased.

"All the time."

Their feet were sloshing through grass and leaves in the place they had talked so often before. And it suddenly seemed only right to her to be honest with him.

"Now. I want to know what happened to that confident girl I said goodbye to in September. The one who set out to the Rio Grande Valley knowing she had so much she could teach those children."

"I suppose I was wrong...if I was so confident." She spoke slowly, doing her best to explain herself to him, to verbalize her feelings for herself. "Maybe there wasn't much I could share with them. Maybe I was the one who needed to go down there to learn."

"Tell me, Jamie, what it is you have learned."

A scene flashed before her eyes, an image of Daniel the night after *Las Posadas* surrounded by third graders begging him to show them how to play baseball. "That giving yourself to people can mean a great many things." Jamie wished she could say this to Daniel, too. But now, with him, it was too late. "Sometimes when you have nothing left of yourself, it's better not to try it."

"I don't remember when I've ever heard you being so cynical."

"I learned I couldn't be two places, two parts of myself, at once," she said smoothly.

"There was a time," William reminded her, "when you would have told me how you were feeling without my prodding. Remember when we used to be best buddies?"

"I thought we still were." She smiled at him. He could just barely see her expression in the darkness. Then she began to tell him more. "I thought I could go down there and give the kids my guts and come out of it unscathed. But I didn't. That man they talked about on TV tonight. Daniel Salinas. He is the INS officer I wrote you about. He is friends with one of the little boys in my class, Miguel. Daniel insisted I was wrong to even try. And, in the end, I proved him right."

"How? How did you prove him right?"

"Because I had to leave."

"And so..." he confronted her gently. Her grandfather's voice had the wisdom of his years in it. "...You opted for a past here with me and decided to forget about the things you want for your future."

"No." Jamie was horrified that he would perceive it that way. "It isn't that way at all."

"But you left behind a lifetime of possibilities. I know it by what you tell me about the children and the place where you lived. And you've been lost since you came here. You must know what you are giving up for me.''

It was ridiculous for her to do it. Medicare and his teacher's pension paid these folks a fortune to take care of him.

''I had to give things up. You're right. But it's worth it.''

William leaned against an oak tree and eased his weight off his cane. He loved his granddaughter. More than anything, he wanted to know he had given her the gift of her own life. ''It wasn't worth it, Jamie. I think you've given up on it because you think you've failed.'' It was a contemptible thing to say to her. But he knew what she was doing. She thought she had to stick around and pay him back for everything his sheltering meant to her when she was fifteen. She owed him nothing. She had been a joy to him then. And she was a joy to him now.

''I didn't fail.''

He had to continue. He didn't want Jamie waiting around while the doctors tried to kick start his old body over and over again. He knew his health was failing. The doctors wanted him to start kidney dialysis in January. And the high blood-pressure medicine they had given him made him sleepy and slow. ''If you didn't fail, then what is happening to the children you care so much about now? Are they suffering because you left them?''

Jamie wheeled toward him, tears in her eyes at last. ''I don't know if the kids are suffering,'' she told him. ''But I know that I am.''

''Jamie, precious Jamie.'' He leaned on his cane and tried to move toward her. But she saw what he was doing and she moved to hug him instead. "Can't you see the answer yourself?"

"I can only see how much you've given me over the years."

"I didn't drag you through your teenage years so you could sequester yourself at Oakhaven with me." Then he grinned. "I've got a question for you. Remember that dress you brought home from the store your sophomore year that I wouldn't let you wear to the dance? The black velvet one with the red sequins all over the front of it?"

"Yeah." She was laughing. "I do." It had been a horrible dress. She wouldn't wear anything like it today. But she had bought it because she thought it made her look sophisticated. "I thought you were so mean to keep me from being glamorous."

"I wanted you to have such a sense of yourself, Jamie. So you could go out into the world someday and know who you were and *be* that person."

"I am."

"No," he said, "you aren't. Or you wouldn't be wandering around Dallas with a long face looking as if you've just lost everything in the world that matters to you."

"I made my decision."

"You didn't make the right one." He hated pushing her away. He missed her so much when she was gone. But he loved her enough to urge her to follow her own heart's bidding. "You owe those kids in Roma a lot more than you'll ever owe me."

She studied his face, so near to hers, the jutting lines, the skin folded in jagged, leathery wrinkles around his eyes and his mouth where he smiled.

"I am not your future. I fight against it, Jamie, but I am an old man. Are you going to hang around here and wait for me to die?"

"That's a horrible thing to say."

"It isn't. It's all in the plan of things." In a flash of insight, he fingered the woven wool of the serape where it hung across his chest. "You did such a beautiful job of weaving, Jamie. In and out. Parts of this and that."

"But I didn't do it myself," she reminded him. "I had help from Sarita and Elena."

"It is often that way," he told her. "We do not weave the fabric of our lives on our own. We depend on others. We *need* others, just as we need to know when to depend upon ourselves. And, my dearest—" he hugged her to him now, leaning on her as she supported him, with her strength as well as with her love, it was something she had done for so long now "—you cannot weave a life without somehow binding your past to a future. You have to be smart enough to tie it all together."

"I know that," she said. "It was what I wanted to teach the children in Roma."

"That's good. Very good. And now," he said, still holding on to her, "it is time you listened to your own lessons."

She wanted to refute his words, but she couldn't. "I can't leave you."

"I will always be a part of you, Jamie. Don't turn away from what you want most in the world. Don't turn away from yourself. Go back to the borderland and teach the children who need you most."

She was silent then, looking at him as tears pooled in her eyes without falling, feeling sad, but knowing, at last, that it was right for her to go.

JORGE GALINDO BOUNCED ALONG on the northbound bus. The lady sitting in front of him was traveling with a piglet. The stench in the vehicle from the little pig and the sweat of the passengers and the rotting fruit someone was carrying in a crate in the back created an assault on his senses that was almost unbearable.

But, Jorge reminded himself, he was a man now. After being separated from his parents for so long, he should be able to bear anything. He didn't feel dejected. This was the way of life for many of the people he knew.

Jorge had come many miles from Mexico City. And he could only guess at the number of miles left to go before he found himself in Matamoros. He carried a leather pouch in his pocket. It contained an envelope with a hand-drawn map on it. It was smudged, but he could still read it. The man who had come to the door with it had told him it was drawn for him by his father. It would direct him to the place where he would live.

The pouch also contained many *centavos* tied up inside a piece of linen his aunt had cut from the sleeve of one of her shirts.

Jorge had not eaten since yesterday at two o'clock, when the bus had stopped to let off passengers and pick up crates in Antiquo Morelos. He was afraid to use the little bit of money he had brought with him.

He was certain he would be robbed if anyone on the bus saw where he kept it.

He had worked hard for the money he had with him. And anything he could save, he wanted to take to Texas with him so that he could repay his father. Felix Galindo had sacrificed so much. Jorge knew his father was even sacrificing his future in Texas to send the money so that Jorge could be with them in Roma, and with his sister, the little American girl his mother wrote about whom he had never met.

Jorge was very excited and very, very afraid. He was thirteen years of age. And, already, he felt very, very old.

MIGUEL CANALES SANK his chin into his hands. He hated this class. The new teacher made him read things he already knew. "*La vaca* grazes on the brushlands when it hungers." He had known what the cow eats ever since he was a baby. And now he had to learn about it all over again. It made him mad.

The door to the classroom swung open and the principal entered. Mrs. Ybarra was speaking to his new teacher. He supposed it was about him again.

The music teacher had tried to make him stand up earlier and sing "Jimmy Crack Corn" in English in front of the whole class. He didn't do it. He knew the words. He had learned them in *maestra's* class before she had gone away. But he certainly wasn't going to sing them now.

"The child is defiant," the music teacher had told his new teacher. Fine. *Defiant*. It was a word his father would be proud of. Just as he had been proud of *Las Posadas*. Just as he had been proud of the baseball game Miguel had played in last Saturday in the park with *Señor* Salinas. Defiance and pride walked hand in hand. His father had taught him that.

Mrs. Ybarra was watching him as the teacher moved up the aisle toward his desk. He frowned at her and closed his book. Another trip to the principal's office. He could see it coming.

"Miguel," the teacher said. *"Señora Ybarra tiene una sopresa para ti."* Mrs. Ybarra has a surprise for you.

He got up from his desk and followed her. He didn't know what to expect now. The promise of a surprise was very different. Mrs. Ybarra smiled at him when she took his hand.

He followed her outside and down the covered concrete walkway and around the corner to the second row of third-grade rooms. They stopped outside the door to the room that had once been *maestra's* class.

"Go inside," Mrs. Ybarra told him. "Go inside and find your place."

He turned huge eyes toward her, black, brooding eyes that made Frances Ybarra want to hug him. "Do I have another teacher now?" He spoke English for the first time in weeks. At least, maybe now he would be back in class with Sarita and some of the others who were his friends.

"No," Frances told him. "You have an old teacher. An old, new teacher. Miss Forrester has come back."

Miguel stared at the principal, his eyes even larger. And then he slammed open the door to his old classroom and ran inside. There she was, standing there, looking just the same as if she hadn't gone away at all.

"Miguel," she said softly as she stooped to hold her arms out to hug him. "Hello."

He didn't move.

"I am glad to see you. Would you like to be in this class again?"

Miguel was happy to see her. But he wasn't happy, too. He had been so sad before, when she had gone. He had spent three days moping around after she left, and sometimes he'd even cried. And when he talked about it to *Señor* Salinas, his friend had told him that *maestra's* life was not with them. *Señor* Salinas had been sad, too. He had told Miguel so.

"Miguel?" she asked, seeing all the fear on his face and hoping to erase it. *Have I hurt all the children this badly? Or can it be just this one?*

"*Vayase.*" He said the word deliberately in Spanish because he knew it would make her angry. You go away. "*Su vida no está aquí.*" It was what *Señor* Salinas had told him. Your life is not here.

"Miguel," she said, as loudly as she could, but the boy's name was hardly more than a whisper. "You must give me another chance as your teacher. Perhaps my life *is* here, after all. I have come back to find out."

"No," he said, his eyes blazing with all the pride he had inherited from Pedro. "I do not want to give you a chance. I do not want you to be my teacher."

And then he fled the room.

CHAPTER ELEVEN

IT WAS DARK WHEN Daniel turned the Dodge into the front entryway at *Los Ebanos*. Instantly, he knew something was wrong. Every light in the sprawling ranch house was burning. Pedro's truck was parked at an angle in front of the patio.

"What is it?" he asked the moment he pounded through the front door, his voice as full of authority as it always was on the river.

Harriet met him. "It's Miguel, Danny. He ran away from school this afternoon. No one knows where to find him. He didn't come home on the school bus."

"Did something happen at school? Did they call him into Mrs. Ybarra's office again? It's happened so often since..." He hesitated and changed his choice of words. "...since he entered his new class."

"We don't know. They assumed he was on his way home when Frances Ybarra telephoned Lúpe. She was just concerned that Lúpe be here for him when he arrived. I'm sure she'll call tomorrow to find out what happened. But today she was just so worried, Lúpe's only thought was waiting for him and then finding him."

"Did you see the school bus arrive? Are you certain Miguel didn't make it to the ranch?"

"We didn't see it. Lúpe went out there when she saw children walking by the front gate. But Miguel wasn't there."

"Have you searched the ranch?" Daniel asked. It was possible the boy had gotten off the bus before Lúpe heard the other children. It was also possible Miguel had walked the five miles from Scott Elementary to *Los Ebanos*. Many people in Roma knew him. Perhaps someone had given him a ride.

Pedro stomped in through the back door. "He hasn't come to our house, either. I checked down by the corrals, too. Nothing. And no one along the road has seen him."

They were right to be worried. Even though Miguel was a legal resident of the United States, he might easily be mistaken for an illegal. He would not know what to tell the agent who might stop him. And there were others in Roma, too, smugglers Daniel knew all too well, who might have reason to bother a young Hispanic boy walking alone as twilight fell. "I'll call the station and see if anybody has seen him. Someone who didn't know him might have picked him up."

"I don't know where else to look," Pedro said, shaking his head as Lúpe came up behind Harriet and hurried to dry her eyes with her apron.

"My *Miguelito*," she said bravely although they all heard her voice quiver. "He is still so young to be out after dark and so alone."

Daniel turned to his mother. "Telephone Frances Ybarra at home. Find out why he ran away from school today. I'll look around *Los Ebanos* once more."

There was one place Pedro hadn't mentioned checking. No one had looked in the mesquite grove down by the arroyo, where he and Miguel had shared many talks. Daniel wondered if Pedro even knew about it.

He was out the door quickly and striding toward the corrals, and then past them, as darkness shrouded the trees and cast ghostly shadows around him. *"Miguelito,"* he called as he approached the arroyo and the stand of trees. "It is your friend. *Señor* Salinas."

No sound answered, nothing stirred, except for the constant breeze that always blew, rustling mesquite beans on the limbs where they grew.

Daniel walked closer, silently now, certain the boy would have heard him if he was there. Daniel's eyes were growing accustomed to the darkness. He peered into it. And then he saw him, a small gray figure perched on a rock where the erosion in the sand formed a bank for the dry streambed. "Is it you?"

This time, the boy turned toward him and nodded.

"I thought I might find you here. Your father has been searching *Los Ebanos* for you. He doesn't know about this place."

"I came here because he doesn't know of it."

Daniel climbed down the bank and sat beside him. He didn't say anything for a while. He wanted to give the boy a chance to become accustomed to his presence before he questioned him.

"I didn't want anyone to find me."

"Everyone at the house is worried."

"I left school early. I think I am in very big trouble." Miguel propped his elbows on raised knees and cupped his chin in his hands.

"Not too much trouble. Maybe only just a little bit."

"A little bit is enough in my mother's eyes. She will make it become very big."

"She won't." Daniel was smiling now, he couldn't help it, thinking of Lúpe, so worried at home in the ranch kitchen, and how happy she was going to be when she saw her son. "Mrs. Ybarra called from town to tell her you had left school. Your mother went out to the front gate after the school bus came. But you were not on it."

"I walked," Miguel told him.

"It is five miles."

"I needed much time for thinking."

"And what were you thinking about?" Daniel asked.

Miguel turned dark eyes toward his friend, and all his confusion shone forth in the light from his pupils even though it was dark where they sat. Daniel saw moisture from the tears that the little boy's pride refused to let fall. "I was trying to think about *Maestra* Forrester, trying to decide whether I am happy with her or angry."

Daniel hated himself for his reaction to the boy's words. He hadn't heard her name since he had spoken to Jamie on the telephone a week before. And just the mention of her made him feel as if the fortress he had managed to construct around himself against her was being battered at, attacked, not by some huge, forceful army but, instead, by his own yearnings for her. *Damn her! Had she hurt Miguel that much, too? How could the child still be thinking of her, needing her, so many weeks after she had gone?*

"Miguel," he said softly, not knowing exactly how to be gentle with the boy, but trying. *Here I am, still trying to sand out the damage she did.* "Miss Forrester's life is not here with us. You must reach for your own future. You must work in your new class with your new teacher."

"Perhaps *maestra* should be here with us." Miguel's pride failed him now as the child-size tears began to roll down his cheeks at last. "Perhaps you were wrong about her."

Daniel was losing patience. Oh, to be a child again, to believe with childlike hope, to have faith in people despite their failures. "I wasn't wrong about her." He hugged the little boy to him. "It is a hard lesson to learn. I know you cared for her. You must fight to forget her." *Just as I am fighting to forget her.*

"But you do not know, *Señor* Salinas," Miguel told him, his voice subdued. "I cannot forget *maestra* and go forward in learning with my new teacher. I no longer *have* a new teacher. I have my old teacher. *Maestra* Forrester has come back."

Dear Grandaddy,
Sometimes I think I should have left well enough alone. I was thinking of myself when I left Roma. And I was thinking of myself when I came back. I know you said you wanted me to come out into the world and really *be* who I wanted to be. But, in some way, I'm afraid I've hurt you. And now I know for certain that I've hurt the children.

They looked at me today when they each came into the room, and their expressions were even more guarded than when we all first met. I think what I've done is even worse than not making them trust me. I became their friend and then I left them.

Miguel Canales ran out of the room when he realized who I was. And even Sarita was subdued, although I think she was glad to see me.

Maybe it's just going to take some time.

I love you so much, Grandaddy. And I love you even more for sending me back. At least, that's the good part in all this. I don't have to leave things as they stand.

Take good care of yourself for me.

Know that, in my heart, I will always be with you.

Jamie

DANIEL STRODE PURPOSEFULLY up Estrella Street. He had parked his truck in the town parking lot just past the customs checkpoint, in front of the town hall. He was walking for therapy. He had no idea what he was going to say to Jamie when he saw her. His hands clenched into fists, as if his self-control was a tangible thing, as if the muscles in his hands and his fingers could clasp it.

Go home, he wanted to tell her.

You don't belong here.

You belong in my arms.

Damn.

He reached her tiny house on Estrella, and the flowers she had loved so were still blooming, but a different car was parked near the front curb. Of course. Jamie had given up her lease when she chose to leave for Dallas. She must be living somewhere else now.

He had absolutely no idea where to find her. It made him feel helpless all over again.

The only place he knew to seek her out was the school. He would register at the front office the same way he always registered, just the way he had on the morning in September when he had come to retrieve Gilbert Muñoz. That day, he had practically brandished his gun at her.

Seeing her today was going to be like seeing her for the first time. And he hated himself for the one bit of hope that sparked up inside him. Had she come back for him? For the children? For them all?

Daniel frowned as he made his way toward his car. He didn't need this. More than likely, Jamie had come back to prove something to herself. To prove she could finish what she started. That was the way Jamie Forrester did things.

But could she give a final ending to the feelings she had stirred in him before she had left him at Christmas? Could he?

It was the first time he realized how frightened he was to see her again.

When he arrived at F.J. Scott Elementary, he didn't have to wait for her. "She's in the same room," Frances Ybarra informed him, with her constant gentle smile. She dealt with everyone the same way, whether they were children or adults, in trouble or being commended. She was gentle and loving and kind. But her demeanor did little to quell the hurricane of conflicts that twisted inside him. "She came in early today so she could ready herself for her first full day of teaching again.''

"Thank you, Mrs. Ybarra." Daniel went to Jamie's classroom and flung open the door, expecting her to be at her desk gaping at him. He knew her well enough to know she would meet his anger head on. But, instead, she was turned away from him, stretched tall on her toes to write the day's assignments in English on the chalkboard.

Her cottony hair, the color of pale terra cotta, turned under in haphazard sections against her shoulders. The entire room smelled of her, he thought, or maybe it was just his heightened senses, a feminine scent both sophisticated and winsome, spicy—like Christmas—and floral—like spring.

The familiarity of it probed at him, reminding him of his desire for her, of the way his body responded to hers when she melted against him.

Probably something fancy she bought in Dallas. Some city smell that cost her big bucks a bottle.

Or was it just her?

The fragrance of Jamie.

"I'll be with you in a moment," she said when she heard the door close on its hydraulic spring. "I'm almost finished." She had been expecting the janitor to come and help her move one of the bookshelves.

Daniel said nothing.

The chalk clicked against the board as she continued writing.

"There," she said a minute later, laying the chalk in its bin then dusting her hands off before turning around. They were starting an exciting science project today, a very simple version of photosynthesis. "I'm sorry about making you wait . . ."

She turned and saw Daniel.

"Hello, Jamie."

She stared at him. His charcoal-dark eyes seemed to beckon to her, and she wanted to run into his arms because she was so glad to see him. She couldn't help herself even though she remembered his words from just the week before. *It will be easier if you just let everyone forget you.* For a moment, Jamie felt as if her heart was frozen, iced over and still, she was hoping so hard. "What are you doing here?"

"I'm the welcoming committee from the INS," he said tersely, not quite certain if he was trying to be funny or trying to stave her off. "Seems like I get all the good assignments. Greeting teachers on their first full day of classes in Roma." His gun was hanging at his side. He touched it.

She did not miss the irony of the motion or of his words, but she didn't smile. "And who have you come to take from my classroom today?"

"I should send you away." *Because you'll do nothing except leave again. Because you crossed borders in me I should never have let you cross.* "Back to Dallas."

Now she knew it for certain. He wouldn't forgive her for what she had done to them all. "Where you think I belong."

"What happened, Jamie? I know you too well. Something made you come back . . . some misplaced sense of obligation that made you want to finish what you had started."

"You don't give me much credit." She wanted to sink onto her knees to escape the betrayal and the anger she saw on his face. But she couldn't. She had to focus on the students who would file through the doorway in twenty minutes. "You are the one who finds it easy to turn your emotions off and on whenever it suits your purpose. You are the one who thinks rules and regulations are more important than people. Don't condemn me because the people I love take top priority over the things I may need or the rules I have to follow."

"Is that how you think I live my life?" He sounded like a hurt child when he spoke, and looked almost bewildered. "You make me sound very selfish."

"Maybe we are both selfish..." she said, sighing, giving in a little "...in our own ways."

"A long time ago," Daniel said, "I dedicated my life to protecting this nation's borders. It's a marriage of sorts. You don't forget the rules. To try to get the job done any other way would be too painful."

"So you've said." Jamie turned away from him then, thinking of the documentary she had seen on the local news in Dallas, about his workday on Christmas, and the danger she knew he constantly placed himself in. During their time together, he had shown her so little of his life along the river. And, this time, when she spoke, she found herself echoing her grandfather's words. "Maybe you made the wrong decision when you sold yourself lock, stock and barrel to the United States government. Maybe you should have held something back for yourself. You owe the people who love you a whole lot more than you will ever owe the INS."

"How can you say that?" The anger in his voice slashed out at her. "You don't know the half of it."

"And whose fault is that? Is it because you give out portions of yourself the same way you would cut out portions of a pie? I *could* know the half of it if you would only tell me. You could start by telling me of the bodily danger you place yourself in day after day. You could tell me about the gunfights and the drug runners and the loads of illegal contraband you fish out of the river. That *is* your life, isn't it?"

"Yes." Daniel was wearing his short-sleeved uniform and, tentatively, she ran one finger along the crook of his arm, the sensitive spot where it bent at his elbow.

"It is the part of your life that frightens me most, Daniel."

The light stroke of her finger made him shiver. But what she'd said jolted him even more. They were almost the same words Sandy had spoken so many years before at New Mexico State.

Although he hadn't considered proposing to Jamie, hadn't dared to submit to his need for her, her comment was like a prophecy to him, warning him that she would be like Sandy, too. It gave him one more reason to turn away from her. As he felt her fingers still tracing his skin at the curve of his arm and sending bullets of response to his groin, he knew he needed reasons to pull away from her. Good reasons.

He stepped away from her, his eyes fixed on her face. *I need you, Jamie. I knew it before you ever pulled up roots and headed to the city to care for your grandfather.* "I don't need this, Jamie. And I don't need you."

"I'm not asking you to need me," she said. "I'm only asking you to put your own life into perspective. To give *yourself* a chance before it is too late."

"You could tell yourself the same thing."

"Perhaps I have," she admitted, her eyes on his, her words soft yet filled with a sudden tenderness he didn't understand. "Perhaps that is why I have come back."

CHAPTER TWELVE

FELIX GALINDO STARED out the window. His wife and his daughter were busy in the kitchen preparing a meal for the teacher. But Felix couldn't relax just now, couldn't forget his son, who was somewhere between Mexico City and Roma.

Thoughts of his son's perilous journey alone filled Felix's mind nowadays and his dreams at night, too, when he lay still in the darkness. He thought of how it would be, the day he'd look out the same front window he had peered through for years and see his son coming up the front walk to his new home.

As Felix thought about it, there came a sharp rap on the front door. He froze for a moment, thinking Jorge might be at the door now, the thing he had always dreamed might be happening, he might actually see the son who was growing into a man. But, as he heard Sarita open the door and he heard *Maestra* Forrester's voice, he felt as if his plan was in more jeopardy than ever.

All I have worked for can be lost. If I once let down my guard and forget who I am.

Where do you hide a thirteen-year-old boy who has never been to public schools and never learned English?

Felix supposed he should be pleased that Jamie Forrester was back in Roma. He supposed he was the only person in the little town who wasn't glad to see her. But she was such good friends with his daughter and his wife, and he was afraid the two of them would slip up in her presence somehow, would mention Jorge's coming, or the money they had saved and had spent.

Miss Forrester knew that he and Elena were not legal residents of the United States. But what would she do when they brought someone else in, too? He trusted her the same way he trusted everyone else—when he had to—to an extent. He was breaking laws now, when his entire lifetime in Texas had been devoted to living within them, to never drawing attention to himself or to those he loved.

And, according to what the man named Elizando had told him, his son should have arrived by now.

It had been a long time since Felix Galindo had had a good night's sleep.

JORGE WAS DOING HIS BEST to be brave. He stood in the dingy storefront office before a man who wouldn't tell him who he was. But, minutes before, the man behind the desk had answered a telephone and said, "This is Elmo."

Jorge didn't dare call the man by name.

"Sir. The letter I received in Mexico City told me to come to this address. I am to receive a social security card and safe passage into the United States. It is what my father promised."

"And who are you?"

"My name is Jorge Galindo."

The man called Elmo searched through his pockets for a key. When he found it, he used it to unlock one of the desk's drawers. He pulled out several sheets of paper with handwriting and ran his finger along each one. Halfway through the second page, he stopped. His eyes narrowed. "Here you are. Jorge Galindo." He studied the boy for a moment before he said more. "Yes, you have come to the right place."

Jorge straightened his shoulders. "When will we travel across the river?"

Elmo slipped the papers into his drawer and locked it. "It will be a long time for you, I am afraid. I cannot take you across."

"What do you mean? I have come all this way."

"Your father made a bargain with me. He told me he would send me *dinero* to take you across. He met with my men and gave them some money. He did not give them enough. You must pay me more."

"But I have nothing." Jorge was thinking of the little pouch he carried in his pocket. But it contained only the equivalent of several American dollars.

"Then you must find some. Get a job selling fruit in the market. Or steal some. Money is easy enough to come by if you want it badly. Do not bother me again until you have some. Twenty-two thousand pesos is what you must bring me." A hundred dollars.

"I have never seen that much money."

"You had better start looking."

"I will cross the river on my own."

An evil grin spread across Elmo's face. "I would not advise it. *La Migra* is everywhere. The agents will find you. You are not old enough for them to send you back to try the crossing again. They will detain you in

Brownsville, and keep you in a camp, until someone on either side of the border steps forward to claim you."

"Then my father will claim me."

"But he cannot. He is not a legal resident, either, Jorge. If he steps forward, he reveals himself. Everything he has worked for during the years he left you behind will be destroyed. It happens all the time."

"I have nowhere to live while I work to earn money for you."

"You can live in the streets. In Matamoros, many people do."

Dearest Grandaddy,

I don't want to sound overly optimistic, but I think things are getting better here. There are still those who don't trust me for leaving. But, by and large, the children are my own again, eager to learn and to accomplish everything that I can offer them.

If I've had any surprise at all, it has been from the parents. I think our production of *Las Posadas* made some of them really realize how important it is for the children to be able to fit in in both places, to belong in their hearts to Mexico and Texas, too.

Pedro Canales is much more lenient with Miguel at home now. And, from what Miguel tells me, he may even be trying to learn more English himself.

Miguel is doing much better in class. I think he's forgiven me. And, slowly, we are becoming friends again. I had dinner with Sarita's family the other night. They were all so excited to hear how much you liked your serape. I *wish* Elena would try to sell some of hers to larger stores in San Antonio or Dallas. They are all beautiful. But it's just too dangerous for her.

Our next big project is to get ready for the Charro Days parade in Brownsville. The kids from Roma march in it every year. So, here we have another time when the children know more than the teacher.

I guess the greatest joy of all in being back here is looking at all those notes I left for the new permanent teacher and realizing that *she* is *me*. Ha!

I love you so much. I'll send you pictures of the parade. Did your children from Renner ever march in a parade? I have never seen so many excited eight year olds in all of my life.

Please, if you need anything, let me know. I haven't heard anything about the last domino tournaments. How are they going?

Take care of yourself for me. And know that, in my heart, I am always with you.

All my love,
Jamie

"HERE THEY ALL COME!" Diego's father pointed down the street over the crowd.

Jamie waved to indicate that she'd heard him. She couldn't shout. The Brownsville High School marching band was high-stepping past just then and playing a rousing rendition of the theme from *Star Trek: The Next Generation*.

They were in Brownsville, at the very southern tip of Texas, where the river flowed into the Gulf of Mexico. "Legend has it," Frances Ybarra had explained to her as they rode south on Highway 83 in the school's dilapidated bus, "that the tip of the Rio Grande Valley is where God laid his shoes...after creating Texas and Mexico...before he stepped off to create the ocean."

Frances and Jamie were taking the children to Charro Days. The kids had been excited about the event for weeks. They would all march in the first parade that kicked off the annual four-day celebration, the school children's parade.

The boys from Scott were coming up the palm-tree-lined street now, all dressed in traditional Spanish costumes, little black pants with gold rickrack along the side seams and black felt sombreros that tilted over their eyes and hid their faces. The students from Roma had used the costumes for years. Some of the fathers present today had worn them when they were in elementary school.

The boys were dancing *Los Viejitos*, the Dance of the Little Old Men. And, as they went by, the small group of parents from Roma applauded for them.

"Good job!" Jamie shouted as they marched in stilted time, acting out the traditional movements everyone knew so well. "Hooray for Roma!" Then she thought of her grandfather at home. He would love seeing this. But the thing that had brought him to mind was the dance itself, the movements of the old men acted out by children.

Behind the boys came the small homemade float the girls designed while the boys practiced *Los Viejitos*.

Their fathers had helped them build it out of plywood from Gutierrez Lumber and Hardware in Rio Grande City, and tissue flowers and an old truck.

Two children from the first-grade classes walked in front of the float, each carrying a flag, one the Stars and Stripes of the United States of America, the other the rich red and green banner of the Republic of Mexico.

The float was entitled *Feliz Cumpleaños, El Padre de La Patria*. Happy Birthday to the Father of the Country. The children riding the float and waving ranged from kindergartners to third graders. A fifth grader portrayed George Washington. His wife, Martha, was represented by a fourth grader. They all grinned and threw candy to the hoards of parents and children and winter Texans lining the boulevard.

Jamie had to suppress a grin. She wondered, for a moment, how George Washington would feel, the man who had fought so bravely for his country's independence from Great Britain, to see the child who depicted him now—a scrawny Hispanic boy dressed in red knickers and a white powdered wig that threatened to fall down over his nose. The child was so proud to be waving from the float, so proud to be a resident of Texas. And, as quickly as the thought had come, she decided George Washington would have been proud, too.

She was standing there grinning, watching the students she knew, when she felt a hand purposefully grip her elbow.

It was Daniel.

He had worked the early shift on the river this morning and gotten off in time to drive to Brownsville to see the children he knew from the baseball team march in the parade. He'd seen Jamie standing in the crowd and he'd studied her reactions for minutes without her being aware of him. He noticed the interplay of emotions on her face even as she felt them: the pride, the amusement and, finally, the thankfulness. He knew her well enough to read every nuance in her changing facial expressions. And he was so drawn to her then, despite the resentment he still felt for the things she had done, that he had no choice but to work his way toward her through the throng of onlookers.

"It's been a while," he said simply.

"I've been staying away from you."

"I figured that out."

"I thought it would be for the best. So you could . . . forget."

"Thank you." He had to admire her. Here, in the midst of so many people, she wasn't taking the easy way out. Instead of empty social chatter, she was being honest with him. Nevertheless, for his part, Daniel didn't want her to know that her staying away had done nothing to help him. He thought of her all the time. Miguel talked of the things she taught him in class almost constantly. He perceived daily events through the boy's eyes and then analyzed them, wondering how Jamie would see them. Just knowing she was in the valley made him question his anger. Even though he hadn't seen her for six weeks, her proximity tantalized him. "So . . . how are you doing?"

"I'm okay."

He noticed she was shaking, but he didn't know why. "Miguel tells me your class is going well. He is very happy, Jamie."

"That's good." The pride touched her eyes once more.

She is feeling it, he thought. *She is feeling the things I tried to tell her of. The valley. The border. I can see the pride of it in her eyes.*

He had tried so hard to make her see the conflicts, the brutal trade-offs they all had to accept when they lived in parts of two countries, in a place that required people to forsake their old home to become a part of their new one. *And, in understanding that, perhaps she understands a bit more of me, too.*

"Are you still so angry with me, Daniel?" She had to know what he was feeling as he stood there studying her.

"Sometimes." He paused, waited, surveyed the palm tree above him. "Sometimes not." His voice turned very soft. "Sometimes I forget how mad I am and I just...miss you."

She gave him a sad little smile. "Me, too."

"You look nice."

"So do you. Nice...and dusty."

He grinned now. It was as if a weight had been lifted from him because he had told her how he was feeling. "I just came in off the river. No paperwork today. So I snuck away and came here to see the kids."

Students from Laredo were twirling by. Their bright pink dresses looked like swirling rosettes in the late-afternoon sun. "I don't know what to say to you." She sounded like a child herself, lost and as lonely as he was. "I've wanted...so many things since I came back. Just to talk to you. If only to be your friend." *Or perhaps more. To know you want me. The way you wanted me before I had to go.*

The past weeks without her, since she had come again to live in Roma, Daniel had felt just as isolated as when he was a teenager and the INS had deported Raphael across the Rio Grande. Since he had told Jamie he didn't need her in his life, he had privately recanted his words a million times. He couldn't help himself. Jamie's dedication to the children and to her grandfather struck something strong and deep within his heart.

"Did you come with the students on the bus? May I drive you home? We could talk..." He couldn't keep from saying it. He felt as if his entire being was an empty chasm. He had felt that way for days, and just standing beside her, still holding her arm, made him feel as if some force like gravity or a magnet, was tugging at that loneliness, stretching it up and away from him, until it became larger than him, uncontrollable.

Jamie glanced around, looking for one of the parents she knew or for Frances Ybarra. She didn't recognize anyone. They must have moved off to the next block, following the children. "I would like that," she said softly, unwilling to turn then and meet his eyes. He would see too much of her joy. *I can't let myself be that vulnerable to him. Not now.* "I have to find a couple of people and let them know I won't be returning on the school bus."

"I'll come with you." He took her hand and led her through the crowd.

It took only moments to find the residents of Roma. The group had not moved far down the paved sidewalk. Jamie told the principal of her plans and told the children's parents goodbye. Then she and Daniel climbed into his truck and drove inland.

They drove for a long time in silence before Jamie finally spoke. "Thank you."

"For what?"

"For not cutting me off completely."

I tried to do it. He had wanted to hurt her the same way she had hurt him. It had been painful to accept that her grandfather was still the number-one priority in her life, and not him or the children. But, for some reason, her priorities had shifted. She had come back to Roma. And Daniel still didn't know why.

"I need to know something, Jamie," he said. He verbalized the question that had been playing in his head for weeks. "I need to know why you came back."

"And if I tell you," she said tentatively, after thinking of it awhile, "will it make a difference in how you feel about my going?" There had been a time, when she had first come back to the valley, when she had thought it would.

"I didn't give you much of a chance to explain."

"I know."

"At the time, I didn't think you deserved it."

She gazed at him, this time seeing the vital strength in the man who sat beside her and clenched the steering wheel with firm, big fingers, thinking of the frail man in Dallas who had urged her to come back to this, a life that might be her future, if only Daniel and the others would let her be assimilated into the border life, too.

"He talked me into returning, you know," she said. "I couldn't have left him, Daniel. Not unless he told me he wanted me to."

Daniel's eyes remained focused on the black-paved, two-lane highway, the stripes making little dashes in his mind as the truck passed over them. *So she hadn't come back because she thought they had a chance together, after all. She had come back because the old man had talked her into it.* "So now I know."

Jamie sensed his desperation and knew she had to say something more. "He knows me, Daniel. He looked at me when I came back and he saw how very alone I was. I had written him about the children. I told him about you. And, when I did, he heard so much more than my words."

What was she telling him? He wanted to pull the truck off to the side of the road and just look at her. But he didn't dare. He didn't dare let her see how susceptible he was to her.

"He told me he hadn't spent all his years with me so that I could follow him around because I thought he needed me." She gave a little gesture of confusion with fluttering hands. "So here I am now. Back in Roma. With some regrets..." She swiveled sideways in her seat beside him. She focused on the familiar tendril of hair that always curled against his ear "...and some hopes."

She would have given anything, just then, to have him hold her.

And this time, as if something otherworldly had whispered it, he knew her thought.

She needs me just as badly as I need her.

Abruptly, Daniel steered the vehicle off the road and ground to a halt on the gravel shoulder. "Jamie." He simply said her name. It was the only word that came to him, and it was all she needed to hear, as he held his arms out to her.

His arms encircled her as she moved next to him. Jamie felt suddenly renewed, as if his gesture was a forgiveness of sorts, for hurting him. "Daniel," she said, sighing, as she basked in the strength of him, drawing it into herself. "I'm trying so hard to sort it all out. What's important in my past. What belongs in my future. How to be both parts of myself without losing memories or dreams."

He lifted her face to his, her chin cupped within his fingers. "You sound just like Pedro Canales."

"I know. Like Pedro and many others here."

"Last month—" his words were tempered by fear because it was so very hard for him, and painful, to be honest "—when I saw you in your classroom again and told you I didn't need you in my life...I was lying. I knew it then. I know it more so now. I would like to take the pressure off you. I would like to say it didn't matter what you decided about going home to your grandfather. But I can't. It killed me, Jamie."

She was gazing up at him, her morning-gray eyes wide and full of wonder at his words. He felt as if his heart and his loins were both going to burst as he gazed down at her. She seemed so much a child. Yet the strength he sensed in her made him strong enough to face feelings he had run from before. He wanted to protect her and he wanted her to need him and he wanted so much more, too, a sharing and an intermingled giving in their lives.

"I want to be a part of your future, Jamie," he said to her as he lowered his lips to hers. He was pleading with her now the only way he knew how, his body wanting, needing, to speak to her in a language of its own. His first caress was careful, reverent. He didn't know if she had wanted this as much as he had. There was something very different happening between them now, something so much more intense than the haphazard, off-balance relationship they had shared in the autumn.

Jamie was lost in him, in his need for her, as his lips moved gently and then pressed harder, to take on an almost panic-stricken rhythm against her own. It was the first time she had sensed how very much Daniel wanted her, the first time she knew for certain the things William Forrester had sensed in his granddaughter the moment he'd seen her walk into the lounge at Oakhaven. Something inside her was budding and blooming, something that filled her and satisfied her and made her long for more all at the same time.

"Oh, please," Jamie whispered against his temple as he kissed her throat, her ears and the tender spot where her blood pulsed at her neck just below. "Don't ever stop this. Don't offer me this feeling and then take it away."

He found her lips once again and parted them with his tongue while tendrils of wanting curled down inside her and made her ache for fulfillment. His tongue slipped in lazy circles against the line of her teeth while his hands did the same against her back, moving in spirals, exploring the texture of her. He had answers to the words she was saying to him, promises, but he couldn't speak just now. He showed her with his hands instead, holding his breath in wonder, as his fingers finally slipped beneath her sweater and found the velvet warmth of her breasts.

"I won't," he answered her finally, his voice so low only she could have heard him as he brushed his mouth against her neck, her ears, once more. "I couldn't hurt you."

His fingers traveled erratic, gentle paths, moving against the ripples that marked her ribs as he continued to luxuriate in the sensation of her. Her lungs were heaving. And then his breath caught, too, as he found the satin lace of her undergarment and he slipped his hands smoothly beneath it.

With his thumbs, he sought the roundness of her small breasts and, when he found the fullness there, he began twining his fingers against her until, at last, he found the portion of her he was seeking. When the tips of his fingers grazed her hard, engorged nipples, he knew he was about to lose himself. He sucked in one frantic gasp of air and held it, doing his best to regain his control, as Jamie reached for him with both hands and touched his face. She stroked the dark hair on his arms, his gold watch on his wrist, wanting to somehow touch even the blood and bone and sinew beneath the skin on his arms. Daniel felt as if she was touching everything that he was.

And then, as if in an effort to save them both their composure, Jamie compressed herself against him while his hands remained trapped against her, between them. She held him there until both of their hearts began to slow their volatile pace.

As she lay against him waiting for her pulse to calm, Jamie began to tell him about the television show she had seen at Oakhaven that told of his Christmas Day.

"I was so afraid for you when I saw it. They made Roma sound horrible." She lay her cheek against him, still absorbing the rosy warmth that his caressing had caused.

"There are times it is horrible," he said. Reluctantly, he slid his hands from beneath her garments. Then he circled her with his arms.

"They played it on New Year's Eve. Sort of a year in review thing. I thought I was going to cry when they started talking about you."

Jamie felt him stiffen against her as she spoke. He had hoped it would never come to this between them. Jamie was going to tell him his job with the INS was pure lunacy, that it frightened her, that she couldn't subject herself to caring for him this much, not when he was always in danger.

"I was wondering if you would see it," he said dryly. He was waiting for her to say the words he didn't want to hear—the same words Sandy had said to him so long before. "I knew it was going to be on the air in Dallas. I almost told you to watch for it the day you called about Miguel. But I didn't."

He had hoped she wouldn't see it.

But Daniel hadn't stopped to think that denying him in any way wasn't like her. She was loyal to a fault to the things and the people she believed in. It was a quality she shared with her grandfather. Like him, she remained steadfast no matter the price. "I felt so far away from you when I saw it." She could tell he had mentally pulled away from her. She could tell it by his sudden stiffness as she spoke. "It made me realize there was so much more standing in our way besides the miles between Dallas and Roma and the decision about where I would go."

"Yes. There is much, much more standing in our way."

"It made me realize there is so much of your life you haven't shared with me, Daniel. It made me feel desperate, as if I had no right to be a part of your life at all."

"And now that you know of it, how does that part of my life make you feel, Jamie? How does it make you feel when you know I go down to the Rio Grande every day expecting to be involved in a battle that could cost me my life?"

Jamie searched her heart for one long moment before she answered him. Something about the urgency in his eyes made Jamie realize how much stock he would place in her answer. "It makes me feel a great many things, Daniel. It *does* make me afraid for you. But you've spent years of training for it. I know you are mentally and physically prepared for it. I have come to terms with that."

"Have you?"

"It makes me feel proud of you…knowing you are loyal enough to risk so much. Perhaps it makes me understand why you go down there each day and turn people across the border to return to lives of poverty. I see that maybe, in a way, you are keeping them safe, too."

He touched her face once more, running one finger straight down from beneath her eye to her jawline. "And does it make you want to turn away from me?"

It was a concept she couldn't fathom. The thought of rejecting him was so foreign to her that she almost laughed. "It makes me want to say extra prayers for you, so God will keep you safe down there by the water." She looked in his eyes then reached for him, sensing what it was he needed most for her to say. "No, Daniel. It doesn't make me want to turn away. It makes me want to hold on to you even tighter."

CHAPTER THIRTEEN

"I'M SURPRISED THE SCHOOL BUS from Roma hasn't passed us," she said, laughing, as Daniel steered the truck onto the highway and shifted gears until he had reached full speed.

"Maybe it passed us while we were kissing." He grinned mischievously.

"If it did," she said, giggling, "then every kid in my class saw us. I'll never hear the end of it."

"Oh, well. I guess it was worth it anyway." He couldn't resist it. He loved teasing her.

"Thanks a lot."

"You're welcome." Daniel glanced across the cab at her. "Anyone who is willing to sit awake and watch a late-night news special about me deserves it."

"It was New Year's Eve. I always sit awake on New Year's Eve." Jamie was still laughing but she suddenly sobered. "Your life in the INS is a part of what you are, Daniel. A part I don't know very well." She was urging him to open up now, hoping he would talk to her. "It is something I will have to learn about you if we have a chance together at all."

He was watching the road, his expression serious. "You're right. Very right." And then he glanced at her and smiled. "Something I haven't always been lately."

"So tell me," she said, and this time she felt so lighthearted she grinned again. "Tell me all about this." She reached toward his short-sleeved shirt and touched the nameplate he wore on his chest.

"Okay," he nodded. "I will."

It had been a long time since he had told anyone this story. But he knew, as she scrunched up beside him on the seat and straddled the gear shift, that he had no other choice. He had to face his pain. She had been right all along. Their sharing now meant everything.

"I was thirteen," he told her, his voice wavering slightly, as he fixed his eyes on the highway. "And Roma had a championship baseball team."

"It was a long time ago."

"I was on that team. All the bats and gloves and the ball I have stowed away...they're all memories for me...some of the grandest times in my adolescence. My best friend, Raphael Ortega, was on the team, too.

"Besides my parents and now—" He didn't say it. He was thinking of the people he had cared for during the years and had loved, his parents, Raphael, the Canales family and now...now perhaps Jamie. "Raphael was one of the few people I have ever loved. I used to stay at his house forever, and his mother would feed me lunch, and his little sister would cheer for me at every home game."

He was talking in a monotone, reliving it all as if it had only just happened, as if a lifetime hadn't passed for him, even though it had.

"I had a bad crush on his little sister, Juana. She was in the fifth grade when Raphael and I were thirteen. And we did everything together. They were my adopted family. Until the INS found out that they were living in Texas illegally and subjected them to deportation hearings. They were brave about it. They didn't hide or run the way so many Hispanic families do. That was back in 1971. I guess they figured they could fight it. They had been good citizens of our community. And everyone they knew told them they would be willing to testify and tell the INS that.

"Raphael was the best player on the baseball team. He could bat the ball clear over the bleachers and out into the street. He always made home runs. And he could catch, too. His big dream, his *only* dream was to stay in the U.S. and play for the big leagues some day.

"It didn't work out that way. His family was worse off, in some ways, because the Ortegas dared trust the system. They thought it would protect them. And it didn't.

"One morning I got off the school bus and went by his house so we could walk the rest of the way together. But the house was empty. Everything was gone. I felt so helpless. But I still had my hopes. The last thing he had told me before he left school the day before was that he would play baseball in Mexico and then try out for an American team and that he would return."

"Did he come back then? He must have. He would be a man like you now, Daniel. Thirty-one years old."

But Daniel was shaking his head. And when Jamie saw the tears in his eyes, she realized there must be much, much more to the story.

"He won't be coming back, Jamie. Ever."

"Tell me why."

"I'll never know all the details. The Ortegas were from a *colonia* called Peñon Blanco. They had no car and not much money. And, after it happened, the stories went around. Everyone knew about it. But no one could prove it or enforce the laws. While they were still on the Texas side of the river, an INS agent tried to rape Juana. She was ten. Raphael heard his sister screaming and he came in to find them before the agent had harmed her. It was Raphael who, with bare fists, defended his little sister's honor."

"Oh, Daniel."

"There are good men and bad men on both sides of the law, Jamie. It was a hard way for a teenage boy like me to learn such a lesson. Raphael protected his sister. And he was badly beaten for it. The family had barely enough money for food to get them back to Peñon Blanco, much less to pay a doctor to care for Raphael. He died during the long walk to the *colonia* with his family. He was a strong youth, but evidently not strong enough to survive the internal injuries the INS agent gave him in Rio Grande City."

Daniel was crying now, openly, something he hadn't done for years. It felt so good to be telling Jamie at last, to finally make her understand the pain he had faced so long ago, when he was still so very young.

"I'm sorry." She didn't know what else to say.

"When I started hearing the stories, I put my baseball in the closet. I never wanted to play the game again."

"But now you have."

"Miguel Canales brought me back to life a little bit." This time he smiled, even though his cheeks were still wet, and Jamie used one hand to wipe some of his tears away. "I saw Miguel born a United States citizen. I saw him born with everything Raphael Ortega wanted, yet never had. And I had to stand behind Pedro and see the man's pride battling against everything the boy was born with. So," he stated matter-of-factly, "I got out the baseball one day and started pitching to him."

"And you joined up with the INS," she commented.

"I knew I could do a better job than some of the others. I knew I could be fairer. I knew I could follow the rules. And I knew I could be kinder." A cloud of some dark emotion passed over his face. "Even though I've come to find that many of the rules aren't fair."

"What happened to the man who accosted Juana Ortega? Do you know?"

"It doesn't really matter, does it? I was only thirteen. And a boy who is just past puberty doesn't have much political clout. I visited the station in Rio Grande City. I wanted to talk to the chief patrol agent in the McAllen sector. I wanted the INS Office of Professional Responsibility to conduct an investigation. But there was no evidence anywhere. And you can't convict a man with words. He certainly wasn't going to come forward on his own. He knew he was protected by the border rules, by the lack of rules. What belongs to one side cannot belong to the other. The man may still be patrolling the river, Jamie. But now," he said softly, "I am patrolling the river, too."

He looked at her and smiled, a sad smile. "And perhaps that is the only way I know to care for people anymore."

"It isn't." She had seen his capacity for giving. And she realized he had totally turned that part of himself away. "What about your friendship with Miguel? And now, the new baseball team? You deserve a lot of credit." It was a pep talk, and they both knew it, but it was one Daniel desperately needed.

"Maybe I am learning to let a part of myself come out again." He paused, waiting, wondering if he should say it. "Maybe you are the one who is teaching me."

And he is teaching me so much, too. About commitment and priorities and meshing my life together into something that can be my own.

They were almost at her new apartment in Rio Grande City. "You'll have to give me directions to your new place," Daniel said.

"This is the exit." Jamie directed him through the correct turns and, when he parked the truck in a space below her door, she turned and barely brushed his arm once more.

He watched her, saying nothing, feeling free because of the stories of his life he had finally been strong enough to tell her.

"Come in, Daniel. Just for a little while. It's a long drive. Maybe you need a rest before you go on up to Roma."

"I'd like that."

"I'll give you the grand tour of my studio apartment."

He couldn't keep from grinning. "Now *that* should take all evening."

"You think so?"

"We could make it last that long."

Jamie felt something begin to heighten inside her. Her pulse quickened as he put the truck into park and flipped the keys off in the ignition. She saw his bare arms, his dark, downy hair curling around his gold watchband, as he reached for his wallet on the dashboard and slipped it into his pocket.

"Okay," she said after they had climbed the stairs and she had unlocked the door. "Prepare for the longest tour of your life. This—" she gestured inside "—is the living room, the guest quarters, the bedroom and the dining room." She stepped inside and he followed her. "That—" she pointed in one direction "—is the kitchen. And that—" she pointed in the other "—is the closet and the bathroom. Impressed?"

"I think so," he said, laughing. "But maybe I should take a look at the closet first."

The apartment was just as she had left it, quaint and homey, with a blue serape thrown over the couch that made down into the bed. A glass-topped coffee table with gnarled mesquite legs stood beside it. And her favorite part of the apartment was an adobe window seat covered with blue and maroon and sand-colored pillows.

Daniel surveyed the pictures displayed on the coffee table. One showed an attractive couple standing behind a tiny girl. They had to be Jamie's parents, he thought. In another, the girl was older and she was standing, arms spread as if affecting a fashion-model pose, in order to show off the bright purple pants she was wearing for the camera.

"My first pair of bell-bottoms," Jamie said, grinning.

The other photograph was of a stately old gentleman saluting the camera.

"My grandfather."

"He's a handsome old man."

"Of course," Jamie said, studying the picture, too, and letting the love for the man who had raised her during her teen years pour forth in her words. "I come from handsome stock."

"You sound like you're talking about cattle."

"You just say that because your father is a rancher. And you'll probably be one someday, too."

"I'd like that." Daniel's eyes had a faraway glint in them for a moment. "I know all about handsome stock." He turned toward her then, in the middle of the little room that was her new home, and held his arms out to her. "Jamie. Let me hold you."

She moved toward him with abandon, grinning at him. "I thought you'd never ask."

"Oh, no." He chuckled. "I think you are trusting me too much."

"I don't think I could ever trust you too much after the story you told me today."

"There you go," he said, still teasing her, "making me into a hero."

"We talked about heroes once, remember? And you said you didn't know if you really wanted to be one. I'm not making you into a hero." She hesitated ever so slightly, her tone turning serious. "You are just a very special man. To me, at least."

"Thank you for making me share so much of myself with you."

"You have the ability to give so much, Daniel. Don't stop with the things you have just told me. I need for you to give that much of yourself to me, too."

"Oh, God, Jamie," he said, desperation in his voice as he stroked her hair. "You know I'm dangerous. It's like I have a borderland inside myself. I might as well guard it with a gun the way I guard the Rio Grande."

"I know," she said, her voice low and calm as she lay her head against his chest again and basked in the feeling of his arms enveloping her. "I know how much I am risking."

And I care enough for you to take that risk.

It was the first time Jamie had admitted it to herself, and now that she had done it, she knew it was so. She gazed up at him, marveling at the things they had just begun to share with one another.

"Jamie. I don't know if...I..."

"...Could drop the barriers long enough to let yourself be everything I need?" She finished his sentence for him. She had silently understood.

"I don't know if I can care for you the way you deserve to be cared for."

"Perhaps you can, in time. But, if you can't, it doesn't matter, Daniel." It was part of the risk she was taking. She knew him. And she knew she had to show him she trusted him by freeing him from obligation.

"And if we take every day just as it comes? You could be satisfied with that now?"

She nodded, knowing full well the things he was afraid of. "It is what I want, too."

"Are you certain?" He was searching her face, not wanting to subject her to the many things that continued to tear at him inside. "It frightens me. It frightens me for you."

"We will do it the way you taught me when I first came to Roma," she said gently, wanting him to realize how strong she was, wanting him to see that perhaps he was the one who had made her so. "We will give to one another what we are capable of giving. And if the time comes to cross a line, to give more, to commit everything, and neither of us can do it, we will know we haven't failed one another. We have just been ... who we had to be."

He cradled her head against his chest, one of his huge hands encircling her hair, and then, almost frantically, she turned her face up to him and found his lips with her own. She wanted him to accept her so desperately, on whatever terms he could.

"Oh, Jamie," he murmured against her lips, "I have wanted this for so long."

"As have I."

He reached behind her then, as she melded herself against him, and with fingers that had found her flesh once before he pressed against the small of her back, circled there and found her again.

Jamie pulled away from him only inches, so that she could help him ease the sweater up from her belt. She raised her arms for him as the garment came up over her stomach, her breasts, and at last over her head. She shook her head once, to free it, and then she stood there, watching his expression, looking at him, her skin gleaming, her hair disheveled, not making a sound.

Daniel's eyes swept over her, taking in the proportions of her, the wide breadth of her shoulders, her small breasts, the lines of her figure where they dipped in at her waist and then flared to fuller hips.

"You are beautiful . . ." he said to her, his voice so soft and full of awe she had to strain to hear him ". . . so beautiful. Just as I imagined you would be."

Jamie found so much pleasure in seeing him admire her that she could scarcely bear it. And, at last, she took one small step toward him so that she could unfasten the buttons on the shirt of his INS uniform. She did so, one by one, with trembling hands, while he bunched her hair in his hands, kissed the top of her head and whispered her name.

She reached the bottom of the row of buttons and tugged the shirt out from his pants. She stopped then and turned expectant eyes on him, seeking his approval now as she began to run feather-light fingers through the damp, dark curls of hair on his chest.

Daniel bit his lip from the sheer pleasure of her childlike expression. Tenderly, he nodded at her. She grinned at him. Their touching was a cross between a necessity and a game as she pushed the shirt so it fell away from his bare shoulders and wrinkled down his arms. And when everything fell to the floor, the shirt and the uniform and the INS badge, it was as if his clothing had represented everything in their lives that had once stood between them, everything that had held them away from one another, until now.

He held her face in his hands again briefly, watching her, enjoying the look of expectancy in her huge eyes, marveling at her trusting smile.

God, I want to deserve everything she wants to give me.

"You can do this?" he asked her and he was almost afraid of what she would answer. "You can give yourself to me knowing who I am? What I stand for?"

"I think..." she whispered as she buried her head against his bare chest and reveled in the texture of his bronze skin there. It was like smooth, fine, wet sand. "I think that you are the one who needs to forget what you think you stand for. I don't."

He had had it in his mind to warn her once more. She was so open to everyone. She gave herself like a gift whenever she found the chance. He had seen her do it for the children, and now she was doing it for him, too. But words of love replaced words of caution.

"Oh, *querida*." He bent then and kissed the top of her head again. "I do hope you mean what you say."

"With you," she said, "it can be very easy."

He gave her a wry cockeyed grin. The expression seemed so endearing and familiar to her that she felt fresh emotion rising within her, something new and joyous and focused and certain.

Jamie was afraid to give it a name. She couldn't, not now, when they had just talked about not committing, not crossing borders. Yet it was everything she could do to keep from shouting at him, proclaiming her love for him, for it was such a new emotion and a precious one. She could only share the feeling with him by doing what she was doing now, by touching him and showing him how treasured he was. "I love it when you grin like that," she said instead. "You look like a little kid about to open presents."

"Ah," he said, as he sat down on the narrow couch swathed with the serape that made down into her little bed. He pulled her down on top of him and finished, "Maybe, Jamie, that is exactly what I am doing."

She draped her arms around his shoulders and bent toward him again, the joy gone from her face, only the raw physical need there, and when Daniel saw it his breath caught in his lungs. She looked so beautiful to him then, and seemed so much so absolutely his, as he flipped open the snap on the waistband of her jeans and eased them down over her hips.

"There you go," she said from above him as she moved to straddle him. "At last."

"You think *you've* had to wait for this?"

"Forever. I've waited forever."

He tried to grin again, but this time he couldn't quite do it. His expression was more like a bittersweet smile, for his mouth felt thick just from wanting her. "I'm glad you think I'm worth waiting for."

He slipped his fingers into the lining of her silken underpants. They were beautiful and blue, like the Gulf Coast sky outside the window. And, as he tugged them down and viewed the rest of her, she moved down beside him to draw his garments down, too. He bundled her up beside him.

"Jamie Forrester," he said to her, his eyes registering all the awe and delight he was feeling as his eyes and his hands and his heart absorbed every inch of her body. She was dainty and lithe and all sand-colored and satin, like her hair. "You are a splendid woman."

"Thank you." Her lips moved against the hairs on his chest as she burrowed there.

Daniel couldn't hold himself back from her any longer, not when he was tasting the saltiness of her skin and hearing the melody of her words and running fingers along a torso that reminded him of the softness of spun honey.

His tongue slipped down her throat and then found her ear beneath her hair. Suddenly he was licking, tasting all of her as her head fell back against the serape, her hair a fan against the rough wool. His mouth moved lower then, down the side of her neck to one delicate white shoulder, as she clung to him. This time, he found the fullness of her breast with his teeth and he encircled it on both sides of her ribs with his hands. He was holding himself at bay so his touch would feel tender to her, but he wanted to grasp at her now, he was so filled with yearning and need.

Daniel tightened his grip on her ever so slightly, holding her breasts so that their breadth was gathered there, her nipples dark and tight and ready for him, as she gathered his shiny curls in her hands, running her fingers through them. The roughness of his hair was so dear to her as she guided his face to where her breasts were rising, falling, waiting for him. She longed for him to wet her nipples with the fervor of his mouth, his lips, his tongue.

He did so at last as she guided his head. He circled her nipples with little licking motions that made her want to sing. "Don't stop," she said to him. "Don't ever stop. I want you always."

But Daniel couldn't say anything, couldn't answer her, as he raised himself above her at last and parted her legs with his own.

"Yes," she whispered to him. "Yes. Please."

"And so this," he whispered, his voice filled with a sudden shot of whimsy, "is making love."

"Yes," she said again. "Making love. Giving love. Sharing it."

And it was true, they were both lost in the observance of loving as he pulled her close and filled her with himself, each of them giving the things they were able to give, each of them receiving, as the breeze blew in from the Gulf of Mexico outside. And as they made love over and over, the water in the mighty Rio Grande rolled silently by, a great barrier in motion—only someone else was guarding it now, as night darkened the water and it moved continuously toward the south.

CHAPTER FOURTEEN

"I DO NOT WANT YOU TO GO, husband." Elena Galindo waved a wooden spoon at Felix. "There are other ways to find out what is happening in Mexico than to sacrifice your family's freedom and your own."

"I have no other choice. Jorge should have been here by now." Felix Galindo shouldered his travel bag. "We have worked so hard, spent all our money. Someone is cheating us. This could be my only chance to find our son. I know he is near to us. I can feel it in my heart. And my sister says he left Mexico City many weeks ago."

"It saddens me to see you leaving."

"Father..." Sarita was tugging at his arm "...will you be very, very careful?"

"Yes, Sarita." He reached down and gave his daughter a friendly pull on the back of her hair, a gesture he had used with her ever since she had been tiny. "I promise you."

It was a promise Felix made to himself, too. In many ways, Elena was right. He was a fool to cross the border now, to bring attention to his family. But he had no choice.

Felix kissed Elena on the cheek and hugged his daughter. "Goodbye, family."

He did not take the truck this time. He couldn't drive it over the border. The INS would check his citizenship status at every crossing.

When he reached the highway, he stuck his thumb out whenever a likely looking car came by. It had to be an old one, rusty and large. It had to look like it might belong to another illegal Hispanic. It scared him that he might flag down someone of authority.

Felix had learned long ago what the immigration authorities looked for. Most of the agents boasted callously that they could spot an illegal by the way his polyester clothing clashed, by the way he smelled, by his black-patent shoes *hecho en Mexico*. Made in Mexico. He knew he didn't look the part. But, no matter how well he had adapted himself to the American mainstream of society, the fact remained. The social security card he carried in his pocket was not a valid one.

He accepted three rides to the north along Highway 83, the Texas Tropical Trail, to a desolate area just south of the Falcon Dam. His last ride let him out near the tiny Texas town of Salineno. From there, he walked directly west until he found the Rio Grande. It would be an easy crossing. The water was low coming out of the dam this time of year.

Felix glanced up and down both sides of the river before he stepped onto the sand by the water. He was alone. He hoisted the bag containing his things high above his head and waded into the current and it seemed so unbelievably easy. When he reached the other side, another country, his Wrangler Jeans were only wet to his hips.

From there, Felix turned southwest. It took him two hours to walk to the Mexican town of Nuevo Guerro. He asked for a ride south to Matamoros on Highway 2.

"I'll take you there," one man in a little *cantina* volunteered. "All the way to Matamoros for only sixteen hundred pesos." The man shot him a sly grin that displayed three missing teeth. And the teeth that remained were stained brown with tobacco.

Felix shook his head. "It is too costly." He had expected to pay half that, only thirty-five or forty dollars instead of seventy-five. He did not have that much money with him.

"You will walk a long way then."

"Here," Felix said stubbornly, "this bribery is a way of life. In the United States, it is not. I have good legs."

"You will use them."

He started off to the south then, alone, and even though he found a ride, the trip took him hours longer than he had anticipated.

But he had to find his son.

It was the end of February, and something was terribly wrong. Felix hadn't panicked until he attended Charro Days in Brownsville with Sarita. He had seen *Los Viejitos*, the Dance of the Little Old Men. It reminded him of the last time he had seen his own first-born son, how it felt to wave goodbye to the stoic child with dark eyes that spoke, even when he was five, of understanding misery. How desperately he wanted to give Jorge a chance at life in a place where growing and learning and dreaming could mean something. In

Mexico, if you began caning chairs when you were a young boy, you died caning chairs after you were old.

At last, he found the storefront operation in Matamoros. A huge placard in the window advertised shamelessly. "False document papers made here. Social security card eleven hundred pesos."

Felix stepped inside.

"I am Felix Galino," he said to the man who sat behind the scratched old one piece desk. It was the only furniture in the room. "I have paid your men to bring my son across the border. I want to know where he is."

"Ah, hello, Felix Galindo." The man produced a key and unlocked his drawer and produced his lists. He sounded as if he had been expecting Felix to arrive for days now. "Your son's name?"

"Jorge. Jorge Galindo."

The man smiled. He remembered now. The boy had already been here. And he knew he could expect much, much more money from the father. He checked the list. "Here he is. I will bring your son to you after I collect the money you still owe me."

"I owe you nothing. I paid your men everything you requested."

"That isn't what my men told me."

"Then they cheated you."

"Or perhaps they only cheated you."

"I paid them everything I had." Felix was ready to use his fists and grapple with the man.

"Your son is here in Matamoros."

"Where is he? Can I see him? Is he well?"

The man behind the desk did not smile. He was not supplying information as an act of friendship. He wanted to coax Felix into spending more. "He is fine as can be expected after such a long journey alone. He does not have a place to live. Perhaps he is working to make enough money himself for our coyote to get him to your home."

Felix wanted to bury his head in his hands and weep. "How much more does the coyote need?" He had scarcely enough to get him back home to Roma. "And how do I make certain all the money gets directly to the coyote who requests it?" He stared coldly at the man. "I am tired of people lying."

"I am the coyote who requests it. Pay me forty-eight thousand pesos today, and your son will be in your home tomorrow."

The sum requested was more than two hundred twenty-five dollars.

"I do not have it now." Felix raised empty hands as if to prove his impecunity to the man. "I worked for years to give your men what I gave them."

"You might check in the market for your son. Perhaps you will find him peddling vegetables. He is afraid to cross the river on his own. If he is detained, he will be held in a camp in Brownsville. And he knows you will not be able to claim him."

The smuggler had the best of him, and Felix knew it. "Very well," he said softly. "I will take your name and your address. I will send you what money I can. I will expect to see my son within days."

"I cannot give you my name. And the mail in Mexico is not very reliable."

Felix was furious. He wanted to beat the man up. But he held himself in check. He would be no good if he landed in the Matamoros jail. He would go to the market today and ask after Jorge. Perhaps someone had seen him. Perhaps he could find another way to bring Jorge across the river. The coyote did not have him cornered yet.

"If you expect money, you will have to rely on the mail. It is the only way I can get it to you. I will not trust another man." Felix pulled a pen out of his pocket and jotted down the street address of the dilapidated office.

"Just a minute," the man said, at last deciding to protect his own interests. "If you send money in the mail, make certain it comes to Elmo Elizando. That is me. The coyote."

"Fine." Felix stuffed the paper into his pocket.

After he left the dingy office, he walked to the market. It occurred to him, as he surveyed all the people there, peddling goods, bargaining and buying, that he didn't know if he would recognize his son on the street. He approached several teenaged boys and asked for their names. But not one of them was the teenager he sought.

Late that afternoon, with a silent prayer for the safety of his son, Felix turned north again on Highway 2. He walked most of the way that night, his mind racing with possibilities. How could he find his son and help him across the river without sending Elmo Elizando the money he was asking for?

When Felix reached Ciudad Camargo at daybreak, he had to decide whether to continue north to the place he had crossed the river before or to cross the Rio Grande much closer to Roma. If he crossed closely to Roma, it would be much more treacherous. The INS patrolled the river regularly. But the shortcut would save him hours. And he was exhausted.

Felix turned east. And he reached the river just as the sky across it above Texas shone rich and red with the sunrise. He hid in the mesquite trees, kneeling low against the sand, as he surveyed the riverbank.

He saw no one.

He stood and walked onto the sand, his bag hoisted high above him. The water was much deeper here. He would have to swim. And just as he moved to the water, Felix felt a knife pressed against the side of his neck. Someone wrenched his bag down and caught his arms behind him.

"Buenas dias, señor," a voice growled at him. "I see you are crossing into the promised land this morning. Men seldom do that without bringing their life savings with them. I would like to have yours, please."

"I have nothing. Only about twenty dollars. And you may have it." Felix's only concern was to get away unharmed. He yanked his arms free and grabbed the bag and tossed it directly into the bandit's stomach. He knocked the man off balance. The act bought Felix a few precious seconds. He ran toward the water, leaving his clothes and his money in the bag behind him. The bandit followed him, probably thinking that Felix had money hidden in his shirt pocket or his jeans.

The Mexican bandit slashed out at him three times with the tiny knife. Felix heard the rending of fabric, then he felt a ripple of pain down his back. But, as he dove into the river and the tepid water closed over his head, he knew he was safe. *Santa Maria.* He didn't even realize he was praying as he swam, holding his breath under the water. He only knew that someone was watching for him, caring for him today, Mary or Jesus or his patron saint for it was as if he'd been through a thousand perils unscathed. And, as he felt the rocks and the sand beneath his feet, the river was growing shallow. Only a few more strokes and he would be on the other side, Felix thought, thanking Heaven.

"COME ON, BUDDY." Daniel aimed his gun at the bandit across the river. He knew he couldn't fire the shot. It would only frighten and disorient the other man, who was fighting for both his belongings and his life. Daniel had no jurisdiction on the opposite side of the river. He looked on, helpless.

He did not recognize Felix Galindo until Sarita's father rose from the current on the Texas side and began to climb onto the sand.

"Felix Galindo." Daniel holstered his gun and ran to his acquaintance from Roma. "Are you hurt? Did he rob you?"

Felix stared at the uniformed man. And it wasn't until Daniel saw the raw fear on Galindo's face that he felt his own heart freeze, too. What was Sarita's father doing crossing the United States border by way of the river?

"You are not okay." Daniel moved toward the man, seeing the rips in his shirt and the stains of blood there. "Have you been cut?"

"My wife, Elena, will patch me up," Felix said in terse English, "as soon as I arrive at my home."

"Wait." Daniel was embarrassed because he had to detain the man. "I'm sorry, *Señor* Galindo. But this is my duty. I have to ask you if you are a legal resident of the United States of America."

Felix raised himself to his fullest height and stared at Daniel's collar. "I am."

"Good," Daniel said. "Show me the papers to prove it and I can let you go."

Felix reached into his wet pocket, struggled for a moment to get his fingers in. His documents were false. But they were good copies. And at least he had them with him.

But his pocket was empty. He held out his hands and shrugged. "Mr. Salinas. My documents are in the bag I left on the opposite side of the river. I have lost everything I carried with me."

Daniel had no other choice but to take Felix in and check out his story. "You are going to have to come with me. It won't take long. I hope you understand that."

And so we have all come this far. For this. Felix could only think of his family then, of Elena, who had given up her chance at legal residence because she was frightened for him, and Sarita, the only one who was safe among them, and Jorge, who might be lost forever now. His lips quivered as he stood before Daniel. His eyes were those of a frightened, cornered animal.

He did the only thing he knew to do. He turned and ran.

"Felix! No!" Daniel shouted as he pursued him. He fired one warning shot straight into the air. "Don't do this."

The man's situation was becoming clear to him. He and his family had lived in Roma for years. And he would not be running if he were a legal resident of the U.S.

Daniel was directly behind Felix now. He only had to reach out to grab the man, tackle him, and he would have him.

Instinctively, he did it. The two men tumbled to the ground as dust flew into Daniel's face.

"Don't fight me, Felix," he shouted. "I have no choice. I don't want to hurt you. This is very, very hard for me to do."

At Daniel's honest words, Felix stopped struggling. The pain in his back was excruciating now. The surface cuts were embedded with sand and thorns from his dash through the brushland foliage.

"I do not want to do this."

"Tell that to my wife, my daughter and my family," Felix spat the words at him. He had almost said *my son*.

Daniel pulled the man from the ground and cuffed his hands behind him. He led him through the brush and the cactus to the waiting truck. Daniel radioed to the sector station in Rio Grande City and, when the information he sought came back, he realized his worst fears. Felix Galindo was breaking the law because he lived here. His wife, Elena, was not a legal resident, either. But Sarita, their daughter had been born in Texas.

More than anything, he wanted to set the man free.

I am not strong enough anymore. Or maybe I see too much.

By the time Daniel and his captor reached the station, he had made his decision. He turned to Felix in the truck cab just before the two of them left it. "I did not apprehend your wife or your daughter crossing the border. I only apprehended you." His eyes were as dark as Felix's, unreadable. He would not say more, and he only hoped the man beside him would understand. "You must sign voluntary papers and return to Mexico immediately, Felix." If he waited for a deportation hearing, it could take days. And the INS would investigate his entire family.

This was the first rule he had ever broken. But Daniel intended to leave Sarita and Elena alone. He had known them for months and had never been suspicious of them. Sarita played on his Saturday baseball team.

"I understand. Thank you, Daniel."

"Do you want me to talk to them for you? Is there a place in Mexico they can contact you? I can tell Elena what happened between us, how I found you, because of your fight with the Mexican bandit."

"Do not tell Elena about the cuts."

"If I am to tell her anything, I will expect to tell her everything." It was his only condition for doing what he was doing now. He wanted to be as honest as he could be.

"I will stay with friends in Nuevo Guerro," Felix said. "When my wounds heal, I do not know where I will be."

Daniel knew where Felix would be. He would be on the river again, trying to cross, so that he could rejoin his family.

"Tell Elena I was unable to find..." Felix hesitated "...what I was looking for."

"I will."

Daniel held the door open for him and then kept a tight rein on the man's handcuffs for appearance's sake as the two of them walked toward the building. Daniel stood with his friend as Felix filled out the necessary papers and signed his name.

Another INS officer took over the process now, as Daniel watched from the corner, mentally going over the words he would write on his own paperwork to avoid any mention of Felix's family.

There were at least forty illegals waiting to go back that morning. They had all signed voluntary return papers, and they were all wearing bright orange jumpsuits and waiting in a locked area for the bus to come. And when the bus arrived, a white one with the green insignia on the side that read United States Immigration and Naturalization Service, the illegals filed on and sat with heads poked through open windows.

This bus was like any of the buses the INS sent across the border each day. There might as well have been a party on board. The men hung from the windows and waved at the agents who had entrapped them and at the pretty women who happened to be walking by on the Texas streets. But when this bus went by Daniel saw Felix sitting there. Felix was the only man not smiling. Felix Galindo was staring straight ahead, and Daniel wanted to shout out at the injustice of the man's plight, as the bus pulled onto the street and made its way south toward the International Bridge.

Dearest Grandaddy

I am so glad to hear that everyone envies your serape. I made it for you so everyone could look at you and know how special you are to me. And I'm glad you've decided to wear it instead of hanging it on the wall. Since I'm not there to give you hugs, I wanted you to have something that would keep you warm.

I have lots of things to tell you. But the best thing I can tell you is that I am very happy. Enclosed is the picture you asked to see of my Daniel. You were right in your last letter. You *do* have a right to see what sort of ''fellow'' is ''courting'' your granddaughter. And I'm here to tell you that he's a very wonderful fellow. Do I sound like I'm on cloud nine? Maybe he can come with me to Dallas the next time I come. I'll talk to him about it. I really would like you two to meet face to face. Grandaddy, I am falling in love with him.

Thank you for giving me all this.

Speaking of coming to Dallas, I am looking at my calendar and planning on flying up there for spring break. Does that sound okay with you? And don't worry. I will heed your advice in the last letter. I won't ''set up camp'' in Dallas like I did the last time.

Well, there's somebody knocking on the door. It's probably Daniel now.

Let me know if those dates look okay to you for a visit.

Give yourself a hug for me. And take good care of yourself for me. Know, always, how much I love and miss you.

Jamie

Putting down her pen, Jamie ran to let Daniel in the front door. She always felt sorry for him when he stopped by her apartment on his way home from the river. He always arrived both physically and mentally exhausted from guarding the Rio Grande. But today, as she flung her arms around him and kissed him, she saw an almost unfamiliar distance in his eyes. She had almost forgotten what his eyes could look like when he erected his inner bridges between them.

Something had happened today that had ravaged him. Even the angles on his face were sharp and hard, as if his face were carved of ebony instead of skin and bone.

"I'm not staying," Daniel said, his voice devoid of emotion. He seemed like a robot, programmed to perform without feeling. "I still have something I have to do. I want you to come with me."

"I will." She didn't want to ask him what had happened. "Where are we going?"

"To the Galindos. I had to send Felix Galindo across the border into Mexico this morning."

It took a moment for the words he said to register. She stood there staring at him. And when she realized what it was he was telling her, Jamie wanted to strike out at something. She wanted to strike out at him.

"Why? Why did you do it?"

"I apprehended him coming across the river. I am going to tell Elena. I want you to come with me. It will be easier..."

"For you?" she screeched. "Why would I want to make that easier for you?"

Her anger stabbed into him like a knife and lodged, twisted, in his heart. The wounds she gave him now were every bit as real as the cuts on Felix's back. "Forget it then, Jamie. Just forget it." He had come to tell her how desperately he needed her by his side for this. But Daniel's pride was as intense in some ways as Pedro's. He wasn't going to beg her for this. He turned to go.

She glared at his back. She wanted to hit him, to hurt him. Didn't he know what he had done? Yet she couldn't say anything. She clung to the kitchen table. And then, just as he was about to close the door, she made her decision. Her words were crisp, honed to a keen edge, formulated to injure him. "I will go. But I'm not going for your sake. I will go for Elena." Jamie slung her purse over her shoulder and then just stood there, looking sheet-white, as if she had wept away all her energy, even though he knew she hadn't had time to cry.

In some ways, Daniel had expected her reaction. He had even prepared himself mentally for it as he drove toward her apartment. Yet, when she rejected him in righteous anger, it was harder for him to accept than he thought it would be. He ached for her to understand what he'd had to do. He ached for her to hold him, to strengthen him, even while he knew she couldn't.

He told her about the knife wounds on Felix's back and about the Mexican bandit.

"Couldn't you have just forgotten the rules *once* and let the man come across the river? He was hurt, Daniel. And the bandit obviously stole everything he took with him."

"He has friends in Mexico. He told me so."

"Couldn't you have just let him come across to his home?"

"And is this his home, Jamie?" Daniel was furious at her for upbraiding him. And mad at himself, too, for even considering that she might be right. Maybe it took strength or stupidity or compassion to bend the rules. Maybe those just weren't qualities he could boast of. "Think about it. Does Felix Galindo really have the *right* to call Texas his home?"

She squared her chin and looked at him. "I believe any man has the right to follow his dreams, to prove he can be who he wants to be, regardless of his birth-place."

"I don't like it when you accuse me of screwing up other people's lives." *You do it so easily. I needed you to strengthen me. Because, this time, what I've done hurts me, too.*

Jamie stood behind him in the foyer while Daniel told Elena what had happened to her husband.

"Ah, *madre de Díos*," Elena cried, clasping one hand over her mouth and then struggling to regain her composure so that Sarita wouldn't see her weeping. "He promised he would not let this happen. He is a strong man, *Señor* Salinas. But I am frightened for him because of his wounds. He has no money with him to pay for a doctor in Nuevo Guerro. And our friends there won't have any to lend him."

"He did not want me to tell you about the knifing. He was very lucky to get away from it alive. He wanted me to tell you not to worry, that he is okay." Daniel stood his ground, erect and expressionless as a statue, as he spoke to her. "He will be back soon. I know it. But he could not tell me that."

Elena took his hand while he stood, rigid, with Jamie behind him, wanting to scream out to both of them. *This is a farce. This man just sent your husband back to a place that must be like a foreign country to him. This is his home. Because you and Sarita are here.*

Jamie stared at Daniel's neck, at the point of curly black hair that lay against the collar of his uniform, thinking how sad she was for Daniel and how vulnerable he was. And how stubborn.

She felt her soul go out to him, even as her anger would not subside. Jamie knew there was nothing she could do to help him to make this easier. There was no part of herself she could offer him just now. Not in honesty.

"Elena," Daniel was telling the woman, "I don't think there is anything more I can do for him. But it might help if you can tell me why your husband was crossing the Rio Grande this morning. Why did he go into Mexico? What was so important that he felt he had to jeopardize the security you have built for yourselves here?"

Elena opened her mouth to explain it to him. She wanted to tell Daniel about their son. He had been so kind to come here, so brave to face Felix's family and tell them what had happened. But then she saw his uniform just as she was starting to speak, and she realized she couldn't say anything about Jorge.

"I cannot tell you," she said. "I believe I can trust you with the truth. But I cannot betray my husband's faith."

"It is your choice, Elena." Daniel's eyes traveled to Sarita. The little girl stood behind her mother clutching the woman's skirts. She seemed like a different child from the boisterous little girl who only last Saturday had made her first hit on the baseball diamond. "I only wish there was something I could do to help him."

"There is not a way." Elena was almost whispering. "Not as long as you wear the uniform of the INS. I am the one who regrets that I cannot call you friend. Because, deep inside, I know you would make a trustworthy one."

"Yes. I would."

Daniel turned to Jamie. She took one step away from him. She was clutching her purse as if she were clutching a weapon against him. "Are you coming with me?"

She shook her head. "No."

"It's your choice, Jamie." But, inside, he wanted to scream at her, *Why can't you trust me, too?*

"I want to stay here."

His eyes met hers for one long moment. They were like black onyx, hard and pure, unyielding in the questions they silently asked. And she couldn't answer.

She knew she was failing him.

How can you care for me, his eyes were asking. *How can you touch me the way you did, make love with me and now turn away?*

We are lovers, Daniel, Jamie wanted to say aloud to him, but she didn't dare, not here in front of Sarita Galindo and Elena, *but will we ever be able to belong to each other's souls?*

CHAPTER FIFTEEN

"HE SHOULDN'T HAVE left us, Mama," Sarita wailed. "You were right in what you said to him. I only want to see him again. Do you think he will be able to come home to us?"

"Of course he will, *niña*. We will see Papa again. And Jorge will come, too."

"Elena." Jamie moved toward them then. "I am sorry for what Daniel has done. I want to do something to help you."

"There is nothing, *maestra*," Elena said to her, and her voice was full of compassion for the teacher who was trying so hard to assist them. "There is nothing anyone can do for my husband now except pray."

"I can do that."

Elena turned to Sarita. "We will go to the church now. For benediction and vespers. Perhaps Father will say some prayers for all of us, too." The woman turned kind, wise eyes to Jamie. "I thank you that you have come to be with us. And I know the best thing you can do now is to go to *Señor* Salinas. From the sadness I see on his face, he needs you very much."

"Oh, Elena." Jamie sat beside them on the bench beside the loom where she had done her weaving and buried her face in her palms. "I want to go to him. I cannot go to him. I cannot stand by his side. I cannot agree with what he has done.''

"You must find a way to be with him. Within your own heart, *maestra*. I know you think that, by sending Felix back, he was being cruel. But I can tell you that, during his cruelty, he was also being kind.''

"How can you say that? When he could have *helped* Felix?''

"It was Felix's choice to swim the Rio Grande and go into Mexico yesterday. My daughter and I begged him not to go. But, in our lives, it has continued to be inevitable. The going. The coming. The searching. The needing. It is how our lives must be. It is who we are. A part of two loyalties. A country that is our past. And another that we pray can be our future.''

"No man, regardless of whether he wears a uniform and carries a gun, has the right to take that from you, Elena.''

The woman brushed Jamie's hair from her forehead as Jamie gazed up into Elena's weathered, dark face. "My husband will return to us as soon as it is possible for him. No man can stop him from that. No gun. No law. That was the message Daniel Salinas brought from him today. That he is nearby, waiting and loving us.''

"You live by so much faith," Jamie whispered. "I don't know if I could ever do that. Faith in the man you love. Faith in God.''

"Faith in God is easy," Elena whispered. "God's strength is so obvious. He always provides the faith for us, holding it there, for us to grasp, whenever we seek it. Faith in a man is not nearly so easy to find. But it, too, is something worth seeking, something worth needing."

"I want to believe that." Jamie gripped Elena's hand as if she was gripping a rope that was pulling her out of danger. "I want to have faith in Daniel. I want to love him, Elena."

"Find your faith, then," Elena told her. "Search for it in every place you go with him. See the many things he did for us today, the kind things, despite the rules he had to follow.

"When Felix did not have the papers with him to prove he was a legal United States resident, the INS agent who detained him would have run a check on his entire family." She sighed, a weary sigh, and leaned back on her heels. "When that information came back, Daniel had to know that *I* am not a legal resident, either. And, although Sarita is a citizen, she should have been sent to Mexico to live, too, because we are her parents. She has no legal guardian in Texas. Daniel should have come here today with his truck and other men and his handcuffs and he should have carted us all away."

Jamie wanted to cry for Daniel then, for the courage she had not recognized in him, just thinking of how alone he was now and how quickly she had condemned him.

"I believe he protected us," Elena said in a hushed, tender voice. "But maybe, *maestra*, that is for you to decide."

I see a man I love. Doing things I try not to hate. But perhaps I do not see more than I want to see. Perhaps I do not see his most obvious acts of caring because I do not look for them.

"It must have been difficult for him to come to us and tell of the things he has done."

Jamie nodded. "I know it was."

There were tears in Elena's eyes now, for the man she loved who was hurt and stranded somewhere far away from them across the river. "It was probably one of the most difficult things he has done in his life. And I look at you, *maestra*, and at how much you have taught the children here. I see the way you hurt for everyone. And I have to believe you are the reason *Señor* Salinas was strong enough to come to us."

Dearest Grandaddy,

I don't know where to start to tell you what is happening here. It's very painful and very sad for all of us, but I think it is the worst of all for Daniel.

Daniel stopped Sarita's father while he was crossing the river to come back into Texas. Daniel had to turn him in. And then he went to Elena and Sarita to tell them what he had done.

I don't know if I could have been strong enough to do that.

I don't know if I would have sent Felix Galindo back to Mexico knowing that his home and his family are really here.

I don't know what I can say to Daniel. We just see people and rules and reasons so differently from one another.

And it frightens me because we are so different, and because I do love him so much.

Elena says Felix will return to Texas soon. I hope so.

In school, we are finally starting on the part of Texas history that I like best, the battles that lead to Texas's independence from Mexico. And we are finally getting around to doing those oral reports.

We will see you soon, Grandaddy. Take good care.

All my love and hugs,
Jamie

"JIM BOWIE FOUGHT at the Alamo, and so did Davy Crockett." Rudi was reading aloud from his Texas history report. "They were fighting for Texas's independence from Mexico. They tried to beat Santa Ana and his men. But they lost. They all died."

Jamie's class was learning to present oral reports. She had decided to begin with the famous Texas battles. The little boys adored them. The girls enjoyed them, too. And, in a way, the stories represented much more than the battles themselves. In some ways history represented what the children were facing now, gaining independence by learning English and math and science. Despite their Mexican heritage, they were, by choice, truly children of Texas.

Jamie was thrilled with their progress. She and Frances Ybarra were campaigning with the Starr County School Board to fund a field trip for the third graders to San Antonio. She wanted them to touch the cold, gray stone walls of the Alamo and see the display of Jim Bowie's famous knives.

"Excellent, Rudi," she told him as he sat down.

A hand shot up at the back of the room.

"Yes? Inez?"

"One of my ancestors fought in the Battle of the Alamo. But he didn't die. He fought for Santa Ana's army when he was just a boy. Mama says he was very brave."

Jamie sat on a desk in the first row. She was consciously bringing herself closer to the eye levels of her students. "You can be very proud of him, Inez. He fought for something he believed in. That's something we can all do. Now, tell me. We are learning about history from one point of view because we live in Texas. But do you think Santa Ana was wrong for fighting? For wanting to hang on to what he thought was rightfully his?"

Francesca's hand shot up, and Jamie nodded at her. "No. Because he just wanted it, too. Everybody sees their own parts of life differently than anybody else sees it."

The little girl's words echoed in Jamie's mind that afternoon. She heard them over and over again in her head. They made her think of the things Elena had told her about Daniel.

Everybody sees his own part of life differently from the way anybody else sees it.

Out of the mouths of third-grade kids.

Perhaps I have been right. And I have been wrong, too.

Jamie walked into his office at the station at 4:55 p.m.

Daniel had apprehended only one man that day, a "mule" who had been transporting marijuana across the river in a backpack. Daniel had had to bring him in at gunpoint. The man spoke no English. And he refused to tell Daniel who paid him to transport his load. Daniel felt utterly depleted, as if a part of his essence had been sucked from him during his day on the river.

Jamie stood in the entry to his office and watched him, remembering times long ago when she had first come to apologize to him or just to talk to him about Miguel. The two of them had come a far way together. "What happened today?"

He glanced up from his paperwork at the sound of her voice. He frowned. "What are you doing here?"

"I'm here because of Santa Ana and Jim Bowie and the Battle of the Alamo," she told him frankly. "And I'm here because Elena told me you could have sent her and Sarita back across the border, too."

He lay his pen down. "How are they?"

"Okay. As good as can be expected. They are waiting to hear some word from Felix. But they are better off because you are the one who apprehended him. I know that. They would all be in Mexico by now if you had followed your rule book."

"Are you telling me I did the wrong thing still? Or the right thing? Or just—" he paused for effect, letting his words sink in "—a part of the right thing?"

"I should have seen how hard it was for you to go to them and tell them what you had done."

Daniel walked to the door and closed it. He didn't want anyone to hear what they were saying.

"Why didn't you send them all away, Daniel?"

"There was no point in it. I didn't apprehend Elena and Sarita. I only caught Felix. I won't patrol people's lives twenty-four hours a day."

"Could you lose your job for what you did? Not sending the entire family away?"

"No. It was just a matter of . . . judgment."

"A judgment I condemned you for."

His eyes were hard again, like rocks. She couldn't read them. "You have every right to your own opinion. I see what you do. You build up your loyalty to something brick by brick as if you were building a fortress." The sadness in his expression was almost tangible; it was so intense on his face, so poignant. "I only wish, Jamie, that you could build one of your fortresses around me. That someday you could feel the same loyalties toward me."

"Daniel . . ." Suddenly Jamie wanted to weep for both of them. He was right, and she knew it, for she had proven it to him by her words and actions only the night before. "Is loyalty something different from loving?"

"I don't know." He knew how much his words must hurt her. But he owed it to both of them to be honest.

She buried her head against his shoulder and stood propped within his arms, against the steel of his chest and the muscles there. "I don't know, either." And she allowed herself to cry at last.

THE TELEPHONE RANG at 2:00 a.m. Jamie scrambled up so she could reach it. The blanket fell in folds around her waist.

"Miss Forrester. This is Dr. Rankin calling from Oakhaven in Dallas. I'm sorry to have to wake you."

Jamie shot straight up and was wide awake immediately.

"Your grandfather is very ill. He has had a stroke."

"What?" She wanted to shriek at the doctor. He couldn't be talking about William Forrester. She had talked to him just yesterday, and he had been fine. "He can't be. He has to be okay."

"He isn't. I'm sorry."

She was furious and frightened and sad all at once. "Couldn't you see something like this coming? Couldn't you have done something to stop it?"

"No, Miss Forrester. Unfortunately, strokes often hit their victims with very little warning. We couldn't have predicted this. The nurse here was helping him into bed, and he had some sort of a seizure. He suffered another bad fall. The nurse was unable to hold him up when he passed out."

"Why did this happen?" Jamie couldn't help raising her voice as the tears began to stream down her face. "I just don't understand. A stroke. Was it bad? Will he come back from it? Can you do anything more for him? Is he asking for me?"

"I'm afraid I can't go into details over the telephone," the doctor said. "I can tell you that it was a massive stroke. We haven't had time to evaluate everything yet. And we are never certain. But I can tell you that we are not terribly hopeful about his recovery."

Perhaps the worst feeling Jamie could have experienced right then was guilt. And she felt it, masses of it, squeezing down on her, pushing the breath out of her lungs.

She had deserted him when he needed her most.

If only I hadn't let him talk me into coming here. If only I had stayed with him. If only I had hidden my

*feelings about the children and Daniel. If only he knew
how much I loved him, he wouldn't have given up.*

"What can I do for him, Dr. Rankin?"

"Not much. But perhaps you would like to come.
To be with him for a while."

"I'll be there tomorrow. It will be late morning before I can arrange for a substitute for my class and get
a plane out of here."

"Thank you." The doctor hesitated. "He can't say
so but, if he could, I know he would want you by his
side. And, if it helps you to know, he has been in very
good spirits lately. We had to fight with him to put him
on kidney dialysis this winter. He kept telling us we
couldn't run new gas through an old engine."

Despite her devastation, Jamie smiled. It sounded
just like something he would say. "He always thought
that about everything. You keep things going just as
long as you possibly can with maintenance and love
and care. And when everything starts falling apart at
once, he always said that you just stop tinkering and
go on to something else."

It was the same thing William Forrester had done
for her. He had loved her and cared for her and, when
he sensed she had found the chance at something more
for her life, he had urged her to go and had gently
pushed her away.

The sky was still dark as she packed a bag with a few
of her belongings. She called to make her plane res-
ervation at six o'clock. And then she drove out to *Los
Ebanos* to tell Daniel that she had to fly to Dallas.

When he met her at the front door of the ranch
house, her eyes were great pools of sadness. It had
come around again, Jamie thought, having to choose

between them, the two focal points in her life. It would always come to this, no matter how hard she tried to escape it.

"Oh, Daniel," she cried out to him as she grasped his bare shoulders and clung to him like a frightened child, and he cradled her in his arms. "Grandaddy's had a stroke. It was massive. And Dr. Rankin won't tell me anything else over the phone. I have to go to him. I have to be with him."

"I know...I know," he whispered over and over again into her hair while his family disappeared into another room and he rocked her in his arms the same way he would have rocked a little girl who had fallen down and scraped her knees. He felt so helpless, seeing how she was hurting. "Go ahead and cry. I know...I know..."

Jamie tilted her face up to him. And when she spoke, her tone was so bleak, she sounded as if there was no hope left for anyone in the world, anywhere. "I'm leaving again."

He caught her face with his hands then and held it, steadying her, strengthening her with the certainty in his gaze. "I know you have to go, Jamie. But, this time, you aren't going alone. If you'll have me, I'd like to go with you."

"Oh, Daniel, Daniel..." She was sobbing now, and she sounded as if her heart was breaking, and maybe it was, but she thought she could face anything if he was by her side. He could only have guessed how much she needed him. "Can you come? Will you? What about your job?"

"They've been trying to make me take a vacation for the past three months," Daniel told her. "I'm glad I saved the time for you."

Jamie telephoned Frances Ybarra and arranged for a substitute for her class only hours before the plane was scheduled to leave. The first Southwest Airlines flight out of Harlingen departed just after noon. Daniel held Jamie's hand without speaking during the flight. It took almost three hours for the plane to fly northeast, land in Houston then head north to Dallas-Fort Worth International. Daniel rented a car after they had landed and negotiated the Dallas traffic while Jamie sat silently beside him, her face grim. But her composure didn't crumble until they walked together into the front hallway of Oakhaven.

There was no domino game in progress on the round card table in the corner. The leather armchair where William Forrester always waited to greet her was empty.

Jamie wasn't crying. Her eyes were dry. But when she spoke, her words came out in little choked sobs that made him want to take her pain away. Daniel was glad to see her display any of her feelings at all just now. He had been frightened for her because she had remained so stoic during their journey. The long hours of emotionless resolve were something he had never seen her experience before.

Jamie should never have been made to live like this for so long. For a moment, Daniel blamed her grandfather for it, that she had become so dedicated to coming here to this place that smelled of disinfectant and ammonia and age and death.

He marveled at her strength.

"Dr. Rankin's office is down the hallway," she said, directing him feebly. "He said he would be here this afternoon waiting for me." Jamie stopped walking. She didn't really want to go on. She wasn't ready to face the truth yet, wasn't ready to find out the fate of the man who she loved and who had raised her.

"It's going to be very hard," Daniel said. "But you can do it."

She looked at him then in silent thankfulness. She led him down the hallway past the nurses' station and knocked on the doorway marked Robert Rankin, M.D. with a gold placard. She began asking questions when the doctor walked into the room.

"Where is he? Have you evaluated him yet? Are there tests you can perform?"

Dr. Rankin approached her, his arms outstretched, without answering.

"How did he sleep last night? When can I see him?"

"Hello, Miss Forrester," he said, his voice full of compassion for her. But Daniel heard pity in it, too, and it was everything he could do to keep his composure. *Stop feeling sorry for her and answer her questions, man. Please.*

"You may see him as soon as you would like. He's been admitted to B.B. Owen Medical Center. One of our nurses is with him. But perhaps," he said cautiously, "we should talk first."

"Tell me. I want it. Now."

"It's bad, Miss Forrester," he said, his tone brusque, as if he'd already cut himself off emotionally from the entire ordeal. "Very bad."

Speechless, Jamie sank down into the huge office chair opposite his desk, defeated.

"He's lost control of the right side of his body. I doubt very seriously if he'll ever speak or move again."

It was almost worse than if he had died. He was still here, and she still loved him, but he might be lost to her.

"I've heard enough," she said. "I've heard all your doubts." She struggled to rise to her feet then as if she, too, were very old. She reached for Daniel. "Get me out of here."

It didn't take long to drive to the hospital. It was only miles north of Oakhaven off Central Expressway on Campbell Road. And when they arrived, they found him just as Daniel had guessed they would, motionless, in a sterile room. He didn't make any sound or even turn his head when Jamie walked into the room.

She knelt beside the bed and took his hand, and Daniel wanted to weep for her. William Forrester stared straight ahead from the bed, with eyes that were not quite empty. His head lolled heavily to one side. "It's okay, Grandaddy," Jamie whispered to him as she reached out and stroked gray strands of what was left of his hair. He made no motion, no indication that he heard her. "Everything's going to be all right now. I'm home."

CHAPTER SIXTEEN

THE KNOCK ON THE GALINDOS' door was loud enough to wake them all. It was 3:00 a.m. Elena stumbled from the bed without even thinking. She found the front alcove and threw open the door. It was Felix. She fell into his arms.

"Ah, my Elena," he said softly as she began to whimper and lean against him. "At last I am home. Tell me if there has been news of our son."

She told him nothing as she guided him into the kitchen. It was warm there. She handed him a towel. His clothes were still wet from the swim across the river. "Take your shirt off, Felix. You will warm quicker that way. And I want to examine the wounds on your back."

"They are not terrible," he said. "I was lucky." He shrugged out of his shirt, turning his face in the opposite direction so that Elena could not see his grimace of pain. "Only flesh cuts."

"Did you see a doctor in Nuevo Guerro?"

"No." He shook his head. "But time can heal many things that doctors cannot."

The shirt fell off his shoulders and into Elena's hands. She traced her husband's back with one time-worn, loving hand. "They are worse than you said."

"Tell me, Elena. Has there been news of my son?"

She answered him only because he was pressing her. "No, Felix. There has been no news since you left. Jorge has not come to us. I was hoping you had found him...hoping...that since God and fate had sent you back across the river..."

"On the day *Señor* Salinas sent me back to Mexico, I went to see the coyote. He says Jorge has not come to us because the coyote did not receive enough money for our son's crossing. But, long ago, I paid his men the full fee.

"Jorge is in Matamoros, he said, trying to find his own way to come to us. But he has frightened the boy with stories of deportation camps. And, in a way, I am glad. Jorge is inexperienced and alone. I do not want him to try to come on his own. I even searched the streets in Matamoros, stopping boys in the market and asking them their names..."

Felix buried his face in his hands. He had nowhere left to turn and he knew it. And he couldn't stop the horrible sense of desperation from flooding his spirit, even as he sought to be brave, for his wife's sake.

"I agreed to send the man more money. But I have no money left. And because, in living here, we are breaking a law, there is no law here that will protect us."

"I do not think everything is lost yet." Elena bent beside him and stroked his knee. "We must seek someone on the side of the law who knows us and is willing to help us. Perhaps *maestra*."

"The teacher can do nothing."

"Yet she has already done so much for us."

Felix frowned at his wife. "Where is your pride, Elena?"

"It is somewhere across the river, in Mexico, with my son. While I am waiting for him, I cannot afford to be proud."

She turned toward the little kitchen window that looked out on other tiny houses to the west. She was peering toward the river, which ran through a deep ravine as it bisected Roma and La Ciudad de Miguel Aleman; two towns, two peoples. Elena couldn't see the Rio Grande from where she stood, for it was shrouded in darkness and too far away, but she knew it, felt it. It ran like a mighty force, and swept along the lives of the people here with it.

As Elena thought of the river, she thought of something else, too, a friend she had found, the kindness of the INS man whose duty it was to guard the border. If Felix would agree to it, it was the perfect way to show Daniel Salinas that his kindness meant much to them. It was the perfect way to show the man that they knew they could trust him.

"I know what we will do." The doubt was gone. They could turn to Daniel Salinas. As he patrolled the river each day, perhaps he would be willing to search for their son.

"If I could not do it, then how could he?" Felix asked her when she suggested the plan.

"Because of who he is." The INS agent was free to go back and forth across the river as he pleased. Perhaps he already knew of the coyote they had commissioned.

"And what reason do we have to trust him so much?" Felix queried. "If we tell him about our son, we are giving our future into his hands."

"He has been very kind to us, Felix. You know that. And *maestra* trusts him. I think it would be nice for him to know that we do, too."

"I don't know."

"He is a good man. Even if he is not willing to seek out Jorge, he can tell us what to do, yes? And, even if we tell him the truth, he will know we have done it of our own will. I do not think he will take what he has found to the authorities."

"Are you willing to wager that much, wife?"

Elena did not hurry to answer him. She weighed her own words, considering her choices, before she spoke again. "Yes," she said to her husband. And she wanted to shout it, she was so certain what they were doing was good and suitable and right. But when her words came out they were scarcely more than a whisper. "I am."

JAMIE FOLLOWED DR. RANKIN outside the room. He had just finished examining William Forrester. "I've spoken with him," she said matter-of-factly. "He doesn't want to go back to Oakhaven, Doctor. I'm going to take him home."

"Miss Forrester. I said he had recovered enough to be moved. I meant moved back to another health-care facility. I did not say he had recovered enough to go to your house."

"His house. He is going to his house." Jamie held her ground. It was the way she would always fight for the people she loved. She stood beside them no matter what the cost. "I've checked into it, Dr. Rankin. You cannot legally fight me on this."

"Hold on, Miss Forrester. You certainly don't need to threaten me."

"I'm not threatening you. I'm telling you the facts."

Her grandfather could not speak. But his eyes remained as clear and bright as his mind. She had mentioned his homecoming to him this morning. She told him that Daniel had agreed to help her. And she had been able to read all the aching happiness in his eyes. Looking at him was the only way she could communicate with him now.

"You go to him, Dr. Rankin. You ask him what he thinks. He will make the final decision for himself. He will answer you with his eyes. He cannot argue anymore about my life and what he wants to give me. I look into his eyes and I see sheer, raw feelings. He needs me."

"It's impossible." Other than recovering strength physically, William Forrester had made no progress at all. "He can sit in a wheelchair. But how are you going to get him into bed? How are you going to lift him and turn him?"

"I have a friend who will help me when we first get home." Daniel had asked to stay with her in Dallas, to help her as long as he could. When the time came for Daniel to go back to the valley, Jamie would hire someone. But, meanwhile, he was here with her, and that made her strong. "I'm not frightened by it."

"Your grandfather needs rehabilitation. How will you cope with that? How will you get him to the hospital as an outpatient?"

"The same way the nurses at Oakhaven would cope with it." If Dr. Rankin thought she was playing a game, he was mistaken. Jamie had thought everything through. "I will telephone the senior citizens' van and have the driver help us aboard."

"Miss Forrester," the doctor said, his tone suddenly softening. "You will destroy yourself. You have no idea how much it will take from you if you bury yourself to care for him. It isn't what he would have wanted."

"His mind is still sharp, Dr. Rankin. You told me so yourself. He still hears things and sees things and feels things. I want him with me. I want him at the house where he can hear the katydids in the trees and see the neighbors walking by. He'll do nothing at Oakhaven now except stare at the wall."

"You are not being reasonable, Miss Forrester," he told her.

And Jamie just shook her head. "I am being who I have to be."

"IT'S SUCH A NICE little house." Daniel hugged Jamie to him as they both gazed out the window toward the oak trees in the front yard. The lawn was just beginning to turn lush again now that it was springtime in North Texas. "I can see why you were so happy here."

"I was." Jamie turned away from the window and began unloading more of her grandfather's belongings from the box.

Daniel watched her as she squared her shoulders one more time. He had noticed the gesture more times than he could count today. And Daniel couldn't tell her, but he was worried about her.

He had to let her do it. He had to let her go, had to let her perform this one act of great love for the old man she cared so much about. But Daniel didn't know what it would do to them, having her so far away. Nothing had really changed between them. Jamie was still returning to the life she had belonged to before she had come to teach the children in Roma. But, just now, setting her free was the one way he knew to show her how much he cared about her, too.

Daniel took a mental inventory of the man's life as he watched Jamie unpack William Forrester's things. A bottle of after-shave so dusty it was obvious he hadn't used it for months. A red toothbrush with bristles in soft, worn whorls. The Mickey Mouse alarm clock Jamie had told him she had given her grandfather for his birthday the year she was in the tenth grade.

"I don't think a man can ever be unhappy when he has so many friends," she said, pulling more of his belongings from the box. Many of his friends had stopped by the room before she had moved his things out of Oakhaven this morning, to tell her how much they were going to miss him, now that he was going home. "It was one of the things that made me able to leave him at Oakhaven, too. I know how much everyone cared about him. And he could always round up enough people for a domino game there."

Jamie pulled the brilliant red serape from the box and unfolded it. She spread it on the bed and ran one hand along the double selvage where her grandfather's neck had always been. "I guess I'll keep this on his bed. He told me that he couldn't ever decide whether to wear it or lay it there."

"That's a good idea."

He saw tears pooling in her eyes again and he knew she was doubting everything again.

"Oh, Daniel. I'm so afraid that time will pass and everyone will forget about him. He can't play dominoes anymore. He can't even talk."

He gathered her into his arms again, aching for her, aching for himself because, in two weeks, he would no longer be near enough to hold her. "Your grandfather has been a part of many lives here, in much the same way he has been a part of yours. Asking his friends to forget him now would be like asking the children in Roma to forget you. Your love. The pride you have given them. *Las Posadas*. And what they know of both sides of the Battle of the Alamo. You will always be a part of them." And then he gazed at her, thinking of the lessons that loving her was teaching him, too. God, he was thankful for her presence in his life. And he knew now that it was time to tell her so. "Just as you will always be a part of me."

She turned doe-soft eyes toward his. "Will I?" She wanted to believe him, the things he said, about her grandfather and about herself. "Oh, Daniel, will I?"

"Yes," he said, his eyes riveted to hers even as he held her. And she felt as if she was drawing something from him, burning with it, as he told her. "Always, Jamie. In my heart, I will never leave you."

She searched his face. "You can make that commitment to me?"

"I can."

She threw her arms around Daniel's neck and kissed him, a kiss that encompassed them both, surrounded them, bonded them. All that each of them was, tied them together at that moment, as, once, it had torn them apart.

This time, it was Jamie's turn to take slender fingers, cup them and encircle his face. The nameless emotion she had been feeling for him suddenly found its expression. "I am in love with you, you know." Her words were scarcely more than a whisper.

"I think—" Daniel touched her nose and gazed down at her with such longing that she almost couldn't bear it "—that if we ever have a chance to be together, to belong to one another, that I could love you, too."

He had said it then, something she had once only been able to dream he might say. "But we promised we wouldn't expect it from one another."

"And we didn't expect it. But I love you." He said it again, just tasting the words on his tongue, marveling himself at what they might mean. "My only wish is that I had a lifetime to learn about loving and giving and sharing as only one little schoolmarm can teach it." He winked at her. "I think that you are the most stubborn, loyal, wonderful thing that has ever come into my life."

The house was empty. They wouldn't pick her grandfather up at the hospital for another two hours.

Jamie gripped his neck again. It was easy to forget that, soon, their time together would be over. Daniel had a life in the Rio Grande Valley. And, this time, her life in Dallas would encompass her completely. She would be so busy nursing William Forrester that she wouldn't have time to think of anything. Except for how much she missed them. Because, in a way, both of them would be gone, and not just Daniel. But

Daniel was here with her today, and for now that was all that mattered.

She gazed at him solemnly, her eyes brilliant and alive with wanting. "This is it for us, then. Everything that we can share..."

"Yes, *querida*." Little loved one. He swept her up into his arms and carried her to the bed. "It is."

Daniel lay down with her and drove both hands into her hair, holding her, as she tightened her arms around his waist and pulled him on top of her. Her fingers moved to the buttons on his shirt and then, when she was finished, to the snap on his jeans.

His hands traveled down her neck to her shoulders, then down the length of her arms to her thighs, and then he eased away from her just far enough so he could undress her and, as he did, he felt as if he was opening a gift, something pure and fine and precious, as she lay waiting for him, needing him, but—more than that—loving him.

She kissed him with the innocent straightforwardness of a child and with the gentle intensity of a woman. And, when she did, Daniel was lost in her. He looked into Jamie's face and saw everything she was feeling, joy and certainty and tenderness. He saw himself there because her feelings were his own. And this time, when he filled her with everything that he was, everything that he could be, it was as if their lovemaking encompassed their very souls.

CHAPTER SEVENTEEN

THERE WERE FOUR domino hands set up, all around the little table on the sun porch. It was the place where Jamie and her grandfather had always played. Forty-two was a game played with four people. But it was easier to teach Daniel this way. And this way, she could keep her grandfather sitting beside them in his wheelchair.

William Forrester stared straight ahead at the domino hand Jamie would play for him.

"Look at my hand, Daniel. It's horrible. I have fours but not one of them is high. I would pass—" she grinned at her grandfather "—because I've been told before that I'm a chicken and I often pass on hands I should have played." She hugged her grandfather. He didn't move. He never did.

"Grandaddy never misses a bid," she continued, "no matter what his hand looks like." She turned William's domino hand around so Daniel could see what she would be playing. He had a double deuce and several other high twos to accompany it. "This is a good trump. But look at his off. He wouldn't want to bid over thirty-one or he might go set."

"Right." Daniel was confused. He ran fingers through already tousled curls. "And any man who knows the ins and outs of this nation's immigration laws should be able to figure out how to play this game. But I can't."

"You will. It takes practice. And time."

"I hate it when people tell me that." He couldn't help grinning. "It's exactly what I told the kids who had trouble hitting the ball on the softball team."

Her grandfather was still facing forward, and as she bent over, Jamie kissed him on the cheek. She was standing behind him, talking to Daniel. "So it's hard to swallow your own advice."

"Jamie..." The somberness of his tone stopped her domino lesson. And this time, when she looked at him, she began to comprehend the unfathomable darkness in his eyes. Deep and frightening. It was the same way his aloneness felt, deep and frightening, whenever he remembered he was leaving her soon, in three days, and perhaps for forever.

"What is it?"

He waited before answering her, uncertain of how much he should say in front of William. "I'm going to miss you."

She ran a hand over the shoulder of the man who was now her ward and she gazed at both of them, sitting side by side, the man who had been her future, the man who was her past, one so vital, the other so brittle and small. Her grandfather's skin seemed pearlescent, it was so pale. And then she turned away from both of them, but not before Daniel had noticed the regret and the look of raw longing on her face.

"I will miss you, too," she said hoarsely, to nothing, to no one in particular. Jamie might have been speaking to either of them, for her words sounded as delicate, as fragile as spun glass, even as the Texas breeze wafted into the screened-in sun porch and seemed to hurl them away.

Daniel could only think of Jamie now, and not her grandfather, as he spoke to her this time. "I will not wait for you there forever," he said in a tone the same texture as her own. It was their deepest feelings, their deepest sense of love and fear, they were discussing now. And Daniel was almost afraid. "But I will wait awhile."

Jamie was facing all that had once meant so much to her. The cracked walkway that had always led to this home. The mimosa tree with the pink, fuzzy flowers that floated in the air like feathers when the limbs moved. A woman taking long, casual steps along the sidewalk as she pushed a baby in a stroller.

"I don't want you to give up a single day for me, Daniel." She was whispering but she knew he had heard her. And she sniffed once and that's how he knew she was crying. "Perhaps both of us have already wasted enough time."

"No," he said urgently, knowing now that she still couldn't comprehend how much their time together had meant to him. He had found in her a love and a friendship that he had been denying he needed ever since he had been a boy. He wasn't going to be able to let go of it quickly. "You mustn't even think it."

"I can't help *but* think it." She turned toward him again, not wanting to face what she wanted to say, yet knowing she had to tell him. "You say you love me enough to understand why I have to be here. Let me love you enough now to tell you that I know why you must go."

As she spoke, there was a slight movement at the table. Neither of them saw it. They sensed it. Her grandfather was sitting in his wheelchair right there beside it.

"That must have been the breeze," Daniel said.

Jamie whirled toward William. "Grandaddy? Daniel, I don't think it was the wind. I think he moved. Did you see it?"

"I don't know."

The red serape slid off William's lap.

"Grandaddy?" Quietly, so as not to startle him, Jamie moved to kneel beside him. She picked the serape up and smoothed it and placed it across his legs. "Are you trying to say something?" She waited, hoping for a sign, a word, a flicker in his eyes, anything, but nothing came. "Did you want something?" She kept hoping... hoping...

"I think it must have been the wind, Jamie. *Querida*. I don't want you to get your hopes up."

"Don't you think he might be trying to tell us something?" She turned eyes full of childlike hope toward Daniel, seeking reassurance. "Perhaps if something was important enough, he wanted to say badly enough, he might try."

The sound started from behind them. It was a guttural, indistinguishable moan, but it was a sound just the same. William had lost all control of his mouth, his lips and his vocal chords. But the moan erupted from much deeper than that. It sounded as if it had come all the way from his heart, as Jamie ran to him and knelt again and gripped his knees.

As she sat before him, he made another attempt and, this time, it was more like a little chirp, while slowly, slowly, one hand rose from where it rested on the padded arm of the wheelchair as Jamie watched. She was too breathless and full of hope to say anything more, as her grandfather just barely managed to reach out toward Daniel.

"IT COULD MEAN ANYTHING, Miss Forrester," the doctor told her. "A sound. A gesture. My guess is that it was involuntary. A flinch in a muscle he has absolutely no control over anymore."

"You don't even want to see him?"

"His regular appointment is next week, isn't it? Remind me of this when I see you. But there's no reason to make a big issue of it. I don't think you understand how much damage was actually done."

She hung up the telephone. Maybe when you become a physician, you saw so much heartbreak or just felt so helpless that you gave up being optimistic about things. Maybe she was wrong. Maybe she should stop hoping.

Jamie stood at the window and peered through the sheer curtains. Daniel was jogging up the street toward the house, his long, fierce strides powerful and sure as he moved up the sidewalk. Every time she looked at him, she throbbed from wanting him to touch her, from wanting him to satisfy the new and certain desires that loving him had aroused in her.

It was time to wake her grandfather. She went to his room and knocked politely. He couldn't answer her. But she thought it only right to let him know she was coming. And, this time, when the door creaked open, she knew immediately that something was wrong.

She couldn't distinguish it. The room seemed much colder than usual. As she moved toward the bed, she felt a horrible dread rise like bile in her throat.

"Grandad?" She called out to him once and then she was beside him. She touched skin that was cold and the same texture as gray, cracking parchment. "Grandaddy? *No!*"

She rolled him over with one hand and stroked his hair. When she saw his eyes she knew it was certain, for all the light and life had gone from them, and that's when she knew he was gone.

It was strange. At that moment, she couldn't cry or call out for help. She only sat beside him as a horrible numbness washed over like a gigantic dose of morphine, as if everything she was capable of feeling had died along with him. And, as she touched his face, she could only think of his mind and how it had been trapped inside his body and that now it had been set free. She loved him so. And she saw him now in her heart the way he had always been, walking with her, his fishing rod slung over one shoulder, telling her about the students at the little Renner school where he taught.

"Thank you," she said to him then, knowing that somehow, from somewhere, he could still hear her. "Thanks for being a part of my life."

She felt Daniel's tentative touch on her shoulder. "Jamie? Is he gone?"

She nodded to him and she was still dry-eyed. She felt like everything around her was spinning just beyond her grasp. Everything she had once known was gone now, orbiting away in a haphazard pattern of its own. She had never felt this devoid of emotion as she reached out to smooth her grandfather's hair one more time. "It seems like I'm always having to tear parts of myself away. Why do I always have to tell parts of myself goodbye?"

FOR DAYS, JAMIE FELT as if she had died, too. She moved through the hours as if she was mindless.

She accomplished tasks. She telephoned her grandfather's friends. She scheduled the funeral and picked out a coffin and arranged for the flowers and music she knew he would have liked. She checked into his insurance coverage. And she might as well have been someone with no heart at all, and no feelings, for there were days she couldn't remember, as she moved through them.

Every part of her seemed to be made of lead, tugging at her and weighing on her. She couldn't stand and walk, she could only drag herself along, her hands, her feet, her hair heavy as rocks whenever she tried to move.

Daniel stayed beside her every day before the funeral. She remembered him later as a distant shadow. He didn't hold her. She didn't want to be held. He made her lie down when she was exhausted and he made her eat when she hadn't even realized she was hungry. From somewhere, very gently and quietly, he functioned as a part of her. But then came the day after the service and the hugs and condolences from friends when it was time for Daniel to go.

"Tell me what you are feeling, Jamie," he asked her as they stood together on the concourse at Dallas Love Field. "I have to know where I stand in your life now that he is gone."

"I don't have any feelings. I don't want to feel anything." She had cut herself off from everything. "Don't push me, Daniel, please."

There was so much to do at the house still. She had to get it cleaned. She felt like Humpty-Dumpty, shattered and irreparable, as she watched Daniel walk from the Southwest Airlines counter where he had purchased his ticket. There was still too much of herself to hang on to here in Dallas, still too much to put away.

When Daniel held his hands out to her now, she wanted to run away from them. She wanted to run away from everything that threatened the rock-hard nothingness inside her.

"Just say the word, Jamie," he said, hating what he saw on her face. "Say one word. And I won't go. Or I'll buy you a ticket, too."

"I'm not ready for that, Daniel. I don't know if I'll ever be."

"You've got to live your own life." He was angry at her, and she understood why. But she couldn't summon the bravery now or the love to follow him.

"I've just—" her eyes found his as they stood there, with people milling around them like a current "—turned myself off."

It was what he had tried to do for years after Raphael had gone. It was the thing that loving her had pulled him away from.

Gingerly, sadly, he reached out to touch her face one last time. She had done it at last. He had warned her about it from the beginning. She had fought against it for months. But now, something inside her was gone. And it could be forever before she found it again.

"You've turned your emotions off, haven't you?" He wanted to strike out against the hardness in her eyes. *And was it this easy for me, too, when I cut everything else away?*

Her expression was blank. "I can't help it." Jamie despised herself for her feelings but she vocalized them anyway. "It just hurts too much to care."

"A long time ago, you told me it was worth the hurt. Damn it, Jamie, you *proved* it to me. Don't turn away from yourself now, Jamie. Just because he died..."

"I could have done so much more for him." Her eyes were vacant, a reflection of everything she couldn't feel in her heart just now. "I should have stayed, Daniel. And now it's too late."

"No." He had lost her then. It was over between them. She was just like him. Because, along with her numbness, she was carrying an incredible burden of guilt as well.

"It's ironic," he said dryly. "We've traded places."

"I'll miss you," she whispered. "I already miss you."

But you don't have to miss me. He wanted to shout at her but he didn't. *You can come home.* But he was talking about his home and not hers and he knew it. And then, he couldn't stop himself, he had to tell her because he loved her. "You have to let yourself grieve for him. You have to let yourself hurt because he is gone."

"I can't."

"I have faith in you, Jamie. You will," he said. "In time, you will." He smoothed the hair from her temples and gazed at her. "Jamie. Never forget how very much I have loved you."

But she didn't say anything, she just stared at him with uncomprehending eyes. And perhaps she was right to not say anything now. When at last she did speak, she merely said, "I do know." But her tone was clipped, as if she really didn't want to acknowledge him. "And I thank you for that."

"Goodbye, *querida*." Daniel turned and handed the stewardess his boarding pass without looking back.

FELIX GALINDO KNOCKED on the door at *Los Ebanos*.

Daniel answered it.

Felix was trembling, he was so frightened. He had no idea what the INS agent would do when he found out Felix was back on this side of the border. But he had no other choice. Elena's original plan had been to contact Salinas through *maestra*. But Jamie Forrester was gone now. And Daniel Salinas was their only hope.

"And so," Daniel said, "we meet again."

"I know I have endangered myself coming to you. But my family is desperate for someone who is on the side of the law."

"I don't understand, Galindo. How can I help you?"

"Our son is lost."

Daniel glanced behind him to see who was listening. No one was there. He was working the late shift today, and Harriet and Lúpe had driven into Mexico to shop at the market. "Come inside. I don't know if I can do anything for you. But at least we can talk."

Felix was too frantic to sit on the couch. Instead, he paced the floor while he told Daniel his story. "We need someone trustworthy to help our son. He is in Matamoros. When we came to Texas many years ago, we had to leave him behind. We have saved money in the cookie jar for years. For all of Sarita's life. And, at Christmas, I gave it to a coyote who said he would help us. But now the coyote says I must pay him more money. I do not have more money. And, every day, I grieve for my son."

The INS agents had known of coyotes for years. They were ruthless men who cheated both the laws and the people who paid them. They had very little regard for human life. They brought people north in trucks or in unventilated railroad cars. And when it looked as if they might get caught, the coyotes disappeared, leaving the people who had paid them to fend for themselves.

Daniel was surprised that Felix had taken so drastic a measure. "I cannot legally find your son," he said. "But perhaps I can search out the coyote who took your money and capture him. Do you have a name? An address? Anything?"

"I do." Felix produced the paper scrap from his pocket. He had been carrying it with him for weeks. "Here is his address in Matamoros. His name is Elmo. Elmo Elizando. And if you find this man, perhaps he will lead you to my son. And if you find my son, you can tell him we still wait for him."

Three months before, Daniel would not have considered helping the Galindos. But there was something new within him now, something that knowing Jamie, loving her, had brought to life within him. "Okay, Galindo," Daniel said at last. His voice was low and ominous. It frightened him, too, what he was about to do. *Yet I do it for Jamie. I do it because she once loved Sarita. And because she once loved me.* "Go home. If anyone sees you here talking to me, he will question our motives."

"Do not send me away without agreeing to help me. Please."

"I will do what I can." Daniel was beginning to formulate a plan. It was one that might work for both of them. "I need to speak to some INS men about this. I will come to your home when I can and tell you more."

"Oh, thank you." Felix grabbed Daniel's hand, and there were tears in his eyes as he pumped his arm so hard Daniel thought he might pull it off. "Perhaps all is not lost to us after all."

"I WANT TO TRY a setup to get this guy." Daniel didn't bother to sit in the huge chair across from the chief patrol agent's desk. He was too excited and too shot full of adrenaline to sit. It was wonderful to do something again, to have something to take his mind off missing Jamie. "It's been a long time since everything has fallen into place like this. An anonymous tip came in yesterday morning." He wasn't going to tell them that his information came from Felix Galindo. Felix had risked everything by coming to him. "David, I know it will work. There's another coyote working out of a storefront office in Matamoros. People here have commissioned him to bring relatives over, and he is bilking them. We could siphon more money to him, have him make a run, and I can find out through my source when he is coming. It would be easy to lay a trap for him."

"Interesting," David Gonzales commented. "But dangerous. Both for you and for the people this man may bring over. If he realizes he is going to be caught, there's no telling what he might do."

"I know that. But I'm willing to risk it, David. I've got this guy's name and address. And I'm ready to throw a wrench into his business. I don't want coyotes plying their human trade along this part of the river."

"Very well," the man behind the huge mahogany desk told him. "I'll authorize it. But be forewarned. It could get nasty down there."

"I know it," Daniel said. "I am taking my gun."

FELIX AND ELENA walked hand in hand toward the storefront office where Elmo Elizando conducted his business. Felix carried two hundred twenty-five dollars with him. It was money Daniel had given him from the INS in order to set a trap.

"You should not have come with me," he told Elena.

"I want to see this man face to face. I want him to have to meet my eyes. And after what happened last time, you know I would not let you come alone."

Sarita was in school with the new teacher Frances Ybarra had hired to replace Jamie. It had been relatively easy for Elena to leave her daughter and accompany her husband.

"I sometimes wonder if Jorge really made it to Matamoros." They had been at the market for hours already, checking in every stall, asking boys names and showing people Jorge's picture. "This man has told us so many lies."

But when they entered Elizando's office, they did not speak of his cheating. They knew what they had to do, for Daniel had instructed them. They were both businesslike and polite as Felix placed the money on the table.

"We are most anxious to have our son with us. Here is the money you requested. Two hundred twenty-five American dollars. I came here to deliver it personally. It makes me feel good to know you received the amount that you asked for."

"Very good. Very good indeed." Elmo Elizando smiled, an evil smile that revealed tobacco stains across what teeth he had. Elena wanted to be sick, just knowing they had entrusted their son's life to this man. "I will deliver your shipment now."

"I want to know what day." Felix's tone was bland, and he seemed composed, as if they were talking about groceries or dry goods out of a catalogue instead of a boy's life.

The man closed his eyes and leaned back in his chair. He calculated his schedule in his mind. Then he leaned forward and leered at Elena. "Next Tuesday, *Señor* and *Señora* Galindo. You can expect to see your son next Tuesday."

CHAPTER EIGHTEEN

DANIEL PULLED ANOTHER electronic sensor out of its storage box and positioned it on a bush near the ground. He was going to get Elmo Elizando. And to do it, he was tapping every possible vehicle crossing on the river within fifteen miles of Brownsville.

He didn't have much longer to wait. It was eleven o'clock Monday night. Yet he would work thirty-six more hours, if need be, to catch the human smuggler and find Jorge Galindo.

Daniel hadn't decided what to do when he found the boy. He had in mind only to speak with him, to tell him that his family was waiting for him and to find out if he was well. He had promised Felix and Elena he would detain him and speak to him long enough to find out where they could contact him in Matamoros.

Everything was in place. David Gonzales had put extra agents all along the Rio Grande for the next twenty-four hours. But Chief Patrol Agent Gonzales knew that Daniel wanted to be the one to apprehend Elizando. It was a matter of principle. This was his setup. And he wanted to be the one to take it to the ground.

Under cover of darkness, Daniel set the last sensor, then drove his truck inside an arroyo to hide it. He spit on his binocular lenses and polished them. Then he climbed in the truck, turned his radio on and waited.

AT FIRST, CLEANING OUT William Forrester's house had seemed hopeless to Jamie. There were constant decisions to be made, what to keep, what to throw away, what to donate to charity. And she was surprised, when she was finished in his room, that there was very little she was holding onto for herself. She kept the serape she had made him. There was a box of pictures of her parents and mementos her grandfather had decided to keep when her parents had died, and to it she added photos of her grandfather, old ones and more recent ones. There was one she especially loved of him standing in front of the Renner schoolhouse surrounded by grinning, mischievous students.

Jamie kept his box of ivory dominoes, too, and she kept his fishing pole and several of his favorite spinners. But, out of an entire household, that was all. The rest of it wasn't worth much any longer, except as memories.

She folded the last of the ragged flannel shirts he had worn into a paper sack and added his favorite fishing shoes.

It shouldn't be so easy to throw away these parts of a man's life.

Jamie cleaned out the old rolltop desk in the den and the junk drawer in the kitchen. By the time she got to her room, she found herself grieving for her own life even though she couldn't grieve for William Forrester's. The feelings of loss and inadequacy and disappointment rose in her like tumultuous currents. She felt as if she had been gripped by an undertow in the ocean. She couldn't breathe, she couldn't think, she could only ache—for who she had been once, for who they all had been—as she crammed boxes full of her old green and white pom-poms and corsages from dances and stuffed animals.

Jamie hadn't decided what to do with her own things. Her grandfather had left the house to her. And the school district in Carrollton had offered her a teaching position. And she was planning on staying. But she didn't know if she could live in the old house without him.

She walked through the house, and as she did, she saw something she had missed. Her grandfather's sweater lay draped over the back of an armchair in the family room. It was where he had always left it before he moved to Oakhaven. When he had worn it home from the hospital, she had draped it there again without thinking. It looked as if it belonged there. She must have walked by it a hundred times until this time, when she stopped to finger it.

It still held the faint scent of him, the hint of cigar smoke he always came back with after playing dominoes with his friends, the clean spiciness of soap, the mustiness of age.

Jamie folded the garment across her arm. Perhaps she should keep it. It had been one of William Forrester's most treasured possessions. But like so many items she had packed away during the past days, the object seemed like nothing now without the man to wear it.

She set it flat on her bed so she could check the pockets and fold it to put in the bag for charity. And, as she checked the first pocket, she heard something crackle and she felt a piece of paper with her fingers.

She pulled it out and opened it.

"My Dearest Jamie," she read. It was a letter to her, dated the day William Forrester had suffered his stroke.

Jamie began to tremble. She plopped down on the bed that had been hers ever since she had been a little girl and read his words.

My Dearest Jamie,
I just got your letter telling about Daniel and Felix Galindo. My heart goes out to you and to Daniel and to Sarita's family.

I *do* miss you so much. But I am so glad you went back to Roma. When I read your letters, I sense a joy in your words that I did not see in your eyes when you were here with me.

Know only that I feel so lucky to be your grandfather. You have always been such a gift to me. You always tell me the difference between how I acted when you were in high school and how your friends' parents acted. But I know teenagers well enough to know that I can't take all the glory for that. Most of them are embarrassed to even admit they have parents or grandparents. And, Jamie, you were always willing to be there for me, even though it might have meant that you weren't the most popular girl in class.

I was trying to think of what advice I could give you in this letter to make you feel better about the daily conflict you are seeing now between many of the people you care for. You wrote about

Daniel, how you see people and reasons and rules so differently from one another.

I have been around a long time, little one. I've seen people change. I've seen reasons change. And, during the past years that measure almost a century, I have certainly seen all the rules change.

The one thing that has sustained me throughout the years has been the loving I shared with my family. Your grandmother and I shared so many happy years together. And I was always so proud of your mother and father, and finally you. When you were born, I thought I had never seen a more beautiful young lady. Little did I know that you were going to grow more beautiful each year and that, someday, you and I would be best, loving friends the way we are.

I challenge you never to let rules and reasons and other people stand in your way of finding relationships as precious and fine as ours.

I love you, Jamie. You are my joy.

All my best to you,
Grandaddy

Jamie placed the letter in her lap. She buried her face in her hands. God, how she missed him. And how she had loved him. And, at long last, she was able to weep.

With her tears came her final, merciful release from the guilt and pain that had crippled her after William Forrester had died. And, after the emptiness, the other things that were a part of her flooded in to fill the spaces... Her hopes, her heart came rushing back to belong to her again.

And with them came the love for Daniel that she had only just begun to know.

I want to go home.

The thought came unbidden, from a new, stronger part of her. Almost unconsciously, she glanced at herself in the white French provincial mirror that had been hers since she was a little girl. She still looked the same as she had looked this morning. But, somehow, she'd experienced a wonderful resurgence of faith.

She trusted Daniel. He had given her so much by coming with her, standing beside her, and then by letting her go. She trusted him with her life. She trusted him with her love.

She was happy again and humming a Spanish ballad when she picked up the telephone and dialed the real estate broker who had already contacted her about selling the house.

"This is Jamie Forrester," she said when the woman answered on the other end. "Can you have an appraiser come this afternoon and look at the house? I've decided to go home to the Rio Grande Valley. I would like you to list this place."

THE SUN BURNED HIGH overhead. It was one o'clock.

Daniel's radio crackled to life. "Something's tripped the sensor two miles south of you."

"I'm on my way." He turned the key in the ignition. "I'll radio for backups if I need them. Have someone ready just in case."

Daniel knew the exact location. A low-water crossing leading to a makeshift dusty road that was safer to use this time of day because it fell beneath the shadows of the trees that surrounded it.

The vehicle he was looking for would be traveling fast. He drove across the sand, dodging sandstone and traversing clumps of prickly pear. He saw the massive plume of dust it sent up first, then he saw the van. It was a tan panel van, almost completely camouflaged against the sand. There were no windows in the back, and the front ones were shaded. *Bingo. I've got him.*

Daniel gunned the engine. He drove with both hands, his mind on the loaded gun in his holster. He aimed his path ahead of the van a ways so he could be ahead of the driver to intercept him. And when he reached a flat piece of sand where he could manipulate the wheel with one hand, he grabbed his radio.

"I'm on the river-crossing road seven miles north of Brownsville. We're approximately two miles west of the highway moving east-northeast. I'm stopping this guy now. I need backups. There's no telling how many people this guy is carrying."

The van swerved from its course.

Damn. The driver had either seen him or he was monitoring INS radio communications.

Daniel swerved in the same direction and followed. He was gaining. His truck was much more powerful than the van. He was close enough now to guess that there were two people in the cab of the van. He was close enough to see the van's two front doors fly open.

God, no.

The smugglers were going to jump. They could run and hide and pull a gun on him before he could stop his vehicle and climb out to apprehend them. But losing Elizando wasn't what Daniel was afraid of now.

The van was traveling at least forty miles per hour over rocky terrain. And it wasn't going to have a driver. The people in the back of it could be crushed or killed.

Daniel's gut wrenched up into his throat when he saw them do it. The two men seemed to fly from the van, and they rolled in opposite directions across the sand as the van careered out of control. It was as if it was a fleeing animal, a jackrabbit or something else with a mind of its own, as time hung suspended and the van bounced back and forth, zigzagging and straightening. Daniel followed it, saying silent prayers for the people inside.

He saw the arroyo coming. It was inevitable. There were hundreds of them, little dips and crevices that were dry now but became streambeds when the water was high. *Please... God...* He issued another prayer without realizing he was doing it. *Don't let them be harmed.*

The van dived nose first into the dried streambed. Then it flipped over onto its side. It stopped, but the wheels continued to turn. Daniel jumped from his truck and made his way through the dust and the smoke. He could barely see, but he knew he had to reach the door in the back.

The door was padlocked shut. He could hear people moaning and screaming inside. He stood back, aimed his gun and shot at the lock from an angle. The bullet pinged against the metal and blew the padlock to pieces. And then Daniel opened the doors.

It seemed like hordes of people were scrambling from the back of the van. Some of them were bleeding and all of them were frightened and it seemed to

Daniel at first as if there were hundreds of them, but when he counted them, there were only twenty.

He showed them his badge as they cowered before him. "I will help you if you are hurt. Do not try to get away."

The radio in his van came on. "Salinas? This is Larralde."

Daniel backed away from the group of people toward his radio. He kept his gun trained on them. "Salinas here."

"We were on our way to back you up. We've apprehended two men running toward the river. Did you lose anybody over there?"

"Yeah." Daniel breathed a sigh of relief. They had Elizando. "The head guy. Keep him."

One woman from the back of the van moved toward him. Her hand was covered with blood. He pulled a handkerchief from his pocket and knelt beside her, blotting at the open gash on her palm.

As he helped her, his eyes swept down the row of the people standing there. Not one of them had moved. They were like children, lost and afraid. "Are any of you legal residents of the United States?"

One by one, they shook their heads. And when he turned to the woman beside him and waited for her answer, too, there was such a look of sorrow in her weather-lined face that he had to look away.

There was no telling how much money these people had paid Elizando to bring them here.

"I am sorry," he said in Spanish. "I am going to have you all sign consent papers and return you to Mexico."

Daniel's gaze rested on one teenage boy who stood away from the group. The child was alone. He was staring at the INS agent, his eyes clear and hard, the hatred there not quite disguising the fear.

Daniel didn't want to attract attention to the boy. But he knew he had to talk to him. One by one, he moved down the line of people again, asking their names, checking their injuries, helping them sit on the ground.

At last, he came to the child.

The boy stared at him, his eyes bright with disappointment and failure. A man's eyes in a boy's face.

"What is your name, son?"

Seconds...moments of silence. *Please tell me the truth,* Daniel was pleading silently, *so I can help you.*

"My name is Jorge Galindo."

He had found Felix's son. Daniel's body remained rigid. He gave no sign of the relief or the release of adrenaline that rushed inside him.

Until this moment, he had not decided what he was going to do.

"I know your father, Felix Galindo," he said beneath his breath. "We have been searching for you. Are you hurt?"

"No."

Daniel made his decision. It was going to be a life-changing one. "I have too many others here to care for. I will not be able to stop you if you run."

Daniel turned his back to the boy. He did not dare say anything more. He did not look back as he moved to assist the van's other passengers.

He bent to help one old man lying in the dirt. And then he heard something behind him, one slight sound. There was a clicking of rock and then the whisper of the brushland, but Daniel didn't turn around. He didn't have to look, for he knew that Jorge was gone.

THE SOUND OF running footsteps echoed in Jorge's head with the same ringing thuds as his heartbeat. And, for every footstep he made, he heard another, matching it, coming from the distance.

This is the end of it then. I will die here in Texas. They will follow me forever. But I will not go back. I will fight them.

He had been running for what seemed like miles. He was exhausted. And, as he slowed, the footsteps he heard behind him slowed, too. It was strange. They never came any closer. They seemed to resonate from somewhere deep below him in the sand. And, when he stopped, all was silent except for the buzzing of a grasshopper as it flew from a mesquite beside his knees.

And then he knew it. The footsteps had been the echoes of his own. There was no one following him.

Jorge stood alone. Miles of sandstone and prickly pear and arroyos spread out around him. He did not know why the INS officer had chosen to set him free. He did not honestly care. The man in him wanted to shout out in defiance. And the part that remained a little boy wanted to cry in his mother's arms.

And, perhaps soon, he would be able to find her.

He shoved a grimy hand into the pocket of his jeans and fished for the envelope he was carrying. It was creased and wrinkled, and he had read it so many

times during the past months that the ink on it was almost totally faded from it.

Jorge scanned the map and shaded his eyes before
he searched the sky and found the sun. He could still
smell the river just over the draw to his left. And he
knew he didn't dare travel too closely to the highway.
Instead, he used the sky above him to guide him north-
northwest until he came to the place his father had
marked off on the map for him, where the little cot-
tages and the river and the two bridges came together
atop a ridge to form a little town.

Roma.

He was home.

THE BREEZE TRAILED in tendrils across the acres at
Los Ebanos, rattling through the mesquite limbs that
bowed almost to the ground. Jamie stood on the patio with Lúpe and Miguel, and as they talked she
couldn't stop herself from gazing out over the timeless scene of the surrounding ranch land.

The peace of it surrounded Jamie, too. She had
come home at last, not to a place but to a part of herself that welled up strongly within her and remained
firm and good and right.

"I don't know where he is," Lúpe told her. "He's
been out patrolling all night again. He's been working like a fiend ever since he came back from Dallas."

"Do you mind if I wait for Daniel here?"

"No." Lúpe was smiling, and Miguel smiled, too.
Jamie bent to give him a hug and tousle his hair.

"When he comes back," the child said, beaming,
"maybe he will pitch a few balls for me. You can see

how I am learning to hit the baseball very hard and make it fly far, far away."

"I'm so proud of you, Miguel." She remained stooped beside the child, watching the play of lights in his eyes as he talked of the new things Daniel had taught him to do.

"We are playing Rio Grande City kids in a tournament next Saturday. *Señor* Daniel says I will be one of the best hitters."

Jamie heard the crunch of tires on gravel. The familiar light green truck turned in and crossed the front cattle guard. "He's here." Jamie's breathing seemed to stop as she waited for him to drive toward her. And when he climbed out he was covered with dirt and he was exhausted, but he looked so good to Jamie she could hardly bear it.

Daniel walked toward the patio gate, and suddenly Jamie was frightened. She hadn't stopped to think what he would do when he first saw her. She hadn't stopped to think what he might say. She stepped back and stood beside Lúpe, steeling herself against his reaction.

I have my life here. I have myself. I have the children.

She was a part of this valley now, a part of the borderland. If Daniel wouldn't have her, she could still belong to this place that she loved so well.

The gate creaked open, and Miguel ran to greet Daniel just the way Jamie herself wanted to run to meet him. Instead, she remained in the shadows.

"Where's Mom and Dad, Lúpe?" He extended one hand to the housekeeper and intended to follow with the other. That's when he saw Jamie. He stopped. He felt his guts knot together and snag onto his breathing. He felt like someone had punched him in the stomach.

"Daniel . . ." She said his name once, and that was all she needed to say. Her pleading was evident to all of them in the gentle way she called out his name.

He stood, poised there between Lúpe and Jamie. "What are you doing back here, *querida*?"

"I sold the house in Dallas. This is my life now, Daniel. The children. This valley." *And you.* But she didn't say it. "My life in Dallas was over a long, long time ago. Maybe even on the first day I left Grandaddy to come here. The day before you took Gilbert Muñoz from my classroom." She had had to discover that, to acknowledge it, for herself. And, in reading her grandfather's final letter, she had done so. After all the rules were broken and the reasons had changed, it was still only the love between them that mattered. "I loved him so much, Daniel. But he set me free a long time ago. It is time, now, that I go my own way."

Lúpe took Miguel's hand and led the child inside.

Daniel's arms relaxed and fell to his sides. He wanted to reach for her, to clutch her to him, to tell her he loved her, that it had been his dream that she come to him. But he didn't. Instead, he spoke to her in measured tones. "I have to tell you what I have done."

When the INS found out he had allowed an illegal to escape into Texas, the agency would conduct an internal investigation. He would be charged with smuggling. He could be incarcerated in the federal penitentiary for years.

He would not proclaim his love for her and ask her to stand by him while he lived out his sentence. She had already lived out a sentence very much like it on her own.

Jamie felt as if her throat was jamming down into her lungs. What was he thinking? *I have to tell you what I have done. I've fallen in love with someone else. I've made myself forget the things we give to one another. The future. The past.*

She wanted to cry out when she heard the irony in his voice. "The funny thing is, you're going to be proud of me for this one."

"Maybe I don't want to hear it."

"You'll find out soon enough from someone. The Galindos will tell you if I don't. And the INS will prosecute me."

"Daniel. What is it? What have you done?"

"Today I helped smuggle a boy into this country." He had known the implication of his actions for a long time. But as he confessed it to her, the full impact of it fell upon him. All the drilling. All the emotional games. All the rules . . . designated black, designated white.

He had disobeyed them, had failed them, had lost his dream.

"I helped Jorge Galindo join his family. The boy has come to live in Roma with Elena and Felix and Sarita."

"Oh, Daniel." The tears began to stream down Jamie's cheeks now as she surveyed his face. She knew all the things he must have sacrificed for the boy. His integrity. His iron-hard resolve. "You saved a family. A teenager's life. You should be honored as a hero."

"I won't be."

"Why? What made you do it?" She had to know, had to hear him say it. For once in his life, he had let his heart rule his mind. And she loved him all the more for it.

"It seemed a fair trade of sorts. For Raphael's life."

It was Jamie who went to him then. She wrapped her arms around Daniel's waist, drawing him to her. She lay her head against his shoulder, thinking of how it would be if they could only grow old together, sharing things this way.

He stepped away from her. He wanted to tell her he had rationalized it in his mind. He had decided during the drive home that he had done it for Raphael. A life in exchange for a life. But, in the instant he had decided to set Jorge free, he had known it was because he loved Jamie. Loving her had given him a new grip on humanity. In that moment, he had looked at Jorge and had seen a face instead of a statistic. "I will be prosecuted for it, Jamie."

"But you have harmed no one."

"I've broken a promise that I vowed over and over again to uphold."

"But . . . how will they know?" she asked. "Did someone see you?"

"No."

"Then who will tell the INS?"

He gave her one sad little grin before he told her. It was so obvious. Why didn't she see it? "I will."

"You can't do that."

"I can do it. And I will. I have a great respect for the INS and its rules. This is my concession to them." He was standing before her, his fists clenched, determined not to let anyone stop him. And Jamie loved him enough to know that, when he had let Jorge run free, he had let a bit of his integrity go, too. If it was something he needed to do to remain true to himself. She understood. "I will lose my position as an agent." He watched her, and strangely enough, he didn't feel afraid or sad. "And I could lose much, much more." *I could lose you.*

CHAPTER NINETEEN

"I'M SORRY, DANIEL." David Gonzales shook his hand in the corridor outside the courtroom. "You were a hell of a good agent. One of the best. I hated to have to let you go."

Daniel gave the man a wry smile. "But you have to go by the rule book. Don't spend time berating yourself. I knew the consequences when I let the boy escape." The judge and the jury only knew he had let a man go because he felt sorry for him. Daniel hadn't bothered to attach a name or a face or even an age to the illegal person. As far as the jury was concerned, Daniel did not know and could not identify the person he had set free.

"Then you know I can't rehire you even if you are acquitted. But I do hope the trial ends well for you today."

"I do, too, David. Thanks."

They parted and Daniel leaned against the cold marble wall, waiting to go in.

Actually, the time away from the INS had been good for him. He and Benny had spent hours riding on horseback through the black brush, chasing cows and talking. And it had surprised him to find out that Benny was ready to get out of ranching now.

"Your mother and I want to buy a motor home and travel all over the country," his father had told him one day.

"But what could you see that would ever be any prettier than this?" Daniel had asked as he scanned the calloused beauty of the gnarled trees, the spiny prickly pear, the huisache.

"Nothing." Benny tipped his Stetson toward his son. "But I've been looking at the backside of cows for a long time, too."

Daniel laughed. "You might as well travel around the world, then. It takes a lot of sight-seeing to make yourself forget a scene like that."

Besides spending time with his family, Daniel had worked with the baseball team for hours, too. All ages of children had been showing up at the park to watch the third grades play ball on Saturdays. Several fathers had telephoned him and offered to be coaches. Someone at a parish hall meeting had told Father Mac that the teams needed uniforms and equipment, and three days later the director of the YMCA had called to see if his team needed a sponsor. And when the park was occupied, they even played games at *Los Ebanos*, out on the front lawn, where Daniel had taught Miguel how to pitch and hit.

"Mr. Salinas." His lawyer opened the door and held it for him. "The jury is in. Come take your place."

Daniel strolled into the courtroom behind his counsel. He hadn't expected the jury to come back so soon. And he hadn't expected the entire third-grade baseball team to be suited up and supporting him, all of them with huge, mischievous grins on their faces as they lined the front.

Jamie was there, too, sitting just behind Sarita and Miguel, supporting him, even though he hadn't told her he loved her lately. She looked beautiful to him, her hair loose, draped in ribbons around her shoulders. She gave him a thumbs up sign as he walked up the aisle and took his seat in front of the children.

The jury foreman stood and produced a piece of paper. The room was silent as he read it. "We, the jury, find the defendant, Daniel Salinas, guilty of the felony of smuggling..."

The people in the courtroom began talking. Even the children began to chatter. They had found him guilty. Daniel clutched at the back of his chair. The room was spinning. The blood thrummed in his ears. *This is it, then. The end.*

The jury foreman continued to read from his notes. "Although we have found this man guilty, we suggest the judge impose a light sentence on Mr. Salinas. As testimony has indicated, he is an upstanding member of this community. Although we do agree that he broke the law and although his position at the INS was one of public trust, we do not believe it is called for to punish him on the same level that one would punish a repeat offender."

Everyone was still talking.

The judge rapped his gavel on the podium in front of him. He waited for the citizens of Roma to quiet down before he spoke, too. "I quite agree. Mr. Salinas has been through enough. I intend to get this thing over with once and for all. Daniel Salinas, I sentence you to five years in the federal penitentiary for the felony of smuggling. However, I agree to probate that sentence on the grounds that, when you broke the law, you had no intent to gain. You did not accept money or drugs or promises. The world needs more people like you." His eyes met Daniel's. "What you did Mr. Salinas, was not heroic. It was simply very...human." He rapped his gavel again. "This court is adjourned."

Daniel tried to sit down, to let the shock and the joy soak in, but before he could find his chair, his lawyer was clapping him on the back and someone else was shaking his hand and the entire baseball team was bobbing up and down around his knees.

"Son." Benny stood there before him, and his mother, Harriet, stood right behind. She looked flushed and beautiful and excited, as Benny motioned to Daniel. "Hold out your hand."

Daniel extended his palm to his father. And, instead of taking it, Benny dropped something into it. It was a key chain with several keys and a golden medallion the shape of Texas on it.

Daniel looked at them. "These are the keys to the house, Dad."

"The keys to *Los Ebanos*." Benny hugged Harriet to his side and winked at her. "I'm buying the motor home tomorrow. And you, son, have a ranch to run."

"Dad . . ." He tried to say something, even a simple thank you, but he couldn't. Instead, tears of gratitude came to his eyes as Benny gave him a one-armed hug.

Daniel embraced his mother, too, and then, when he pulled away from Harriet, he saw Jamie standing there, watching him, and the tears were streaming down her face, too.

She mouthed the words to him from across the room. "I'm happy for you." And then she turned to go.

"Wait! Jamie, wait!" He shoved his way through the crowd to follow her. When he reached her, she was already at the door. "Wait up, Jamie. Please."

He had done everything he could to keep from seeing her. He cared so much for her, needed her, loved her, it was torture for him to look at her, still thinking he would go to jail, that there was no possibility for their future. "How are you?"

"I'm okay. Not wonderful, but okay. And, I'm better now, after hearing your sentence." She had spent the past few nights lying awake, missing him. "I couldn't get my job back at the school. So I'm down in Weslaco working for the Rio Grande Valley Chamber of Commerce. Frances Ybarra has promised to call me the minute something opens up. And I visit Sarita and see some of the other kids often." She stopped talking, searched his eyes and wondered if she should tell him more. "Jorge is a wonderful boy. I'm teaching him to speak English."

Daniel couldn't keep from laughing. "And I'm teaching him to play baseball. He's going to turn out to be a well-rounded teenager like all the rest of them."

He stopped talking. They stared at each other, the silence poignant between them.

"You know," he said at last, while a current of people flowed around them, "how very much I love you."

"No," she said, holding her emotions in check. She was trembling, she loved him so, and she wanted to cry out just to hear him say what he had. "I thought you had changed your mind...when I wouldn't come back with you from Dallas.''

"Well." His lips were dry, his throat parched. He suddenly realized what it was he was doing, and he was scared. "I couldn't very well have taken you to jail."

"No." And then she gave him a tiny, mischievous grin that looked almost like one of the children's. "But I would have come to visit you if I had known you loved me." Her eyes locked on his, and her face sobered. "You know, Daniel, that was all I ever wanted from you."

He grinned, too. He was aching to take her in his arms. But that would come later. "Jamie. Hold out your hand."

"What?"

"Don't ask questions. Just hold out your hand."

She did, and he dropped the keys to *Los Ebanos* in her palm. She drew them to her and looked at them. "What are these?"

"The keys to *Los Ebanos*." His grin grew wider. "It's mine now, Jamie, and I'd like you to share it with me. As my wife."

She gripped his shoulders and tilted her face toward his. And then she couldn't resist playing the game, too. "I don't know," she said stoically. "Maybe I will. If you are willing to meet two conditions."

Daniel was suddenly worried. "What conditions are those?"

"That you let me bring all my students out there on field trips and you let me help you dip cows."

"Ah..." He hesitated on purpose. "I don't know. I might have a condition, too."

"And what might it be?"

"That you let me have baseball games on the front lawn on Saturdays."

Jamie couldn't stand it any longer. She was crying. And she was so happy that she felt as if her heart might burst. "I don't see anything wrong with that. It would be fine." She threw her head back and laughed. "It would be *wonderful*."

"Well?"

She had a home now and a life and the man she loved. "Yes, Daniel," she shrieked. "Yes. Yes. Yes."

He threw his arms around her and swung her around right there in the courtroom. And they were both giggling, and her feet were hitting people, and she was so happy she wanted to sing.

Daniel was holding her high above him, and she took his face in her hands and gazed at him. "I love you, too. So much."

And this time, when he set her feet on the ground and bent to kiss her, neither of them noticed that the courtroom had emptied around them.

WHITE SATIN RIBBONS fluttered in the gulf coast breeze all along the entrance to *Los Ebanos*. Lúpe had laced them everywhere, in and out on the wrought-iron fence that lined the patio and in the trees and even on the front gate high above the cattle guard. Piñatas hung from every tree in the front yard. They were filled with candy and tiny presents for the children.

There were crepe paper flowers bunched on the fences, too, because Jamie loved them. Harriet and Sarita and Elena had made them from paper they'd bought downtown, purple ones, pink ones, turquoise and red.

In town, everything was decorated for Christmas. But, today, the decorations at *Los Ebanos* were in honor of Daniel and Jamie's wedding. Lúpe and Harriet had been working for weeks to prepare for the celebration. And Mother Nature had done her share in the decorating, too. The bougainvillea was blooming all along the front of the house as Jamie stepped out the front door and made her way along the front walk toward the man who would be her husband.

The priest who had come to marry them had constructed a little altar in the grass, with pots of poinsettias arranged around him and a hand-carved ebony cross beside him. He had draped William Forrester's brilliant crimson serape across the lawn in front of him. Jamie and Daniel would use it as a kneeling bench.

As Jamie walked across the grass toward Daniel, Jorge Galindo strummed a soft wedding ballad for her on the guitar. A horde of children went before her. She had asked her students from F.J. Scott Elementary to attend, Sarita and Miguel and the others from last year's class, and the new third graders from the class Frances Ybarra had hired her to teach this year. The children all wore bright colors, and the girls had flowers in their hair. They skipped along in the grass then stood beside her.

When she reached the little makeshift altar and slipped her fingers into Daniel's large, calloused hand, their eyes met for a moment, and the light in Daniel's bound Jamie to him for an eternity as she smiled at him.

"I love you, schoolmarm," he mouthed.

She winked at him. She loved it when he called her schoolmarm. And then she turned serious. "Me, too," and then she whispered, "this is for all our tomorrows, Daniel."

"I want it to be."

"Dearly beloved..." The priest began the ceremony. The two of them exchanged vows and promises and rings. And then they knelt to take communion as, in the distance, the parish hall chimes began to ring. And as the beautiful fine linen of the wedding dress Jamie wore touched the thick weave of the serape beneath her knees, Jamie could feel her grandfather beside her, knowing her and loving her. His spirit surrounded her as the timeless sun shone down white-hot on the brilliant colors of her wedding day.

The priest handed Daniel a loaf of unleavened bread, and together they broke it while the priest made the sign of the cross and repeated the age-old canticle. They sipped wine and joined hands again. As they were married, Jamie couldn't help thinking of the fabric of their lives, how their days would be woven together now, all parts of who they were at last intertwined. She was a whole person with Daniel by her side. And as they rose together and walked arm in arm toward the patio at *Los Ebanos*, the children from her classes were giggling and jumping around them, and Jamie knew she was all she could be now... tied together... who she had once been... who she was destined to grow to be... because of their loving.

Harlequin Superromance

COMING NEXT MONTH

CHRISTMAS IS FOR KIDS

Spend this holiday season with nine very special children. Children whose wishes come true at the magical time of Christmas.

Read American Romance's CHRISTMAS IS FOR KIDS—heartwarming holiday stories in which children bring together four couples who fall in love. Meet:

Frank, Dorcas, Kathy, Candy and Nicky—They become friends at St. Christopher's orphanage, but they really want to be adopted and become part of a real family, in #321 *A Carol Christmas* by Muriel Jensen.

Patty—She's a ten-year-old certified genius, but she wants what every little girl wishes for: a daddy of her own, in #322 *Mrs. Scrooge* by Barbara Bretton.

Amy and Flash—Their mom is about to deliver their newest sibling any day, but Christmas just isn't the same now—not without their dad. More than anything they want their family reunited for Christmas, in #323 *Dear Santa* by Margaret St. George.

Spencer—Living with his dad and grandpa in an all-male household has its advantages, but Spence wants Santa to bring him a mommy to love, in #324 *The Best Gift of All* by Andrea Davidson.

These children will win your hearts as they entice—and matchmake—the adults into a true romance. This holiday, invite them—and the four couples they bring together—into your home.

Look for all four CHRISTMAS IS FOR KIDS books available now from Harlequin American Romance. And happy holidays!

Especially for you,
Christmas from
HARLEQUIN HISTORICALS

An enchanting collection of three Christmas
stories by some of your favorite authors captures
the spirit of the season in the 1800s

TUMBLEWEED CHRISTMAS by Kristin James

A "Bah, humbug" Texas rancher meets his match in his
new housekeeper, a woman determined to bring the spirit
of a Tumbleweed Christmas into his life—and love into
his heart.

A CINDERELLA CHRISTMAS by Lucy Elliot

The perfect granddaughter, sister and aunt, Mary Hillyer
seemed destined for spinsterhood until Jack Gates arrived
to discover a woman with dreams and passions that were
meant to be shared during a Cinderella Christmas.

HOME FOR CHRISTMAS
by Heather Graham Pozzessere

The magic of the season brings peace Home For
Christmas when a Yankee captain and a Southern heiress
fall in love during the Civil War.

Look for HARLEQUIN HISTORICALS CHRISTMAS
STORIES wherever Harlequin books are sold.

Wonderful, luxurious gifts can be yours with proofs-of-purchase from any specially marked "Indulge A Little" Harlequin or Silhouette book with the Offer Certificate properly completed, plus a check or money order (do not send cash) to cover postage and handling payable to Harlequin/Silhouette "Indulge A Little, Give A Lot" Offer. We will send you the specified gift.

Mail-in-Offer